THE GRANITE CLIFFS

Recent Titles set in Cornwall by Rosemary Aitken

THE GRANITE CLIFFS

Rosemary Aitken

This first world edition published in Great Britain 2003 by
SEVERN HOUSE PUBLISHERS LTD of
9–15 High Street, Sutton, Surrey SM1 1DF.
This first world edition published in the USA 2003 by
SEVERN HOUSE PUBLISHERS INC of
595 Madison Avenue, New York, N.Y. 10022.

British Library Cataloguing in Publication Data

Aitken,   Rosemary
    The granite cliffs
    1.   Mineral industries - England - Cornwall - Fiction
    2.   Great Britain - Social conditions - 20th century - Fiction
    3.   Love stories
    I.   Title
    823.9'14 [F]

    ISBN 0-7278-5854-8

Except where actual historical events and characters are being
described for the storyline of this novel, all situations in this
publication are fictitious and any resemblance to living persons
is purely coincidental.

Typeset by Palimpsest Book Production Ltd.,
Polmont, Stirlingshire, Scotland.
Printed and bound in Great Britain by
MPG Books Ltd., Bodmin, Cornwall.

For Ursula

Part One

February – April 1911

One

The morning, which had begun cool and misty with only a slight breeze stirring the grasses on Penvarris cliff, now threatened to turn cold and wet. Victoria began to regret that she had spent so long out idling, watching the waves that crashed into the headland rocks, and then looking for the first buds of primrose in the lanes. For a moment she was almost tempted to turn straight for home – it was probably foolish to have come so far on this errand, all alone – but she saw the twitching curtains all along the hamlet as she passed. It was too late now.

Here it was. Number nine, the last little whitewashed cottage in the row. The painted door faced straight on to the lane. She took a deep breath and knocked.

The door was opened almost instantly, by a girl with a mane of tawny hair who – seeing Victoria – rubbed her hands hastily on her coarse sacking apron. She stared at the visitor in surprise. 'Well, it's that Miss Flower, as I live and breathe! Whatever brings you down Polvidden way?'

Victoria swallowed hard. 'I understood that there was ill-health in the house.' Surprise made her sound unduly prim, even to her own ears. Usually on visits of this kind she was greeted by someone older, one of the stout local women from the village who always presided over births, offering advice and cups of tea in Cornish accents broader than their hips. This girl could not be much older than herself – seventeen or eighteen at the most – and she looked a picture of strapping health, standing there with that great sacking apron, orange skirt, stout working boots and big work-reddened hands.

3

'My sister, yes,' the girl explained. 'Taken bad before her time she was, and bleeding like a pig. Thought we'd lost her altogether, at the time, but they both pulled through and they'll do handsome now.' She stood back against the door invitingly. 'Want to come in and see the babe, do 'ee?'

Victoria hesitated. She knew that it was traditional for visitors to view a new-born child – just as some of the older parishioners expected one to come and see a corpse. She'd often done both with her father, who was a clergyman, but that was quite different of course – he knew what to say on such occasions, and she shrank from going into that stuffy warmth alone. She knew what such cottages were like: poky, crowded little places, crammed with texts and heavy furniture, and smelling of babies, smoky fires and fish.

Besides, the presence of this girl unsettled her. That flamboyant hair and brightly coloured skirt made Victoria suddenly aware of her own boringly neat fawn dress, smart gloves and warm embroidered cape. It made her feel positively drab.

She said, 'No, no. I won't disturb your sister. I brought some chicken jelly, that is all.' She produced a little glass jar of it from her dainty drawstring bag.

The girl took it, doubtfully. 'That's some kind of you, Miss Flower! It's—'

Whatever she was going to say was interrupted by a thin voice from within.

'Who is it, Mollie?'

Mollie answered, calling over her shoulder, without moving from the spot, 'Vicar's daughter, from St Evan church. Brought you some jelly, tempt your appetite.'

'Don't she know that we're all chapel here?' The voice was querulous.

Victoria said hastily, 'Of course I know. But you are within our parish, and I think my father was called here once before. By the quarry-owners, was it? When someone was hurt by a rockfall at the pit?'

The red-haired girl said, 'S'right. My brother Jamie, that

4

would be. Always call on Reverend Flower, they do, when there's any trouble at the pit. And Eadie's Stan was in the choir, one time. Anyway, like I say, it's nice of you.' She looked at the little jar of jelly. 'Make this yourself, did you?'

Victoria flushed. Was the girl making fun of her? Of course she hadn't made the stuff herself. Mrs Roseworthy, the housekeeper, had made it, as she did every week for the 'poor and suffering' of St Evan parish. Victoria rather enjoyed the job of calling on the villagers and dispensing nourishment. People were generally very grateful, too. But though this Mollie smiled and said all the proper things, there was something very knowing in those bold brown eyes. Victoria could not think of what to say.

She was saved the necessity of saying anything. The voice from the interior spoke again: 'Well, if she's give it you, Mollie, thank 'er quick, and then come in and shut the door, do, before me and this 'ere infant catch our deaths. Wind's turning easterly this morning, Jamie says, and I can already feel a bit of spite in it.'

'I'll be going then,' Victoria said, before Mollie had the chance to speak. 'I hope your sister gets well soon.'

Mollie nodded. 'Best hurry 'ome yourself, you had, Miss Flower – before this rain sets in. Thank you again for the jelly.' And she began to close the door.

Victoria hurried up the lane. How could she have been such a fool? It wasn't even as if that household was grateful for her call. It was one thing to visit homes where she was known – the little cottages she'd visited with her father – but whatever had possessed her to come out here with her jelly to this unfamiliar place, unannounced like that, and with the weather turning, too?

But of course she knew the answer perfectly; it was an excuse. None of the regular parishioners was ill, but news of this difficult confinement had given her an opportunity. A reason for getting out of the house, for walking on the cliffs, away from the disapproving strictures of her governess, Miss Boff. She could almost hear that sharp voice chiding now, as shrill and strident as the seagulls overhead: 'It's not *becoming*, Victoria!'

Of course, Miss Boff was not a bad old thing, at heart, though she was thinner than a beanpole and more wrinkled than a prune. Just as well, since she was as much of a fixture in the household as the gas geyser over the bath. She had come to teach when Victoria was young, and somehow had never gone away again, although at seventeen Victoria (in her own estimation anyway) had long outgrown her copybooks.

There was still an afternoon a week supposedly devoted to 'literature', where Victoria was supposed to give an account of what she'd read. They were currently working through *The Pilgrim's Progress*, but since Victoria devoured books with as much appetite as she devoured cream cakes, she was able to do this easily – while still privately devoting delicious hours to more exciting things. Her friend Isabella patronized the penny lending library, and passed the books on to Victoria. Not that Miss Boff knew that, of course.

Victoria had spent many a happy hour up in her room, weeping over the plight of the little match girl or galloping with gallant ladies across Arabia. It was all doubly delightful because it was half-forbidden, and she still had time to satisfy Miss Boff about the dark doings of the Giant Despair.

The only real problem with Miss Boff these days was that Father, being a widower, was still inclined to defer to her judgement in matters feminine, and the governess had a predilection for 'seemly' browns and greys, and an old-fashioned belief that nice young ladies should wear their hair up, and then only in horrid coiled plaits like blonde earmuffs. The girl at the cottage would never have believed it, but the vicar's well-dressed daughter could feel a pang of something very close to envy for that cascade of reddish hair and the bold colour of the coarse orange skirt.

A sudden gust of wind threatened even now to carry off her silly prim fawn hat. Victoria lowered her head against the first stinging spots of rain. If she didn't hurry, she'd be soaked to the skin before she got indoors, although it wasn't far. Here was the burial ground and, on the far side of it, the tower of St Evan church and the square outline of the vicarage, the smoke from its chimneys blown sideways by the wind.

She glanced around. There was nobody about, so she went the quick way home across the graveyard, hitching her skirts ('most unbecoming, Victoria') to climb the big stone stile. Her hems were damp from trailing in the grasses and her bonnet ribbons spotted with the rain, but by skirting swiftly round the gravestones and scampering down the back path to the house, she made it home before the real downpour began.

Miss Boff was waiting for her in the hall. 'You'd better change your shoes, Victoria, and perhaps your gown, since you have elected to come into the house with muddy hems. Your father wishes to see you in his study. And kindly do not gallop in the hall – most unbecoming in a young lady like yourself!'

Mollie Coombs didn't stay to watch her visitor depart. She hurried back to where her sister lay, propped up with pillows on the kitchen settle for her 'first day down'. The baby, whose birth had nearly killed her three days ago, lay contentedly asleep in the wooden crib beside the fire. Wilfred Emmanuel Stanley Tregorran. Mollie smiled. A big name for a very little lad.

But there was no time to stand and stare at him. There was a deal to do before the men got home that night. Three hungry mouths to feed (not counting herself and Eadie): Fayther, Jamie and Eadie's husband, Stan ('big Stan Tregorran' as they were already calling him) who would eat as much as the rest of them together, given half a chance. Great pile of bacon stew it took to fill that lot up – took you best part of half an hour to peel enough potatoes and swede. And then there was the floor to scrub, the ironing to do, and that bucket of nappies to be boiled and dried – there was always washing to be done, when there was a baby in the house. No one but Mollie to do it, either – or any of the other household chores – with Eadie laid up in her bed and Ma (God Bless her) carried off by that awful fever years ago.

Mollie gave herself a little shake. Whatever did she expect? Of course you couldn't expect the men to help, especially after a long day at the quarry. Worse than the mines, the quarry was, for tiring a man. Or so her brother Jamie said, and he should know since he had tried them both.

She sighed and went out to fetch in the washing from the line before the rain began. She didn't think of the chicken jelly pot again until much later on, when the child's napkins were washed and dripping on the rack and yesterday's damp ones had all been hung on strings around the fire to air. 'Nice of that girl to bring you that,' she said, moving the jar aside. She filled the kettle with water from the pail again and set it on to warm.

Edith grunted. 'Aren't a charity case yet, I hope. Don't know why she wants to come down here, her and her la-di-da ways. Polvidden folk can look after theirselves. Tisn't as if we even go to that there church of theirs.'

'Come on Eadie, that's not really fair.' Mollie splashed warm water into the stone sink and swilled the teacups over with the rag. 'We aren't really chapel folk, like lots of them round here. We were glad enough of Dr Flower when Jamie hurt his back, and your Stan did go up there quite a bit, himself, when he was young.'

'Only for the singing,' Eadie said. 'Best choir for miles around they had, one time. But that's all gone now, long ago, since old man Polmaen died – that was the organist. That's all it ever was, with Stan – the choir. Certainly never went to hear the vicar droning on. Worse than the chapel he is, half the time.'

Mollie grinned. It was quite true. Everyone knew that the preachers down Penvarris chapel could get carried away by their enthusiasm and preach for more than an hour. No wonder half the Methodists round here thought cooking on a Sunday was a sin – their dinner would be burnt to cinders every week. And that Doctor Flower wasn't far behind. Must be more difficult for churchy folk, she thought. They weren't all grand families with staff to cook their meals, many of them were quarrymen and miners, like themselves.

She turned to her sister. 'Well, you stop "droning on" yourself, and try to get some rest. That child will want feeding any minute, and they three men'll be home before you know. Now, I've got a bit of raw fry in the pan. I'll leave it to simmer on the hob a bit. I want to just slip down the end of the Row a minute, and see if Auntie Anne wants anything.'

'Well, take a shawl for heaven's sake, it's pouring rain.' Eadie's worn face softened in a smile. 'Not that I s'ppose you'll take a bit of notice. I don't believe it's Auntie Anne you want to see at all. Out looking for that Daniel Olds, that's what. I do believe you're walking out with him.'

'Don't be so daft, I'm doing no such thing. And don't you going saying so to Fayther.'

But Eadie wouldn't let it drop. 'Well, what's so awful if you were? Don't suppose for moment Fayther'd mind a bit. Nice boy Daniel. Always was. Decent habits and a steady job. Not bad lookin', either, if you like that grizzled look. No, Mollie girl, you could do a whole lot worse. And if Stan and me do get that quarry house we're promised, you and Daniel could get wed and have our bedroom here. I daresay Fayther wouldn't mind.'

'Don't know what you're taking on about!' Mollie retorted, annoyed to realize that she was blushing. 'I aren't fixing to marry anyone just yet.' And even if I did, she told herself fiercely, I'd want something a bit better for myself than sharing Fayther's house, in a poky front bedroom with a floor that creaks and nothing of your own around you. And cleaning and cooking for everyone else besides.

But she could hardly say so to Eadie, who had done exactly that. Instead she went on: 'Daniel Olds is nice enough, I'm sure, but there's lots of other herring in the sea. I don't know what's supposed to be so special about him.'

But she did, of course. All the girls in the village knew. Something about grey eyes and a lopsided smile. Not that he would look at her, she supposed. She picked up her shawl. Look at this for instance; it had been Ma's, a pretty thing, only it was faded now and fraying at one edge. Bet that stuck-up Miss Flower from the vicarage never had to peel a potato or wear a hand-me-down shawl in her entire life. Mollie frowned at herself

9

in the mirror. She was beginning to sound as sour as Eadie, who could be a proper harpy when she chose.

Mind, you could hardly blame her, Mollie thought. Washing and scrubbing and cooking and ironing, and mending all the day – you didn't realize how much Eadie did, until she was laid up in bed and couldn't do it. And married to that awful Stan as well – great hairy, lazy lump, snoring on the settle after tea with his braces down and his shirt undone, like a man twice his age. And the way he leered at you sometimes, patted your bottom and called you 'little Moll', it was enough to make a cat sick. And you weren't supposed to mind him, because it was 'only Stan'. No, the sooner he and Eadie got that quarry house, the better.

Only of course, then it would be Mollie who had to slave all day. If only she could get away somewhere – go and be a lady's maid, perhaps, like Auntie Anne used to be. Now, that would be something! Smart uniform, and living in a big house up the town! There'd be a lot of work, she knew, running up and down the stairs, but you could learn to say 'yes ma'am, no ma'am' and hold your tongue, in exchange for three square meals a day and a whole half-day off a week to do whatever you wanted. And four and six a week besides! No half-day a week off if you stayed home here, and no money either. But of course, they wouldn't look at her for anything like that, great coarse girl with patches on her skirt!

One of these days, Mollie told herself, arranging the tattered shawl around her head, one of these days she'd show them all! Of course, she knew it was a dream, you needed money for that sort of thing. But she wouldn't stay here and be turned into a drudge, like all the other girls. She'd find a way. Start with a job as a bal maiden at the mine perhaps, there might be a bit of money then to buy things of her own. That would be a beginning. A new shawl, maybe, and smart brown bonnet like that Flower girl was wearing. And then we'd see what Daniel Olds would say. She tossed her head. Not that she thought anything particular of that.

But when she went out to see Aunt Anne, draped in the

tattered shawl against the rain, somehow or another it was just
the time to run into him.

The reason for the summons to the study was not, as Victoria
half-expected, an invitation to listen to her father's latest sermon
or help him find a reference in one of his many books. She had
been prepared for that: he often asked her help in little ways,
saying his eyes were not as sharp as they used to be. But that was
not why he wanted her today.

'I say that you shall *not* go, Victoria,' Deedee was saying, using
his preacher's voice. 'A vicar's daughter, attending a house party
in Lent. Whatever would our good pew holders think of that?'
He drew himself up to his full five feet six, flipped up the tails of
his old-fashioned coat and seated himself with dignity behind his
heavy desk.

Victoria sighed. It was one of their rare disagreements. Usually
she could 'wind her father round her little finger' as Miss Boff
would say, but Mrs Cardew's invitation had arrived while she
was out, and he had unexpectedly seen this house party of Bella's
as a matter of principle. And on that, as she knew, he would
never give way.

When he put on his determined face – together with his
balding head, high collar and pince-nez spectacles – he suddenly
bore a startling resemblance to the portrait of Mr Gladstone on
the wall. That great man had been a distant relative of a
previous vicar here, and the painting had stared down undis-
turbed upon this same little study for the best part of half a
century. Under its stern and disapproving gaze, Victoria felt
doubly abashed.

She averted her eyes and glanced around the room. The study
itself could have changed very little since the portrait was first
hung. The same dingy bookcases crammed with books; the same
brown leather armchair; the same faded carpet; the same dark-
panelled walls. No doubt even that dratted fire was just the same
– as smoky then as it was now, she thought, with a sudden burst
of irritation. But her father was as implacable on the subject of

11

the study as he was about Lenten house parties. This was his room and he liked it as it was.

Elsewhere in the house he'd let her have her way, provided that the cost was not too much. New rugs, new paint, the heavy curtains opened to admit the light. 'You're so old-fashioned, Father,' she would say. And he would generally give in. But not when he had made his mind up, like today.

She tried again. 'But Deedee, this is not a real house party, just a family affair.' She called him Deedee deliberately; it was her pet name for him, coined in the days when she first read his name 'Edward Flower, D.D.' on his own portrait which graced the dining room. It stood for Doctor of Divinity, of course, though she hadn't known that then. He usually weakened when she called him that. But it did not soften him this afternoon.

'Am I to understand that you have discussed this invitation with Isabella already?'

Victoria flushed. 'Only when the idea was first proposed. It is Isabella's birthday that weekend, and her cousin is coming from Falmouth specially. Isabella's mother told me that herself. I am invited on purpose to meet him.'

'Then I am surprised at Mrs Cardew,' Deedee replied, adjusting his spectacles in what Victoria thought of as his 'affronted' manner. 'She might have chosen a more appropriate moment for her invitation.'

'It is Bella's birthday, Deedee. That is hardly something one can rearrange, simply because Easter's inconvenient this year.'

It was impertinent, but true. Even Deedee had to see the force of that. 'Be that as it may, I do not think it suitable. I'm sorry, Victoria, of course you may see your friend on her birthday. Invite her here by all means if you wish, but I cannot agree to a daughter of mine attending a formal house party – dinners, dances and charades – on the very last weekend in Lent. And as to being invited to meet this male cousin from Falmouth . . .'

'Oh, Petroc Veryan is not invited on my account, Papa!' Victoria was stung into formality. 'He is coming for Bella. Her mother hopes it might be quite a match.'

Deedee regarded her with a twinkle over his glasses. 'I see. And what does Isabella think of that?'

'I really couldn't say. She has met him only once or twice, and hardly remembers him at all – although apparently he was always very struck with her. I daresay she will be pleased enough to see him, and if she likes him that is better still. At least she will have the opportunity of meeting someone of her own age.' She looked at her father, who infuriatingly was toying with his papers. 'And how *I'm* ever to meet anyone, I don't know,' she muttered in an undertone. 'I do believe you want me to grow into an old maid like Miss Boff, with nothing better to do but moon about after her employer.'

She had not intended for him to hear it, but Deedee put down his papers and looked at her sharply. '*What* did you say, Victoria?'

So he had been listening. She said quickly, in her normal voice, 'Nothing, Deedee. Only grumbling that I receive so few invitations. And sometimes it's so tedious here – you can't imagine Deedee, really you cannot. It's different for you. You have a job to do, people to see – and even your collection of old books to think about. But what have I to think about? Nothing! Except what colour curtains would be better in the dining room, and how I can avoid annoying Miss Boff. At least Isabella makes a little change. How I will manage when she marries, I don't know, since I don't suppose I'll ever wed myself. How am I to find a husband, if I'm never to go anywhere or meet anyone?'

'I hardly think that you would welcome it, Victoria, if I did what Colonel Cardew seems to have done. Do you really wish me to produce some unknown suitor out of the blue, so that you can marry him? I rather imagine that you would prefer a little more choice in the matter?'

He was laughing at her, behind the mild rebuke, but Victoria had spoken from her heart and she refused to be teased out of her ill humour. She said crossly, 'There is no question of anyone forcing him upon her, though no doubt he's a pleasant enough young man. However, since I am not to attend the party, I shan't know. But there it is. I suppose it comes of being the vicar's daughter, tied in by convention and neither fish nor fowl.'

She had gone too far. A look of real anguish crossed his face, and she knew the words had hurt him. She regretted it instantly. She crossed to his chair, laid her hand on his shoulder, and gave him a rueful smile. 'But I suppose that you are right, Deedee, as always. Should you write to Mrs Cardew, or shall I?'

Two

Edward Flower watched his daughter leave the room. He sighed. These occasional differences of opinion were a grief to him. And now he would have to write an aplogetic letter to that dreadful Mrs Cardew, who, with her booming voice and hearty handshake, always made him nervous. Not that she was anything but perfectly polite, and she and her family had been kind to 'little Victoria', but he sensed the patronage implied, and knew that she secretly looked down her well-bred nose at him because, although he was a minister of God, his parents had been 'only trade'.

A minister of God! And through the laying on of hands, part of a great tradition dating back to the Apostles. Is that what his parishoners saw when they looked at him? Or did they see beyond the clerical trappings, and recognize the all-too-mortal man? Just now, for instance, he'd raised his voice to Vicki – something he always tried hard to avoid. He always regretted it when he knew he had betrayed, by some human weakness, the high standards which he set himself, and which he felt that his parishioners expected.

Weaknesses like procrastination, for instance. He had been here for an hour, and he had made little progress with the papers on his desk. A few scattered notes for Sunday's sermon, and that was all. This would never do. He took out his pocket watch to see the time, and since there was no mirror in the room – an antidote to personal vanity – idly looked at his own face in the polished case.

It gleamed dully back at him, telling him nothing, beyond the

15

fact that his hair was as dark and well-groomed as ever, though his face was getting lined around the temples. The grey eyes which looked back into his were a little tired, but kindly and intelligent enough – no hint there of the dreadful doubts which sometimes haunted him, or the disillusion of these last few years. What would his father and mother have said to that after all his insistence on a higher calling, and the years of self-denial and study it had meant? They would have laughed at him no doubt, and told him in their no-nonsense way that he should have gone into drapery, after all. Poor souls. How desperately proud they both had been. 'Our son has gone into the church, you know. Become a gentleman. A university degree, and all.' And he had excelled. Got scholarships. The bishop at his ordination had spoken of 'a new breed of clerics from the business classes . . . first-class minds . . . new lifeblood for the church.'

Only of course, it took more than education and a vicar's vestments to make a man a gentleman, and the fire of faith is hard to keep alive in a damp Cornish vicarage, with no new souls for kindling. He looked at his reflection again and found it smiling back at him, amused by the cleverness of his own turn of phrase.

What vanity! More weakness! He put the watch away, and turned back to the papers on his desk. Bills, most of them – the vicarage was old, and inconvenient, and Vicki was right to urge repairs. One bill from White's Emporium in Penzance was for those new curtains in the drawing room. They had been needed too. Victoria had good taste, bless her, and she knew what touches livened up a room. Like her mother in that as in so much else.

He took out his cheque book, and – like the gentleman that he had half-become – signed it with a flourish. Then, more shame-facedly, another to a saleroom in Penzance – another rare book that had tempted him! At least, there was no difficulty in paying these accounts.

St Evan was not a wealthy parish, but there had been enough money in drapery for his parents to leave him well provided for, and the living was adequate for his needs. The church itself was well provided for; most of the better families hereabouts regarded it as part of their social duty to attend matins or evensong on Sundays and make generous contributions to the organ restoration fund – just as their forefathers had subscribed for the new pitch-pine pews and roof fifty years ago. Whether this had anything to do with God at all, the Reverend Flower sometimes seriously wondered. Probably it did. He was being unkind. Some of the older ladies, in particular, were unquestionably devout.

But these charming ladies had their own idea of God. That was clear from the way they spoke about Him, as if He were a sort of benevolent but irascible English country gentleman, inexplicably fond of organ music and oratory, and much concerned with charitable works. Edward smiled again.

The image of a real and suffering Christ: planting sandalled feet in real cornfields; touching lepers; talking to outcasts; feeling the bite of real nails into living flesh; that passionate figure which had so inspired his own youth, would have frightened and bewildered most of them. He had discovered that in his early sermons. Some of the older members of his flock had been affronted by his modernist approach and he had been at risk of losing his congregation entirely. He had learnt the lesson, and modified his tone accordingly – and then, of course, his own doubts had begun.

There had been a choir and a church band once, but that had lapsed when the organist had died, and Edward had neither the talent nor the energy to revive it. They made do now with Miss Boff on the harmonium while he preached comfortable truisms each week to pews half-full of sleek polished waistcoats, lace gloves and prim Sunday bonnets.

A few of the wives of the quarrymen and miners – with their worn faces and patient eyes – would huddle sometimes at the back, neat in their faded Sunday best, praying perhaps for guidance in this world and something a little kinder in the next. Their menfolk rarely came at all unless it was a marriage or a funeral. They preferred the bold speeches of the would-be union leaders up at the mine, calling for labouring men to unite, with promises of better times on earth. Sometimes, though he hardly dared admit it even to himself, the Reverend Flower had an uncomfortable feeling that the Socialists were right. The current system had failed them.

Including the church and Doctor Edward Flower.

He had done his best, he told himself. Done it even after Vera, his young wife, died in childbirth and the dreadful doubts had begun. He'd gritted his teeth and gone on struggling: visited the sick, and helped the poor. Wasn't that what his Master had required of him? And the sick and poor were at last starting to come to him of their own accord, slowly learning to trust him and bring him their problems, if not their souls. That was something – surely? At least his friend Jonathan would tell him so.

There was a letter here from Jonathan somewhere. Yes, here it was: 'From the Office of the Rural Dean'. His friend had done very well for himself. Of course, Jonathan Stokes had been just another student when they met during their postgraduate term at theological college. They were complete opposites in many ways: Jonathan already leaned toward high church practices and favoured incense, confession and sung offices, while Edward himself tended towards the evangelical. They'd argued about it the first time they met, but all the same there'd been a instant bond between them and over the years Jonathan had proved a good – if most unlikely – friend.

Especially – Edward remembered with gratitude – after Vera died, when grief had almost unhinged him, and he had lost his faith. His friend – already making strides in his own career – had taken the time to travel down, offering not only a sympathetic ear, but practical advice on obtaining nurses and feeding-bottles, and proving surprisingly adroit at managing the cook. It was like having a benevolent whirlwind in the house. Before the visit was over, Edward had somehow been persuaded not to abandon the priesthood after all.

The two men had corresponded ever since, and Jonathan had

never mocked his doubts. In fact, in this very letter he was arguing: 'This lack of certainty of yours, dear friend, is a trial of faith. See it as something sent by God to test you, as he has tested greater men than us. This is what ritual is for. A man must take up his yoke and carry on.'

Edward wanted to believe it. He took up his pen again

It wasn't a 'yoke', he told himself wryly, but it was a start. First a letter to the dreadful Mrs Cardew, and then perhaps he would write to Jonathan and share his worries about Victoria. She was turning into such a pretty girl, and growing up so fast he hardly knew how to behave. Was he in danger of spoiling her as Miss Boff said?

But, poor child, she did have little company of her own age, and very few amusements. She was right about that. And that protest about the tedium of her existence had struck him to the heart. Somehow he had never thought of that, yet it was obviously true. Victoria had such a lively mind – she had out-stripped poor Miss Boff at arithmetic years ago, and he had been obliged to put a diplomatic stop to that part of her lessons. But what could he do for her? It wasn't as if she'd had the education to study at the university, as some girls were actually beginning to do. And it was true, her position made her isolated. A vicar's daughter could not consort with miner's girls, while a draper's granddaughter had no place in the company of the aristocracy. Yet poor Victoria was both.

And as for marrying! Of course, there was time enough for that – she was hardly more than a schoolgirl yet – but he would have to lose her one day, and one had to face the facts. It was as she said, how would she ever meet a husband, in this out of the way place? Perhaps, after all, he should seek another parish. Or acquire a curate?

Yes, that was it! Why ever hadn't he thought of it before? He was sure he could afford it, though that was a consideration, since of course he'd have to pay the man himself. Jonathan would advise him, surely, how to proceed, since he had a curate of his own.

Edward was so pleased with his inspiration that he went back to his papers with renewed energy. First this letter about the house party. He dipped the pen carefully into the ink he had prepared, and began to write.

'Dear Mrs Cardew . . .'

Halfway down the page he stopped, read through the lines that he had written, screwed up the paper and began again. 'The Reverend Flower regrets . . .' It seemed too pompous. He was not clever at this sort of thing. Perhaps he should ask Miss Boff for her advice.

His hand was almost on the bell, and then he stopped himself. What was that Victoria had said? Miss Boff 'mooning about after her employer.' Surely not? He had never given her the slightest cause. Miss Boff? The very idea caused him an emotion unkindly close to horror. No, of course not. That was just Victoria speaking out of pique.

He opened the drawer of his desk and took out the miniature he always kept there. Oh Vera! Would our girl have grown up very differently with a mother's care? Perhaps. Though he had done his best. Encouraged the child with her books, supervised her meals, always tried to make some time for her whatever his duties in the parish were. Indulged her too much, some would say. So like her mother in so many ways.

He pressed his lips to the unforgiving glass and put the little miniature away.

But when, a little later, he wrote to Mrs Cardew he didn't ask Miss Boff for her advice.

'Right then!' Daniel Olds had to gesture as well as raise his voice. No one could hear you otherwise, over the din and clamour of the quarry. Always the first thing that struck visitors, it was, the noise: creaking pulleys; clanking carts and pumps; the chip and tap of the stoneworking yard; and over and above it all the constant ring of iron on stone, as teams of men 'jumped' the weighted iron rods rhythmically up and down on granite blocks to shape them roughly into size.

He lifted his sledgehammer again, and called, 'One more for luck, and I reckon that'll do.' His brother Zaccary, the apprentice boy, turned the hand borer another half a turn, gritting his teeth and screwing up his eyes as Dan brought the hammer down.

Dan grimaced in sympathy. He knew what it was like to lie uncomfortably in a dip, holding a piece of iron rod with a steel cutting chisel on the end of it, while two grown men took turns to swing at it with all their force. It sent shocks up your arms and made your every bone vibrate – even supposing that the hammerers didn't miss, which had happened other places once or twice! It was a horrible jolting job, and in some of the bigger quarries the men changed places after twenty minutes.

Not here, though. Prowse's quarry wasn't big enough for that; only fifty or sixty men at most. Here, everyone did a bit of everything – except for the men like Mollie Coombs's brother Jamie, who had an injury, and skilled men like himself with special jobs. But youngsters didn't have the strength when they first came – took a man to wield a sledger – and so they often got the worst of it. Half an hour holding a hand borer till your eyeballs rang, and then swapping with another boy for the thankless task of fetching water, or carrying filthy, awkward tools up to carpenter for sharpening. Daniel remembered it all too vividly.

He was nineteen now, and fully grown, not very tall, but lean and powerful – a look that drew appreciative giggles from the village girls. Daniel didn't care too much for that; he wasn't walking out with anyone, like most lads of his age. Too easy to be 'caught' like that, as several of his friends had been, with hasty marriages and furtive brides. In any case, there wasn't time. Daniel had worked very hard to get to where he was – he walked miles to Penzance two nights a week to evening classes at the Worker's Institute, and then trudged home again. Ma and Dad had been very good, found the fees from somewhere, and Mr Prowse as well – never minded if Dan knocked off ten minutes early on a 'schooling night' so long as he stayed back another time. 'It's the quarry benefits in the end,' he'd said, and even allowed Daniel to stop behind sometimes, with the nightwatchman in his hut. Couldn't do much studying at home, with half a dozen children round your feet.

So here was Dan, a fully fledged 'black powder' man, and already earning more than Dad. Now it was his turn, putting a bit by each week for Zac, who'd do his bit of study by and by. Not that he was as quick as Daniel, by a long way, but he'd have his chance. Then it would be young Jimmy – and any other little boys that came along.

But it didn't do to show that you were soft. He put down the hammer with a grunt, and nodded at the boy. 'Right-oh,' he said, 'let's have a look and see.' Daniel had been at this so long he could judge the position of the cutting edge fifteen or twenty feet down the hole, just by looking at the handle end. 'She'll do!'

He nodded at old Tom, the third member of the team, who had already put down his hammer and was wiping his dusty face on his muddy arm. 'You bring her out, Tom, and get her cleaned up and dried, while I go and fetch the charge.' He flexed his own back where the muscles ached.

They had been wet boring, which was always a messy job – keeping the hole wet while you bored into it – so then of course the borehole had to be cleaned out and dried with a sprinkling of fine dust before you laid the charge, otherwise your powder either wouldn't burn, or – worse – it would misfire. Then it was hell's own delight, trying to bore out the charge again without having the whole thing blow up in your face. More than one man had been killed like that, and several injured, even here at Prowse's. So Daniel was thinking carefully as he walked slowly over to the powder store.

He was calculating the amount that he would need; it was always up to the powder man to indent for that, depending on the particular block he wanted to split free. The way the crystals were lying in the stone, he thought, a four-inch hole, fifteen feet deep, that would need . . . let's see . . .

'Daniel! Danny Olds! Hold on a bit, it's me!' That was Jamie

Coombs hollering as he came hurrying across carrying a broken shovel in his hand. Going up the blacksmith's and carpenter's, most likely, to see if he could get it fixed. Whatever was he doing here? The powder house was miles from the forge. Naturally. Mr Prowse was very careful about that and wouldn't ever let a man take powder until the hole was bored and cleaned. 'Too many accidents' he always said, and told a story about how, years ago, a load of powder barrels had been on a cart, and when the waggoner put on the brake it caused a spark and blew the whole thing to kingdom come.

Something was wrong, Daniel could see that from Jamie's face. The two men had been friends for years. Jamie had even come to the institute with Dan, until half a ton of rock had fallen down and pinned his shoulder to the wall. Poor chap'd had to give up proper quarrying after that, and had gone down the mines, till Mr Prowse'd found a job for him. 'Don't matter to me which arm you use, my handsome, so long as you put your weight behind the tram and get the waste shifted to the spoil heaps.' But Jamie didn't like it, all the same.

It was a little quieter here, but he had to wait until his friend had caught up him, and then he spoke in a muted roar. 'Hello, Jamie, what's the trouble then? What you doing up this end? You look like the man who found a halfpenny and lost half a crown bending down for it!'

But his friend didn't smile. Nor did he grumble about shifting trams as usual. 'Not a right lot to smile about today. Haven't heard, have you? I can see that.'

'Somebody hurt?' Dan was instantly concerned. 'We never heard a thing.'

'No 'tisn't an accident, for once, the Lord be praised. But I aren't sure this might not turn out to be worse, in the long run. No, it's this contract for the paving setts for Portsmouth docks.'

Daniel frowned. That contract had been a great relief. Plenty of work for everyone, for months, just when the other smaller yards were having to close down. 'Don't tell me the Admiralty's reduced the offer price?' That would mean a score of men put off at once, and Jamie, of course, would be the first of them.

Jamie shook his head. 'It's worse'n that. Looks like we might have lost the whole blessed deal, and that's the truth of it . . .'

'Lost it? But how? I thought it was all over, signed and sealed.'

'So did Mr Prowse, it seems. Had the documents all drawn up and signed, and sent them up to the commissioners to get their names to it – and suddenly this morning, back it all came. The Admiralty changed their minds, apparently. Norwegian stone is just as good, they said, and they can get it twenty per cent less. Course it isn't certain yet – I heard it from the quarry captain half an hour ago. Prowse is coming down here later on, they say, to explain the whole thing to the men.'

It stunned Daniel. What would his ma and the family do, he thought, if all the men were off work at once? Bad enough when the weather was too wet, and you couldn't cut stone for a day or two – they'd sometimes had to beg for credit then – but this! At last he said slowly, 'So what happens now?'

'Dunno. Quarry captain thinks they might be bargaining. Prowse is offering to bring our prices down a bit – though that won't be so easy as it was, now he's signed up for this fair wage scheme of yours.'

Daniel sighed. He had been a member of the Stonecutters and Ornamental Masons' Society, and it had been agitating for years for quarries to introduce the 'Fair Wage Scheme' – based on the work required for a job, and not just on the weight of stone produced. Hit a bad seam, or a faulty stone and it could mean a whole day of work was wasted – and under the old scheme that had meant no pay. Prowse had been a stone man once himself, and he'd seen the sense of it and signed. Better a lower rate you were sure of than weeks with nothing to take home at all. But there were disadvantages, it seemed.

'Seemed like a good thing at the time,' Dan said.

Jamie kicked at a kerbstone with his boot. 'No good having a fair wage for the job, if it means no job at all. And that's what it could come to. Those dratted Norwegians haven't got a fair wage scheme, so they can cut it cheaper – unless Prowse sells his granite at a loss. So that's that. I don't know why the Admiralty can't do a simple thing, and buy our own stone for their dratted setts – but no! Scandinavian is cheaper, so they'll—'

An angry bellow interrupted him. 'Coombs! Coombs! What in tarnation are you playing at? Get yourself back to work at once!' One of the overseers was lumbering towards them, his face crimson with anger.

Jamie lifted his broken shovel aloft in explanation. 'Here, I'd best be getting on or I won't have any job to lose. Thing is though, Dan, if it does come to it, you fancy trying down the mines with me?'

Dan shook his head. 'Might do better further up the county. There's big stone quarries there. I'm a black powder man, Jamie lad, don't know what else I'm fit for. Dynamite it is they use, down the mines. All they got to do is make a hole, see, open up the seam – not like us, trying carefully to split off a piece of workable stone without cracking it or blowing it to bits.' He shook his head. 'Anyway, might not come to that. Let's wait and hear what Prowse has got to say.' He nodded at Jamie and strode off, before the overseer reached them.

But Prowse, when he came, was not encouraging. He tried to be. He stood up on a cart and talked to them, the quarry sounding unnaturally still.

'Now, we're not thinking to start putting people off,' he said. 'At least, not yet awhile. We've got local contracts, like we've always had. So really we're no worse off than we were before this contract came about. We can go on selling road stone, and there's the monumental work as well, so don't think that it'll come to closing down. But I can't disguise it from you, it's going to make things hard. We were having trouble as it is, with all this foreign stuff they're bringing in. We cut a thousand tons more stone last year, and still made less profit than the year before. I don't see how we can go on like that – there'll have to be some changes by and by . . . It won't be yet a while – give some of you a chance to look out for something else. And maybe it won't come to it at all. One of the big quarries further up the country got a job last week, I heard, supplying granite for a great bridge somewhere. And there's quarrymen wanted in America – I'll gladly give anyone of you a character. But if you want to stick by me and see, I'll do my best for you.'

He got down from the cart, to general muttering. There was a even a smattering of applause. Prowse was a decent sort of chap, and 'tweren't his fault they beggers at the Addlemonty don't know good stone when they got un,' as Old Tom said. But it was a sober workforce who trickled home that night, though Prowse let them go off early, just this once.

Victoria had thrown caution to the winds. It wasn't really bad, she told herself. She had done everything she was supposed to do. She had practised the pianoforte (dull!), done a little of her sampler (duller still!), met with the chairwoman of the ladies' guild and talked about the flowers for the church (dull, dull, dull, dull, dull!). And then she had spent an hour with Miss Boff, listening to her babbling on about the 'secret meaning of the Pilgrimage' which was so mind-shatteringly dull that Victoria felt she could not bear another minute. She'd even finished the last book that Bella'd lent to her, so there wasn't even reading to take refuge in.

In the end, she'd slipped out of the house unseen, like a dog escaping from its collar, and – despite the spiteful little showers – had set off towards the cliffs again. There was still half an hour of daylight, and even if she didn't venture far, anything was better than being cooped up there, like one of Mrs Roseworthy's chickens in its pen. She was prepared for weather this time too, with sturdy cape, umbrella and galoshes, and she wasn't being disobedient. No one had actually told her *not* to go out walking in the rain.

It was rather nice, in fact. Not the wind and wet – that was just unpleasant – but this feeling of stolen freedom, and wicked derring-do. Quite like one of the intrepid heroines in Bella's books. And it wasn't as if she'd done something really naughty, like taking the bicycle.

Deedee had a old machine, a gift from a grateful parishioner, and she had learned to ride it when she was young. But Miss Boff had vetoed that years ago, after a muddy misadventure with a ditch. 'Well-bred young ladies don't ride bicycles, Victoria! You might have hurt yourself. And just look at the state of your skirts!' So that was the end of long lovely wanders down the lanes, and expeditions to unfrequented cliffs.

Deedee, of course, was not subject to such strictures, and he still used the bicycle for calls around the parish, or even out to St Just to visit Mr Pencarrow on days like this. The household did keep an ancient pony and a trap, of course – or rather the next-door farmer kept it for them – but the bicycle saved all the bother of catching Bluebell and getting her hitched up just for short journeys, Deedee said, and he was getting far too old to walk. Miss Boff strongly disapproved: 'People will think it very odd, a respectable clergyman of middle years pedalling around the parish like an errand boy. Tongues will wag, Victoria, mark my words, and I've told your father so, though of course I would not presume to tell him what to do.'

It wasn't fair, Victoria thought crossly. If she'd been born a boy she could do anything she liked. Ride a bicycle if she wanted to, go out walking in the rain. Look at those two fellows coming now, across the field, up to the tops of their boots in squelch, and not caring about it in the least. Nobody was going to tell them off if they came in with muddy hems, or tramped home across the graveyard grass.

They were two young men from the quarry, Victoria realized, as they reached the stile. What were they doing here, at this time of day? The quarry didn't usually close till dark. It was rather uncomfortable, in fact, coming across them like this. She didn't have any real errand, and they were staring at her – unsurprisingly. Miss Boff could have said 'I told you so!' Well-brought up young ladies didn't go out strolling in the wet.

She hesitated. Would it seem too awfully pointed to turn around and go back the way she'd come? Perhaps it would. Suppose they followed her? They had crossed the stile by now and were standing there, looking at her with undisguised surprise.

She would ignore them, that's what she would do. Walk straight past them without a glance. They weren't really threatening, when you came to look. They seemed to be talking very seriously.

'They're looking for quarry men in America,' the fairer one was saying. 'Might go there if things turn really bad. But I shan't say anything at home, just yet. And I shouldn't either, Jamie, if I was you. Time enough, if it comes to it. No point worrying the womenfolk, my dad always says.'

He wasn't a bad-looking boy, in fact, though he was bold. He hadn't taken his eyes off her all the time he was speaking to his friend. Strong fellow, too, from the way his shoulders rippled underneath his shirt. She averted her eyes, quickly. Whatever was she thinking of!

Whatever it was, certainly she wasn't thinking where she put her feet! Straight into a puddle, over her galoshes and muddy water right into her buttoned boots. 'Ahh!' In her confusion she lowered her umbrella and an unkind gust of wind promptly turned it inside out. She stopped, helpless with embarrassment, and the young man hurried over to her side.

'You all right, are you, miss? Only . . .' he was most polite. A nice voice too, sort of gravelly. His kindness made her feel more ashamed than ever. 'If there's anything we can do to help . . . ?'

'No, no!' she said. 'I was out walking, and . . . as you can see . . .' She looked at her umbrella hopelessly.

He took it from her unprotesting hand, turned out of the breeze, and rearranged the spokes. One of them was broken, but he turned it right-side out, and it formed a sort of cover once again. 'Just don't you let the wind get under it again,' he advised. 'Now, you sure that you're all right? You haven't got a carriage anywhere?'

Victoria wished that the puddles would open up and swallow her. This time from head to toe.

'No, no,' she said. 'You're very kind, but I've come from the vicarage, that's all.'

28

'It is Miss Flower, after all!' The young man turned towards his friend. 'I said I thought so, but we weren't sure. With you out walking like this and everything.' He seemed to recollect himself and pulled off his cap. 'I'm Daniel Olds, miss, by the way, and this is Jamie Coombs. He's from Polvidden, I live further on. We can walk with you, if you like – it's getting dark and 'tisn't really safe, you know, out on the roads like this alone. Tramps, there might be, drunk men . . . anything, or you'll fall into a proper puddle in the darkness and get drenched. Where were you making for?'

There was no possible dignified answer to this. Victoria attempted to deflect the question. 'Coombs, is it? From Polvidden? I think I called upon your sisters earlier. At number nine? I was delivering some nourishing jelly.'

She'd almost added 'to the poor'. She blushed. This was ridiculous. She sounded condescending, like Bella's mother talking to the staff. And her clothes were getting drenched while she was standing here. She was going to make some bold excuse and leave, but Daniel – nice old-fashioned name – put in, 'I suppose that's what you were doing now, Miss Flower? Out on some mission of mercy?'

'No,' Victoria said. 'Or rather, yes. In a peculiar sort of way. But you are quite right, Mr Olds. It's getting late and I am getting wet. I think I'd better leave it for another time. Good day.' And off she limped, though it was hard to be dignified with one boot full of water and a lopsided umbrella with a broken spoke.

She was almost sure those two young men were laughing at her as she went and that felt like punishment enough. But then, when she got home Deedee saw her arrive and gave her the dressing-down of her life.

Three

J amie and Daniel walked back to Polvidden through the rain.
'Odd thing that was,' Daniel said.

Jamie laughed. 'Come out to see you, more than like. Everyone else seems to. Leastways, my sister Mollie does.'

'What're you on about now?' Dan said, but he found that he
was laughing too. Somehow that strange encounter with Miss
Flower had broken the gloom which had surrounded them till
now.

'My sister Mollie,' Jamie said again. 'Surely to heaven you
must have noticed, Dan? Out to see you every night she is,
sure as clockwork, like the weather woman in Auntie Annie's
clock.'

Dan rubbed a roughened hand through his damp hair and
smiled. 'Annie Hoskins ain't no aunt of mine, Jamie boy,' he
said, pulling on his cap again. 'How am I supposed to know
about her dratted clock?' But of course he did. You couldn't live
in Polvidden and escape that clock.

Famous, it was. Annie Hoskins was so proud of it. Poor old
soul lived in a tiny cottage, one room up and one room down –
though she was so crippled with arthritis that she couldn't climb
the stairs. Didn't have two sticks to rub together, apart from the
clock, and that had been a farewell present from her old employer. It came from 'furrin parts' and was wound up by pulling
down a sort of chain. An old man came out when it was going to
rain and an old woman if it would be fine – though people who
had seen it muttered that you could tell more about the weather
any day by looking at the sky.

30

Coombs dug Daniel in the ribs and grinned. 'There y'are, Dan lad. What did I tell 'ee.' They had reached Polvidden Row by this time, and he gestured to where his sister Mollie was walking up the street towards them. 'In this easterly and all.'

'What d'you expect me to do?' Dan said, though he knew perfectly well.

Jamie gave his slow grin. 'Ask 'er to walk out with you one day. Make her day, that would. Might as well, while you've got time – or Prowse's will be closed, and then you'll wish you 'ad.'

'Take her where?' Dan asked.

'Down the lane to look for primroses, or summat. Go out with the May horns – I dunno. You're the one's supposed to be so clever.'

'May horns?' Daniel exclaimed. 'It isn't May time for weeks yet.'

'Well, think of something else then, if you're in such a hurry,' Jamie grinned. 'But Harry Varfell's got his first horns made. I saw one yesterday. Anyhow, you ask her, then you'd see. Bite your 'and off, she would, see if she doesn't.'

'Get off with you!' Daniel said, but he was grinning. In fact, if a man was going to go out playing tin trumpets on a May morning, he could do a darn sight worse than do it with Mollie Coombs. Striking, she was, with her head held high under that great waterfall of reddish hair, and a pair of brown eyes that looked right at you, laughing – instead of the giggly sideways glances that was all you got from most of the village girls.

Jamie nudged him in the ribs again. 'Go on then, afore she wears out the pavement waiting. Or if you don't, I shall do it for 'ee! I'll tell her you were asking for 'er – you see if I don't – soon as ever she comes 'ome.'

Daniel laughed. 'Oh, go on with you!' But he handed his bundle to his friend, took off his cap and put it in his pocket, ran his fingers through his rain-spattered hair, then spat on his hands and rubbed them on his shirt.

31

Jamie turned to Mollie who was just approaching them by this time. 'Hello, Moll. There, look a bit more like, does he?'

She pushed back the shawl a little and looked at them in surprise. 'Look all right to me,' she said, colouring a little.

Jamie grinned. 'There y'are Dan, lad. What did I tell 'ee?' He winked at them ferociously. 'I'm going over the blacksmith's for a minute now, to see can Old Man Varfell fix me a new handle on this blessed spade. I can't seem to do it right, no how. I've broken the damty thing again. Third time this month, that is. Shan't be long.' And he was gone, turning up the collar of his coat against the rain, across the road and into the blacksmith's shop. And he'd taken Daniel's bundle with him.

'What was all that about?' Mollie said. She stood back in the shelter of the wall out of the rain. 'What's got you preening yourself in the street, like something in the musical halls?'

Oh, what the heck, Dan thought. He might as well. He grinned. 'Can't go asking girls to go out with the May horns, looking like a scarecrow, can I now?'

She coloured again, but met his eyes boldly with her own laughing ones. 'Depends who you're thinking of asking.'

He leaned back on his heels in the rain and folded his arms, looking at her from head to toe. 'Just deciding that,' he said, matching her tone. 'Know anyone who'd be interested, do you?'

'Might do,' she said, pretending to step past him. Her cheeks were the colour of her skirts by this time, but her eyes were dancing. 'Well, are you going to ask her then? Or am I going to stand here getting drenched like a hitching post in a puddle?'

'Suit yourself,' Dan said. She made a face at him. 'You'll come then, will you, Moll?'

'Suppose I might as well,' Mollie said. She pulled the shawl up tighter round her face. 'Keep *you* out of worse mischief, at least. Up at the stile outside St Evan church as usual?'

'I suppose so. Haven't heard, as yet. Harry Varfell is arranging it. Made all the May horns last year something beautiful. Not just beating out tin cans, but he does something when he rolls them up – I don't know what. Best Mayhorns I ever heard in all my life – and I've been out every year since I could walk.'

Mollie laughed up at him, the raindrops making little rivers on her cheeks. 'Hark at you. Think it was an orchestra, you would, stead of just a gaggle of boys and girls, tooting like fifty cats in torment. Just as well it's only once a year.'

Daniel was about to make some retort, but at that moment Jamie came out of the blacksmith's. He was carrying a long, thin, tapering cone of unpainted tin, with a crude mouthpiece at one end of it. He waved it at his sister in greeting as he came up to them. ''Ere, Mollie,' he said, with a wink at Dan. 'See what I bought you. Cost me an 'apenny, it did too. Just in case you were thinking of goin' out with the horns, this year.'

Mollie put her hands on her hips and looked from one man to the other. 'Here, what's all this? You two plotting this together?'

'I didn't put him up to it, honest!' Daniel protested, laughing.

Mollie gave him a look which told him that she did not believe a word of it. She took the horn, nevertheless, with a little toss of her head. 'I don't know what you two are like!'

'Don't you pay no heed to him,' Daniel said quickly. 'I'll call for you at number nine then, May morning, soon as ever it gets light. Walk up with you to the stile.'

'I suppose so. Mind you don't go waking the household then. I dunno what they'll think. I haven't been out with the horns for years.'

'Get off with you,' Jamie said, trying unsuccessfully to shelter with them underneath the wall. 'I remember you were going to be a May queen once. You had your dress and everything.'

'So I may've, but I never was. Got the fever, didn't I, and couldn't go. So that was that. Never been out maying since.'

'Till now,' Dan said.

She threw back her head and looked at him, her hair clinging damply to her cheeks and the shawl plastered to her head with damp. 'Till now,' she said. She raised the tin horn to her lips and gave him a derisory toot. 'Still sound like a tormented cat to me!' And then she was gone, hunching her shoulders against the rain.

'What did you want to go and do that for?' Daniel said, snatching back his parcel as he spoke. 'Thinks we two are making a game of her, now.'

Jamie was unrepentant. 'Didn't seem to stop her, did it? Anyway I wanted to make sure you asked. Harry Varfell would have asked her otherwise. He's had his eyes on her for months. I believe that's why he's started on the horns already – wouldn't let me have it, till I said it was for her.'

'I believe that's why you went to see him in the first place,' Daniel complained. 'How didn't you take your shovel up the quarry forge, like you were going to?'

Jamie made a face. 'I tried, but they're too busy sharpening the jumpers, and the chisels for the dressing sheds. When you're just a trammer, they always make you wait.'

That was a danger sign, Jamie starting on about the trams. Dan said quickly, 'Don't know why you bother messing about with that old spade anyhow. Don't the quarry give you one of theirs, these days?'

Jamie shrugged. 'Too damty short and light for me, those machine-made things. Give me a proper old-fashioned shovel any time. Old Man Varfell made a spade like this for Fayther thirty years ago . . .'

'And with two new ends and five new handles it's as good as new! I know! I heard you tell that one a hundred times.'

'Well!' Jamie said. 'If it's good enough for Fayther, it's good enough for me. And Varfell says he'll get it done, tonight – I can pick it up outside the forge first thing, on the way – and pay him Friday when the wages come. Might be glad of that spade, somewhere else.'

'And I'll buy myself a horn and all,' Dan said. 'Daresay I can run to that. Though I aren't made of 'apences, especially now!' They parted at the door of number nine, and Daniel walked on in the fading light, back to the chaos, tea and squabbling that was home.

In fact, they were eating sprats when he got in. Merelda had got hold of some, from that young fisherman of hers, and was giving herself airs over it. She'd fried them up on the skillet, over the trivet on the fire, and was now doling them out a spoonful at a time like a miser parting with his gold.

'Kept some for you, Dan'l,' she said, leaping to her feet as soon as he'd taken off his boots and put his face around the door.

'Should think so and all,' Ma said, looking up from buttering the bread at the top of the table. 'Don't know where this family'd be, without Daniel's bit of money coming in. Move up a bit there, Kitty, let the poor fellow have a bit of bench.'

Nine-year-old Kitty moved her bony bottom half an inch, and Daniel slid on to the seat beside her.

'Two spoons for you,' Merelda said, wielding the frying pan again. 'And two for Father and for Zac, as well, when they get home. And that's the end of that, Jimmy Olds, so it's no good you looking with hungry eyes at me. You've had more'n your fair share already, seems to me. Proper little gannet you are – eating half your mother's meal and all.'

'Don't go on so, Melda. I only gave him one or two. Child needs a bit of something,' Mother said, spearing a thick slice of bread and holding it out towards the youngest child. Lucy, with all the solemnity of her four and a half years, took it from the end of the knife and passed it carefully to Dan, leaving on it the marks of five small stubby fingers, sticky with fried fish.

Melda handed him a plate of steaming sprats. They were a rare treat these days, since Daniel's eldest brother, Reuben, had got himself washed out to sea and drowned last year, fishing with his father off Penvarris rocks. Mother had stoutly refused to let any of them go out there again, though what the menfolk used to catch had often been a welcome addition to the family table. Father had blustered and sworn, of course, and even thrown a saucepan at the wall, but in the end she had her way – as Mother usually did, where household matters were concerned.

'Smells good,' Daniel said appreciatively, spreading the sprats out on his bread, and making a sandwich of his supper. 'And tastes even better,' he added a moment later.

'Don't encourage her, for heavens sake.' That was the eleven-year-old gannet, Jimmy, who – despairing of more sprats – was tucking into bread and jam instead. 'The fuss Merelda makes over a few sprats, you'd think she'd caught the dratted things herself.'

'Language, Jimmy!' Ma said. 'Your father'd make you wash your mouth out with soap and water, if he heard you talk like that.'

'Well, he isn't 'ere, is he?' Jimmy said, indistinctly, through a mouthful of jam.

'Won't be for a few minutes, either,' Daniel broke in quickly, to avoid an argument. 'Bit of a problem on the eastern face. Charge didn't go off quite right, and the piece of granite they were cutting's come out awkwardly. Couldn't get the crane teeth on to her, so the quarry captain got some of the men to stay behind, to set up some ropes and pulleys on the top and ease her down by hand.' He didn't say anything about Prowse's news. Time enough for Dad to tell her that.

Ma paused in her bread slicing to look at him sharply.

He knew what she was thinking. 'It's all right, Ma. It's all straightforward now. Might have been nasty earlier, when they were getting the ropes round her, but they've got her hanging free and she's coming nicely now. Only, of course, you got to take it slowly – specially with the light going, like it is. Zac has stayed behind to be the boy.'

Ma had resumed her slicing. 'Wonder you didn't stop and give a hand and all,' she scolded. 'What with your brother and your father there.'

That was unjust. She'd have worried more if all of them were late. Dad operated the cranes on the stone-shifting team – that was a skilled job too – and a casual pair of hands was more likely to be a hindrance than a help. However, he said nothing beyond, 'Dad said I was to come on home, let you know they would be late. Save you worrying.'

As if anything could do that, he thought. Fear of something happening to one of them was Ma's constant nightmare – the more so since Reuben had been washed away. And she'd worry even more when Prowse's news got out.

'So don't you start worrying for nothing,' he added.

Ma nodded absently, but it didn't help. Daniel could tell that from the way that she went on cutting bread – mechanically, as if her mind was somewhere else. By the time Father and Zac arrived, mud-stained and bone-weary from their task, there was more bread sliced than was ever likely to be eaten at one meal, even with Jimmy the Gannet there to help.

Bella called round to the vicarage a day or two later bearing a copy of *Vanity Fair*. 'My brother says I shouldn't bring you this. He says it's scandalous – about a young woman mad on men, money and power – and isn't at all suitable for you.' Bella gave her girlish giggle and handed Victoria the book. 'I thought I'd tell you. I knew it would make you like it even more!'

Victoria found herself giggling back. 'I will. And I'm sure Deedee wouldn't mind. He thinks well of Mr Thackaray. It's Miss Boff who would find it "unsuitable for Lent". We've finished *The Pilgrim's Progress* now and we're ploughing through *Paradise Regained*, though I doubt Miss Boff even knows it's poetry. I know one thing, listening to it is enough to make you believe in purgatory!'

Bella looked unimpressed by this piece of churchy lore, so she added quickly, 'And thank you for inviting me to "after birthday" tea. What should I wear, do you think?'

Bella gave her dimpled smile. 'Oh, anything you like, Vicki. I expect it will be only you and I.' She leaned forward and gave Victoria's arm a squeeze. 'Only I couldn't have bear to have a birthday without you.'

'I'm not to meet this famous Petroc, then? I thought he was staying in the house. Why, what's the matter Bella? Why the face?'

Bella laughed ruefully. 'Oh nothing – or rather, just something my brother Horry said: how marrying Petroc was mapped out for me. I sometimes think you don't know how fortunate you are, Victoria. Free to do almost anything you like.'

'What, with Deedee forbidding me to go to balls, and Miss Boff with her dragon eyes on me?' She didn't mention that disastrous walk.

Bella had the grace to laugh. 'No, I suppose not. It's just as bad for you. It's just that sometimes . . . oh, I don't know. I feel as my life is like that piece of silk that Mama's ordered for my gown – already cut to shape for me and pinned for sewing up. No doubt it's very pretty, but it would be nice to choose!'

'Bella!' Victoria was surprised.

Bella giggled. 'I know. I'm being silly aren't I? And talking of sewing, that reminds me, I shall have to go. I have an appointment with the dressmaker at twelve, and Mama will be furious if I'm late.'

'Hold on a minute and I'll come as far as the corner of the lane with you,' Vicki said. 'I've got some more of Mrs Roseworthy's jelly to deliver. It's waiting on the hallstand for me now. I'll just put on my hat and cape and come.'

In fact, there was quite a lot of jelly to deliver. After last week's escapade she'd had to cajole Deedee very hard to be allowed out of the house at all.

She hurried upstairs, skewered her hated bonnet on to her head, and flung the fawn cape around her shoulders. She grimaced at herself in the mirror as she picked up her gloves. There was Bella, effortlessly stylish in her green riding habit and perky hat, while she, Victoria, looked like a dowdy rabbit in her muted browns. She stuck out a tongue at her reflection and hurried back downstairs.

Bella was waiting for her in the hall. Miss Boff popped her head out of the morning room as they were opening the door, but seeing Bella she withdrew again. Victoria could not resist a smile. Accompanied by Miss Cardew, she was evidently 'safe' from acts of social impropriety. All the same, Victoria was anxious to be off, and swiftly led the way down to the gate.

Bella had ridden over with her groom, and now she and Vicki

had to wait impatiently while he detached himself from drinking stone ginger underneath the trees with Old Sam Roseworthy, the aged cousin of the housekeeper, who came in now and then to scythe the grass. He came over and untied the horse, and held the reins so Isabella could mount.

While he was doing this, a trap drew up, driven by a dapper fellow in a cloak and hat. Stephen Pencarrow, by the look of it, a friend of Deedee's come about the books.

He doffed his hat to Vicki. 'Good afternoon, Miss Flower,' he said, and smiled at her in his rather leering way.

'Mr Pencarrow. Father's expecting you. I'm just out with a friend as you can see.' Victoria had never liked the man, and she was glad for an excuse to hurry off.

Bella was in the saddle now, and wheeled the horse to walk beside her friend. 'Vicki,' she breathed, bending so that the groom behind them could not hear. 'Who is that man?'

'Mr Pencarrow. You heard me call him that.' Vicki was secretly impatient.

Isabella giggled. 'Yes I know. But *who* is he? I don't remember seeing him before.'

Despite herself, Victoria found that she was whispering back like a conspirator. 'That comes of you going into Penzance to school. The family house is over near St Just, but he plans to buy a farm or two round here, he has some notion of specializing in some special kind of cows, and flowers for the London market. And he collects rare books like Deedee does, and that's all I know about him, I'm afraid.'

Bella sighed dramatically. 'He's certainly a handsome man.'

'Oh Bella, don't be so absurd. Stephen must be thirty-five if he's a day. And he has a lady friend in Penzance, I hear. I don't know when he thinks to her marry her, but they've been walking out for years.'

'Don't make that disapproving Miss Boff face at me. I'm not about to eat him, I suppose. Though I should love to meet him, I confess. You could arrange it, Vicki, couldn't you? You know him socially, and you're such a trick at things.'

Victoria shook her head. 'Nonsense,' she said, laughing. 'You've hardly met the man. And what about this Petroc chap of yours?'

'I've hardly met him, either,' Bella said. 'Oh come on, Vic, don't frown like that, it's only fun. Haven't you ever seen a handsome man, yourself, and thought, "I'd not mind seeing him again"?' She laughed. 'Oh dear, I've made you blush. Perhaps you haven't thought that after all! I have, I assure you – very often.'

The groom had caught them up by now, and Bella said, in a more public tone, 'But here's the parting of our ways. I'll have to go, or Mama will be furious. I tell you what. I'll come and see you properly next week, when we can have a longer chance to talk. On Friday, perhaps, if you're not busy with Miss Boff that day?' She grinned wickedly. 'I suppose there's no chance that your Mr Pencarrow would happen to be calling then?'

'Oh Bella, don't be so absurd!' But she could not help laughing.

Bella turned the horse and trotted down the lane, but Victoria lingered at the stile. This was the very place, she thought, where she had seen a handsome man herself, though she was not likely to see him often. Even less likely than Bella was to get to meet Stephen Pencarrow.

However, she could not seem to be rid of Mr Pencarrow. She saw him again a little later on, driving towards Polvidden in his trap. She wondered if he'd heard about her escapade, and had been sent to see that she was safe. She was almost inclined to think so from the way he smiled so broadly and saluted her ironically with his whip.

Mollie was carrying eggs home from the farm when a trap came thundering past, so quickly that she was obliged to take to the hedges and flatten herself against the dry-stone wall.

'Drat the fellow!' she muttered to herself. 'Covered me with spatters, and just look at my hems! Filthy wet and muddy from standing in the grass! My good blue skirt as well. And I only got it dried and ironed yesterday. Serves me right for wearing it, just on the chance of running into Daniel Olds. Well, at least there's no eggs broken – that's a mercy, anyhow.'

She took the basket from the wall, where she had thrust it for safety, and went on walking back along the road. It was a long way to Crowdie's farm – unnecessarily long, in fact. There were a dozen places nearer home where a girl could buy eggs if she wanted them, but Crowdie it had always been in mother's day, and it wouldn't have felt right to change, somehow. It was worth the extra walk, besides. Crowdie was good to them – always had been – and sometimes slid in a bit of cheese or butter when he knew that times were hard, and he always let you have the cracked eggs cheap.

There was a wizened broccoli in her basket now. 'No good for market,' Crowdie had said, gruffly. 'You take it home, see if it will do your Eadie any good.' Crowdie would never make a fortune, people said – unless it was in friends.

She was so engrossed in her thoughts that she did not notice the young man in the field until he called her name. 'Mollie! Mollie Coombs!' She turned to see a sandy-haired young giant in a leather apron gallumphing across the grass towards her.

'Thought it was you,' he panted, when he reached the gate. He was a large lad, strong and strapping, and his big good-natured face was scarlet with exertion.

'You didn't ought to run like that, Harry Varfell. You'll do yourself a mischief,' Mollie said.

Harry laughed. 'Tisn't you, my handsome, it's that wretched colt. Cast a shoe yesterday, and the lady up the house wanted him cold shoeing, but she couldn't catch him, and her son's away, so Father sent me here to do it.' He mopped his face. 'Well, she couldn't catch him, and no more can I. Half an hour I've been chasing after the damty thing, and I haven't got him now.' He grinned. 'Still, just as well. If I'd 'a caught 'un sooner, I shouldnt've been here, and then I'd have missed the chance to talk to you.'

Mollie couldn't help laughing at this contorted logic. 'Get

off with you! The forge is only just across the road from
number nine. You can talk to me any time you want to, in the
street.'

'Well – no, I can't, so much,' Harry said, suddenly serious.
'There's father with his eye on me, for one thing, and the people
in the village for another, always someone with their curtains
twitching and their ears flapping. And when I *did* want to come
out yesterday and talk to you, there you were chatting to that
Daniel Olds . . .' He paused. 'Your brother bought a Mayhorn
off me a day or two ago. Said it was for you.'

'It was. He told me you'd started making them again. Some
fine job you made of it as well.'

'Yes, well,' Harry said, looking pleased and proud. 'Thing is –
I know it's weeks away and all – I was wondering . . . if you are
thinking to go out with the horns, you wouldn't care to come
with me?' His face was redder than ever now. 'Course, if you
don't want to . . .' he added, as she hesitated.

'Isn't that, Harry, it's just that I already promised Daniel Olds.
Just yesterday,' she said, glad that she had a real excuse to give.
Harry was a nice fellow, but he was so clodhopping – no wonder
that colt had got away from him.

He seemed to read her thoughts. 'Seems I'm too slow, as
usual,' he said.

Poor Harry, he looked so disappointed, she quite felt for him.
'Still,' she said, to comfort him, 'you'll be there, won't you?
Picking may, and watching the procession, and down at the
maypole in the afternoon? I 'spect I'll see you anyway.'

'I suppose so. Isn't the same thing, though, is it. Still, if you've
promised Daniel Olds . . . I didn't know that you were walking
out with him.'

'I'm not,' Mollie said. 'Well, not really, anyhow. Just said that
I'd go out to the horns with him, that's all.' She saw Harry's face
clear and – fearing she had said too much – she added hastily,
'Better get back with these here eggs, though, now. Eadie'll be
wondering where I'm to.'

Harry nodded. 'Perhaps I'll see you in Polvidden, then.'

He was so eager that she smiled and said, 'P'haps.' And when she looked back, a few minutes later, he was still standing at the gate, pulling his battered cap on peak-side hindermost, and gazing after her.

Four

Bella didn't come on Friday after all. She had caught a chill, the note explained, from going riding to St Just and getting caught out in the rain.

Riding to St Just? Victoria thought. More likely hoping to run into Stephen Pencarrow on the road, and then pretend it was an accident. Still, if so, she'd paid the price. The doctor had ordered to her bed, and although he said she'd soon be on her feet again he was coming in to see her every day.

Victoria was doubly sorry to be without her friend. Not only did she miss the company, but Wednesday had seen the start of Lent, and the inevitable dreariness of that. All eggs, butter and sugar were banished from the house, together with red meat and relishes. Flowers had been exiled from the vicarage, too, just as they were taken from the church till Easter day, and though there was no want of anything, and Mrs Roseworthy had a dozen pleasant ways of cooking fish, there was always something drab about the season.

As, of course, there was supposed to be. Deedee believed in setting an example in these things – any delicacies that arrived at the vicarage in Lent were given to the poor.

So, without her occasional companion, Victoria was even more than usually bored. Not even Miss Boff could object to walks, now that the weather was turning fine, and she set out one fine March afternoon, to walk the mile or so down to the cove, with a pot of the famous chicken jelly in a basket, and one of Bella's novels hidden underneath. Miss Boff – spotting the jelly – had even approved the enterprise. But when Victoria got there, it

44

was too breezy by the sea to sit and read, and she found that she was home again by three.

There were none of the additional services for Lent today, not even choir practice or Sunday school rehearsals for the Easter play with which she might have occupied herself. She wandered into the kitchen, but Mrs Roseworthy had banished her from there.

'There's to be a visitor,' she said. 'A most important one, so I've got a deal to do. Now don't ask questions, Miss Victoria. I'm not to say no more to anyone.' And she wouldn't either, though it wasn't like her to be secretive.

Victoria looked into the drawing room. Miss Boff was writing letters at the desk with such ferocious concentration that Vicki tiptoed out again, and gave up any hope of learning more from her.

In the end, she wandered up to Deedee's study. He was surrounded by books, some in piles and some in a packing case, but when she knocked he got up from his desk at once, and came towards her with a beaming smile.

'Vicki. This is an unexpected pleasure. Not busy with lessons or your piano this afternoon?'

'I came to see what you were doing, Deedee. You've started sorting out your books, I see.'

'Looking at the books which Stephen brought for me.' He picked up a volume from the desk. 'Look at this one now, fine binding, and a few good woodcuts too. But I'll need to rearrange my shelves a bit. With Jonathan coming for a visit, I can hardly leave the study as it is.'

'Your friend coming here?' Victoria was surprised. She'd not even had to wheedle the information from him.

'He has agreed to come and take a service here. It will be quite an occasion for the church.' He smiled. 'Of course, we haven't told the congregation yet; there are a few arrangements he has to make. He has his own parish to think about, you know.'

Vicki nodded. 'But you're sure he'll come?'

'He says he will if it is possible – and when he does, I may have other news.'

She looked at him enquiringly.

'I wrote to him that I was thinking of a curate, and since his present one is looking for a change, he's bringing him down here to see the place. It seems to me an excellent solution. It would help me, and it would give you a little respectable companionship of your own age.' He was smiling at her broadly.

'Deedee!' she could not help but laugh. 'One cannot simply like a man to order, you know. He might be simply dreadful when he comes.'

Deedee nodded. 'Jonathan thinks highly of the man – it seems he's very musical as well. Just what the parish needs. And since he's already been ordained, it only needs the bishop to agree. However, nothing is decided yet, of course. We shall discuss it further when they come. Now, would you care to help me catalogue these books? There must be at least an hour before we need to change for tea.'

So Vicki spent a busy afternoon, useful and occupied for once. Whatever the decision about the curacy, she thought, the future visit was already changing things for the better.

The ice had been broken now, of course, and when Daniel saw Mollie again, it seemed a natural thing to stop and chat.

'Well, give a girl a smile then. You look like a month of Sundays all at once,' Mollie said a few days later, when – for the third time in a week – he met her in the street.

Daniel tried to force a grin. 'Truth is, there isn't a right lot to smile about today. I thought you might have heard. You haven't seen your Fayther or Jamie yet?'

Mollie shook her head. 'I haven't been home since they got in. I've been in seeing Auntie Anne all this afternoon. Half crippled with her knees she is, poor soul. Needs a bit of help, this time of day.'

Daniel had a pretty shrewd suspicion that the timing of these visits to Auntie Anne were less to do with Annie's knees and more to do with his return from work, but naturally he didn't say so. What he did say was: 'Well, daresay you'll hear about it soon enough.'

She looked at him sharply then. 'What is it, Dan? Somebody hurt again? Can't be one of ours, or someone would have said. Here, it wasn't your Zaccary or your dad, was it?'

'No, just these talks about the pit, that's all. They're putting people off down there next week.' He saw her face and added hastily. 'Don't you go worrying about me. I expect I'll do – I'm a black powder man and they can't cut stone without.' He didn't point out that there were several others working at the quarry.

She looked a little happier, and he hurried on. 'I daresay your folks will be all right, in any case – even if they can't stay on with Prowse. Always a place for men like them, so long as there are people wanting graves.'

'I suppose so.' Mollie said. Fayther and Stan worked in the stone-dressing sheds, shaping and polishing the stone.

'I know so,' Daniel said, and then to cheer her up: 'Oh, let's not dwell on it any more. Bad enough when it happens, if it does! Come over to the blacksmith's shop with me, and see if I can get one of Harry Varfell's horns.' He thought she would be eager but to his surprise she turned pink and shook her head.

'No, you go on Dan – I'd best get home to Eadie. Those men'll be starved half to death by now, and she's only just got back on her feet again.' She threw him a smile. 'But mind *you* go and get your May horn now. I'm counting on it.'

So, he did go over, though there was not much joy in it. Harry Varfell took his order without a trace of his usual good humour. Even he had heard the quarry news, it seemed. 'Cost you a halfpenny that will,' he said, ungraciously. 'And you'll have to have 'un, if you've ordered 'un. Sure you can afford to do it, are you, with all the problems down at Prowse's now? Wouldn't rather wait a bit and see?'

'No, I don't think so,' Daniel said. 'I'll have worse problems than paying for a ha'penny May horn if the quarry shuts.'

'Have it your way,' Harry said, fetching a stumpy pencil from behind his ear and a grimy notebook from the skirt pocket of his leather apron. He wrote: 'Danniul Olds – 1 May horn' in his large uncertain hand, moving his tongue with concentration as he wrote. 'I wouldn't be a quarryman just now for all the world,' he said, with a kind of awful relish. 'You fellows couldn't think of settling down when you can't see where next week's work is coming from. No, better a solid job like this. Still be farriers a hundred years from now.' Then he escorted Daniel to the door, almost as if he could not wait to be rid of him.

Daniel went out in surprise. Harry was usually the soul of friendliness. What in the world had prompted that?

He was still wondering when someone called his name. He glanced down the street, and saw, of all things, Jimmy hurrying towards him, with Mollie not very far behind.

Mollie had barely had the time to take off her cloak and put her working pinny on before the hammering started at the door.

'Whoever in the world is that?' Eadie said, looking up from darning Jamie's socks. 'Wake little Stanley up, if they go on like that, and I haven't a minute ago got him to sleep.' She put the mending wool aside and made as if to get up from the chair, but Mollie forestalled her.

'You stay where you are. You're looking tired out. I shouldn't have left you on your own this afternoon. I might've known you'd try and scrub the floor or something equally as daft. You take it quietly, or you'll be taken bad again, and then where shall we be? I'll go.' She undid her pinny as she spoke and tied on a clean one in its place. You never knew who might be calling. She went towards the door. 'If it's that Miss Flower with her jelly again, you want me to let her in? I do believe it did you good last time.'

'S'pose so,' Eadie said, ungraciously. But it wasn't Miss Flower at the door. It was little Jimmy Olds, his sparrow-legs looking skinnier than ever in a pair of trousers that had been cut down for him, and socks and boots that were at least a size too big. He wore a man's cap pulled down on his head, balanced precariously on his ears.

' 'lo, Jimmy,' she said. 'What's all the racket then?'

'Sorry, miss,' he hesitated, his big eyes round as plates, 'only I was wondering, is our Daniel 'ere?' She was about to expostulate, when he went on: 'It's just, there's been an accident at home – our Lucy's fallen in the fire – and I've been sent to look for him. Someone said they'd seen you with him on the street.'

'Well, he isn't here. Went over to the Old Man Varfell's forge when he left me. Shouldn't be surprised if he's still there.' Then surprise gave way to sympathy, and she thought about Dan's family. Poor souls. First the trouble down the face, now this. She added, in a softer tone, 'I'll come with you. Just wait while I take my pinny off.' She suited the action to the word, but before she'd finished, Jimmy Olds was gone.

'You heard that?' she said to Eadie. 'I'm just going across to the forge a minute. And don't you think of getting up. There's a drop of stew in that saucepan – just wants heating through. The men can put it to the stove, for once. Where are they to, anyhow?'

'I sent them down the cove to see can they find some driftwood for the fire. I couldn't bear to have them in the house. Restless they were, the three of them, jumpy as a toad on a hot shovel. There's some meeting of the workers' society tonight. You know there's trouble down the quarry?'

Mollie made a little face. 'I heard. As if the Oldses didn't have enough to worry them today.'

'You know what Mother always used to say. Troubles are like herring gulls: when one comes, others follow,' Eadie said, but Mollie was in no mood to listen. She was already out of the door, and halfway up the street.

She saw Daniel just emerging from the blacksmith's place, with Jimmy scampering towards him. She quickened her pace, and reached the pair just in time to hear Daniel say, 'My lor! Poor little Lucy. Bad is she?'

'Bad enough. All her hand and arm. Ma's been doing what she can. She's tried bicarbonate and lavender to try and soothe the pain, and Mrs Brown next door's been very good – but it's no good. Dad says we'll have to have the doctor in. Zac's gone up to St Just to try and find him now. So Ma says can you come home quick, and I'm to go down the mine and fetch Merelda home.'

Merelda worked there on the surface, Mollie knew, breaking down the tin stone for the stamps.

'How's Zac getting to St Just?' Mollie enquired, joining in as though she were family too. 'Last horse bus will have gone long ago by the time he gets up to Penvarris Road.'

'He's set off walking,' Jimmy said. 'Or running, more like.'

'My dear life, it's miles,' Mollie said. 'Be dark before he gets there, and I'm sure the doctor won't come out here then.'

'Oh, he might do,' Daniel said. 'The doctor's very good. Came out when Lucy had trouble being born – nearly lost her then, we did, and Ma near bending the bedposts with the pain – and that was the middle of the night. And he didn't press us for the fee, although it took a month or two before we managed it. No, he'll come, if he thinks it warrants it – though how we'll pay for it's another thing.'

Mollie said, 'Wouldn't Crowdie take you in the cart?'

'He would've,' Jimmy said, 'if he'd been here. Ma sent me up the farm to ask. But it's Penzance market day today, and he's gone in there – and so has every other cart for miles. And I don't know anyone else round here who's got a horse'

'And I can't stand here gossiping,' Dan said. 'I'm wanted home. Not that I suppose there's much that I can do.'

'Well, I'll go on thinking, and I'll try to catch up Zaccary if I can.' Mollie was suddenly aware of Harry Varfell listening to them from inside the forge. 'Here, why not take Harry with you? He knows more about burns than anyone around here. Isn't that right, Harry?' But Daniel and Jimmy had already gone.

Harry lumbered out, his huge frame filling the door. 'Cold water, that's the thing for burns,' he said. 'We always have a bucket handy, just in case. Put it in and keep it there, as long as you can bear – and the sooner afterwards the better.'

Mollie gave him an absent-minded smile. 'Well, you go down and say so to the Olds.' She saw him hesitate. 'Will you do that, Harry? For me?'

He nodded slowly. 'For you then, Moll. And for the sake of that poor child. I'll take a bit of mother's Greasy Balm with me as well – I daresay Mrs Olds won't mind – and Father swears by it for burns. You coming with me, are you then?'

Mollie shook her head. 'Not me. You know the Oldses, you don't need me to come. I'm just thinking who I know has got a pony or a bicycle. Zac's set off to St Just on foot to get the doctor.'

'Pity there's no one here has got one of they there telephones, like they're getting up Penzance,' Harry said. 'Supposed to be wonderful, they are. Just imagine, you could telephone to someone up St Just and they would go and tell the doctor for you. Quick as that. But there you are. No good wishing for the moon. And not many folks round here have got a bicycle – except the policeman, and you can't go asking 'ee.'

Mollie looked at him. 'But I know somebody else who has!' She reached out impulsively and squeezed his arm. 'Bless you, Harry – you're a champion. You've given me an idea. I'll go and see what I can do. You tell the Oldses I'll look in later on.' When she left him to it he was smiling broadly, rubbing his elbow where her hand had been.

Five

'Victoria? Are you there, Victoria?' Miss Boff's voice floated through the bedroom door.

Vicki closed *Vanity Fair* and slid it underneath the bolster case. She smoothed down the pillows and got off the bed.

'Victoria?' the voice enquired again.

'Coming, Miss Boff.' She went to the bedroom door and opened it. Miss Boff was standing there, rigid and disapproving, like a poker in a brown dress.

'What an age it took you to answer me, Victoria. What have you been doing?' She tried to peer around her pupil and into the room as she spoke.

'Reading, Miss Boff,' Victoria replied. She gestured vaguely towards the bedside cabinet, where a copy of *Paradise Lost* lay innocently open. 'I'm sorry. Have you been calling me? I was so engrossed, I didn't hear.'

'I see. Well, if you want to come up here to read at this time of day, you should light the lamps, otherwise you'll damage your eyes. However, there will be no need for that now. Make yourself respectable and come downstairs. You have a visitor.'

'A visitor? This afternoon? For me?' Victoria was genuinely taken aback. Callers at the vicarage were common enough: tradespeople, clergymen, parishioners, and always people wanting help, from local businessmen to tramps. Visitors for Victoria were much less frequent.

Who could it be? Hardly Bella, she was still nursing her chill.

'I will tell the young lady you are coming. I've put her to wait

52

in the drawing room,' Miss Boff said with a sniff, and disappeared in the direction of the stairs.

Victoria made a pretence of rearranging her hair and went downstairs. So, Miss Boff did not approve much of this caller, whoever it was. That was encouraging. Well, she would soon know. She pushed open the door of the drawing room.

She was expecting some respectable young matron from the parish, so it was a shock to find the Coombs girl from Polvidden there. Her long flame-coloured hair had been shaken free, and she had exchanged that orange skirt for a more sober blue, her stockings were darned neatly and her blouse was clean, but she still reminded Victoria irresistibly of the gypsies who came round selling pegs. She was standing by the fireplace and staring into the flames. She looked up as Victoria came in.

'Miss Flower! My name's Mollie Coombs. I don't expect that you'll remember me . . .'

'Of course I do. Your sister was unwell. I brought her some jelly, I believe.' She could hardly have forgotten this striking-looking girl. 'You asked to speak to me?'

It sounded like Mrs Cardew and the cook again, and the girl flushed. 'You'll think I've got some cheek coming here . . .'

'Not at all,' Victoria said, automatically, although in fact she had been thinking something of the kind. 'You called about your sister, I suppose? Is she worse?' Probably wanting another jar of jelly. Well, she could have it, since she'd come for it, but it would have be made gently clear to her that it couldn't carry on – or everyone in the parish would try to follow suit.

'Tisn't about my sister, Miss Flower. It's about a little girl, lives not far from me. She's fallen in the fire, poor little mite, and burnt herself, quite bad. I'm friendly with the brother, that's how I heard.'

Victoria felt instantly contrite. She had misjudged the girl. She covered it by trying to sound crisp. 'Well, Miss Coombs, of course you can have some jelly for the child, but I'm afraid it sounds as if she needs rather more than that. Burns need medical attention. Has the doctor been sent for?'

'That's just it, Miss, that's what I've come about. I know the vicar's got a bicycle . . .' she hesitated. 'Would he lend it to us, do you think, to go and fetch the doctor at St Just?'

Victoria was seriously taken aback. 'I don't know what Papa would say, and I can hardly undertake for him. Perhaps you'd better speak to him yourself. I believe he has a visitor this afternoon, but he should be finished any minute now.'

For the first time since their meeting the girl seemed less assured. 'Honestly, Miss Flower, I wouldn't have presumed – I thought perhaps, if you could speak to him . . .?'

Victoria smiled. She rather enjoyed 'managing' Deedee in that way. She said, 'Very well, I'll see what I can do. If you would like to wait in here, Miss Coombs.'

What had got into her, she asked herself crossly, as she tiptoed up the stairs and knocked at Deedee's door. She was sounding more like Mrs Cardew by the minute. She wasn't usually like this, being pompous to a defenceless girl who'd only come for help. Yet Mollie Coombs made her feel competitive at once, as if there was some rivalry between them. It was absurd. Why should she feel defensive? She was the one with the advantages. Except for those bold eyes and tumbling curls, and perhaps a certain freedom in the choice of clothes.

Deedee's 'Come in' interrupted her thoughts. She pulled herself together and obeyed.

Deedee was sitting behind his desk, and that awful Stephen Pencarrow was beside him. They were talking about books, evidently, from the open brown paper parcel between them. Deedee looked up at Vicki with a smile.

'I'm sorry to disturb you, Papa,' she said, and outlined the request before either man could speak. Only then did she add, 'Good afternoon, Mr Pencarrow,' nodding to Stephen who had scrambled to his feet. 'I'm sorry to interrupt your conversation.'

'Always a pleasure to see you, Miss Flower.' He flashed her his easy smile. However could Bella think of him as handsome? While that quarry fellow down at the stile, with the lopsided grin

. . . She pulled herself together and heard Pencarrow say, 'In any case, we'd almost finished here.'

Deedee was already walking down the stairs, running his hand across his bald spot, as he always did when he was thinking hard. The two others hurried after him. 'Borrow my bicycle? I suppose that's possible. Does the fellow know how to ride a bicycle? Or do you think I'd better go myself?'

Victoria would have given sovereigns to offer her own services, but she didn't dare. Just as they reached Mollie in the hall, Stephen said, 'Perhaps I can solve the problem, Doctor Flower. I'm travelling that way myself. I'd gladly take the young lady in the trap.'

Mollie said, 'That's some 'andsome of you, sir, thank you.'

Victoria was less convinced. 'But Deedee, how will she get home? She can't go walking round the lanes alone at night. There might be tramps, or drunk men – anything.' She was quoting what that quarryman had said to her, and the recollection brought a pink flush to her cheeks.

'Don't worry about that, Miss Flower. I daresay the doctor will bring me back. If not I'll stop and wait for Zaccary Olds – he'll walk back home with me, supposing we don't pass him on the way.'

But Victoria wasn't really listening. Olds? That was the same name, surely? It couldn't be? She turned to Mollie, 'Is . . .?'

But Stephen was hustling the girl away. 'Then there's no problem. No, really Doctor Flower, I'm happy to oblige. So, come along, my dear. It won't take twenty minutes in the trap.'

'Now that was kind of him,' Deedee remarked, leading the way upstairs again. 'He tells me your friend Bella is indisposed. Do you want to come in, and help me with my books a little? I am a poor substitute for lively company, I know.'

Victoria's mind was full of what she'd heard. Olds. That was the same name, surely? But he was Daniel. She remembered that. Probably just coincidence. But Deedee was looking at her strangely. She said, 'Of course I will,' and went to help him catalogue the books.

It wasn't till much later, when she was kneeling by her bed, that something else occurred to her. How had Stephen known about the chill? Bella must have contrived that meeting after all. Victoria shook her head.

She remembered the burnt child in her prayers.

Lucy was still screaming when the doctor came. Ma was almost beside herself by that time, cradling the child in her arms and trying desperately to rock some comfort into her. She had dipped a bottle-teat in next-door's parsnip wine and was trying that – 'knock out a bull with two glasses of that' people always said – but nothing seemed to help. Dan and the others stood by helplessly.

'It's all my fault,' Ma wailed, for the hundredth time. 'Should have kept a better eye on her. Oh, my precious girl. Hush. Hush.'

But Lucy didn't hush. They had managed, with some difficulty, to immerse her arm in water, and smear the blistering flesh with Harry's greasy balm, and that had seemed to give her some relief. But the pain was terrible, all the same, and she screamed so piteously and long, that it was all that they could do to make her drink.

That was Harry Varfell's doing too. 'Got to get fluids in her,' he kept insisting, so Melda warmed milk and water in a pan and Ma fed it to her in a borrowed feeding bottle. Daniel wasn't sure it did much good – Lucy wasn't drinking much of it – but it gave the womenfolk something to do until the doctor came. Supposing that he ever came, that is. Zac seemed to have been gone for hours, and still there was no sign of them at all.

Then, all at once there was a commotion in the street. Half the village was on the step by now, but even Daniel could detect the sound of horses' hooves and a respectful shuffling at the door. And next minute Zac came in, with the doctor following at his heels. There was an instant murmur of relief – you could sense the tension easing in the room – though it was stupid, Dan was well aware. The presence of a doctor was no guarantee.

'Well,' the doctor said, 'what have we here?' He was already on his knees, examining the child's blistered arm as closely as he could through Harry's grease.

Ma began her lament again. 'Left her alone for half a minute to get a bit more wood, and over she went. Caught her foot on the hearthrug, by the looks. Didn't have my mind on it, that's what, not since Dad and Zac came home. Thinking about them, I was, and all this worry about the quarry pit, instead of keeping watch on the child. And now look what's happened. She will recover, won't she, doctor? I couldn't live with myself else. Burns can be awful things.'

The doctor did not answer her directly. 'Well, it seems you've done the proper things. Had it in water, by the look of it, and that will have taken down the heat, and kept the air from it with grease, that's good. Now, let me have that feeding bottle here.' He took off the teat and added a few drops of something from his medicine bag. 'A little laudanum to help the pain. When she's a bit calmer I'll put a dressing on. Aloe and paraffin ointment would be best. I'll leave you some, and a bit more laudanum as well.'

It did seem to be having some effect. Lucy's screams had tempered into sobs, and he took her gently from her mother's arms.

'I'll need to put her on a bed for this. You –' he turned to Daniel – 'show me where, and you –' to Melda – 'can put the kettle on. I think your mother needs a cup of tea, with something stronger in it, if you can.' He gave his bag to Jimmy, who staggered under it. 'And you, young fellow, carry this for me. Now, lead the way.'

It was astonishing, Dan thought. The man had not been in the house ten minutes, and already he had restored a sort of calm. Even Lucy, in those unfamiliar arms, was only whimpering now. The doctor laid her on the bed, on top of a clean towel which Dan found for the purpose, and dressed and bandaged up the injured arm. Then the doctor propped her up in Ma's bed, with the arm resting on the bolster, with Jimmy Gannet sitting guard with her. Lucy, Dan was relieved to see, was almost nodding off between her sobs.

'She should be all right in time,' the doctor said, as he went downstairs with Dan. 'Provided she doesn't get infection in the burns. It's bad, but it is only surface blistering – it's fortunate the child was only in her vest. If the clothes had caught fire and stuck to her it could have been much worse. Now . . .!' he led the way back into the kitchen.

Harry Varfell had disappeared, and so had Zac by now, and one of the neighbours had taken Kitty in, but Dad was there sipping a cup of tea and Mother was toying mechanically with her empty cup. There was a little more colour in her cheeks, though, Daniel saw.

She started up as soon as she saw them. 'How is she now?'

'Almost asleep,' the doctor said. 'Give her a drop or two of laudanum in milk if she wakes up again. The pain will be savage for a little while.'

'I'll go up to her.'

'Do that, but don't disturb the child.' He waved aside a cup of tea, which Melda was trying to press into his hands. 'I shall need to see the child again. Those dressings will need changing. Now try to get some rest, all of you. The child will be wakeful in the night. But you did well – her recovery will be largely due to you. I'll see myself out.'

Dan followed him to the front door all the same. 'Thank you for coming, doctor.'

'I'm sorry it took me so long to arrive. I was out attending to another call, but the young lady and your brother found me, all the same.'

'Young lady?' Daniel echoed foolishly.

'The red-haired young lady who came back here with me. I believe it was she who commandeered the trap to come and look for me. I think you have much to thank her for. Without her, I rather fear, you would not have found me yet. Well, goodnight. As I say, I'll look in within a day or two. And tell your father not to worry. Pay me when you can.' The doctor unhitched his sulky and trotted off.

Daniel looked up and down the darkening street. There was no one to be seen. No sign of Mollie, or of Harry either. Even the curious bystanders had gone. Of course, Dan remembered suddenly, there was that Stoneworkers' Society meeting called tonight. He should have gone himself. But somehow, this evening, he had no heart for it. He turned and went slowly back inside.

Mollie had not followed the doctor into the house when they arrived. It didn't seem fitting somehow, butting in, and instead she'd joined the little gaggle waiting on the steps. It was not long, however, before Harry Varfell caught sight of her through the open door, and came sidling out into the street.

'The doctor's seeing to the child upstairs,' he announced to the little gathering. 'Given her something for the pain, and hoping she'll sleep. Nothing else that anyone can do tonight.'

'You sure? I should go to the meeting otherwise,' someone said. There was a general ripple of agreement, and bit by bit the little group dispersed. Mollie found herself alone with Harry in the street. It was almost dark by now but she could see his face, smiling shyly in the dim light from the house.

'You found the doctor, then. That's good,' he said.

'You did well yourself. All the right things. If she gets over it, it'll be down to you, I heard the doctor say.'

Harry shuffled. 'Yes, well . . .!' But her praise seemed to have given him confidence because he said a moment later, 'You going home, are you? 'Cause if you are, I'll walk up with you. Can't have you walking on your own, this time of night, you can't see where you're going. 'Ere, you'd better take my arm, the lane is full of holes.'

Molly was about to protest that she was perfectly all right, but Harry had already seized her hand and tucked her arm in his, and somehow it seemed churlish to refuse. But he hugged his elbow tightly to his side, so that he squeezed her hand against his chest. It felt too intimate, so when they reached the bottom of the dip, where the lane was muddiest, she seized an excuse to disengage.

'I'll have to have my hand back, Harry, to hold up my hems. Can't afford to get my best skirt in the mud!' Even in the moonlight she saw his face, and so she went on gaily, to minimize the hurt: "Just as well as I was wearing it today! That's three big houses I've been in – and driving round in carriages like Lady Muck.'

'Three?' He looked impressed.

'I went up the vicarage at first, see could I borrow the vicar's bicycle.'

'You never!'

'Yes, I did, and he'd have lent it, too, only there was a fellow there who had a pony trap. Ever so good he was, took me to St Just, and picked up Zac on the way. Course, when we got there, doctor wasn't there – the woman said that he was out this way all the time, over at Lower St Evan House seeing to Miss Cardew. So Mr Pencarrow turns around and brings us all the way back there. Wonderful, he was.'

'I suppose he was.' Harry sounded less than delighted about that.

Molly laughed. 'Don't think that la-di-da Miss Flower thought much of it. Found half a dozen reasons why it wouldn't do, and when I answered them, you should have seen her face! Shocked as if I'd sworn in church!' She smiled at the recollection. 'I dunno why. Suppose she didn't like it – girl like me. But Mr Pencarrow took me all the same. And then the doctor brought me home. You'll have to pay half a crown to speak to me, before long, all this riding round in carriages.'

They had reached the row by this time, and were outside number nine. 'Well, here we are then,' Mollie said, but he made no move to go. He just stood there silent in the dark, like some sort of standing stone. Poor Harry. Such a nice fellow, but so lumbering and slow – always two scats behind, like Tregony band.

'What is it, Harry?' Mollie said, although she thought she knew.

Harry cleared his throat. 'Thing is, Mollie . . . I know you said you aren't walking out with Daniel Olds. Not proper walking out, that is. And I know you've promised him to go out with the horns. Only, I was wondering . . . If you aren't walking out with him, would you consider walking out with me? I think a lot of you, you know, and I've got a lot to offer with the forge. Only I wanted to ask you, before you got too serious with Dan.'

She was trying to think of something kind to say, but he seemed to read her thoughts.

'Don't need an answer now, of course. But think about it. Don't just say "no" off hand. You will do that, won't you Moll? Think about it? Promise me you will?'

He was so earnest and serious that she found herself saying, against her better judgement, 'I'll think about it, Harry. Can't promise more than that.' And then she went inside and left him on the step.

'What was all that, then?' Eadie said sharply from her stool where she was feeding little Stanley by the fire.

'Nothing, only Harry Varfell. He's been down helping at the Olds'. It's bad, but not as bad as might have been. I'll tell you all about it later on.' Molly was reluctant to confide. There was so much to do before the men came home from their meeting: the supper things to wash, her own food getting cold, and the washing to be taken from the rack and damped and rolled ready for ironing, that, as she half-intended, the matter was forgotten and she didn't have to say another word.

Much later, when she went up to bed and there was no one there to see, she took down the Mayhorn from the shelf and cradled it, like a baby, in her arms. Then she put it down beside her on the pillow, and it was still there when she went to sleep.

Part Two

April – May 1911

One

The day of Bella's tea party had come at last and Victoria could hardly wait to go. Partly, she recognized guiltily, because St Evan House kept Lent less strictly than the vicarage, (so that although there might be no chocolate or cream in deference to the season, there were still likely to be buttered splits and jam, and a dozen kinds of dainty sandwiches) but also because it seemed a long time since she had seen her friend.

To start with Bella had been in a bed for a week, nursing that chill, with the doctor coming every other day. 'Mama says one cannot be too careful, especially with the house party coming up,' she had written, in one of her many notes. 'And I suppose I must submit, because my head still aches a little. But it is very tedious lying here.'

It must have been, Victoria thought wryly. That was the seventh missive in as many days. Bella was not usually such a committed correspondent.

Victoria had missed her friend enough to go up to the House, accompanying her father, to enquire after the invalid. But Isabella had not 'been well enough to come downstairs', and after that she hadn't liked to call. One could hardly turn up there, unannounced, with pots of Mrs Roseworthy's jelly as though the Cardews were poor parishioners and Bella might be in need of nourishment!

At last another note had come, excited pages full of news. Bella was recovered now, she wrote, 'but we have been so busy, first with preparations for the house party and then with the event itself, that life has been a whirl, and sadly there's been no time for other visiting. But, oh Victoria, the birthday ball! I stood up for every dance, and my new gown was a sensation' (underlined three times) . . . 'even Mama agrees!'

So the house party had been a great success. As for the famous Petroc: 'So much has happened, darling Vic, I am positively bursting to tell you everything. I'm dying for tomorrow and for our private tea. Do come as early as you can, otherwise I'm sure I shall explode with all my news!'

Indeed, when Victoria was shown into the room, her friend did seem genuinely glad to see her. Bella was looking more than usually pretty, sitting in the window seat, wearing a beautiful pale green tea gown with roses round the hem and her hair up as befitted a young woman now 'out' in society. It made her look suddenly very grown-up and elegant indeed. But as soon as she saw Victoria she leapt up like a child and came rustling towards her with both her hands outstretched.

'Dear, dear Vicki. It is so good to see you. It seems such an age.' She seized her friend's fingers in her own and squeezed them enthusiastically. 'Now you must come here and sit down here by me. There is so much to tell!' She settled herself back into the window seat, and patted the cushions invitingly. 'Thank you, Alice,' she added to the maid, who was still loitering beside the door. 'That will be all. You can bring tea up in half an hour. We have a great deal to talk about.'

Bella certainly had a lot to tell. All about the dance, the supper, the orchestra – six pieces and a pianist – which gentlemen had invited her to dance, how her dress had been the sweetest thing imaginable, and how Petroc would have filled her card from the first waltz to the last, if good manners had permitted it.

Vicki sat and listened, trying to nod and smile and not to mind too much that she had missed all this. As it was, since Deedee had been called out that night to visit a bereaved parishioner, she'd been obliged to spend a dreary evening with Miss Boff, over a Lenten supper of sardine sandwiches and fruit.

'And what did you think of Petroc, then?' she said, with an attempt at good humour.

Bella smiled. 'Oh, he is quite agreeable, I suppose. Good-looking in a florid sort of way, though I have never quite liked that fair, blonde-headed look. But he has nice eyes, and perfect manners, and he dances splendidly. And it is always flattering to be adored.' She gave the gurgling little laugh that she reserved for matters of the heart. 'But honestly, Victoria, he is so very grave and staid, you'd take him for a man of thirty-five. Didn't you see him at matins yesterday? Almost all the house party accompanied us to church.'

'Exactly!' Victoria exclaimed. 'And since I was occupied with Sunday school, I didn't get a chance to find out who was who.'

'Well, if you don't run away too soon, you shall meet him properly today. Being family, he's staying for another week or two. He's gone out with my father this afternoon, to look into a horse he wants to buy, and –' Belle dimpled at her with a knowing smile – 'that is not the best of it, you know. You will never guess who's with them, talking about men of thirty-five!'

'Don't be a tease. You know I've no idea!'

'That dashing Mr Pencarrow of yours, that's who! Now, what do you think of that!'

Vicki shook her head. 'He's not my Mr Pencarrow, as you know very well. I didn't realize he knew your family – remember you required to be introduced. I did guess, though, that he must have had your news, since he knew all about your chill! Your acquaintance seems to have grown apace.'

Bella smiled. 'That was all your doing, clever girl! Sending him round to call on me like that!'

Now Vicki was genuinely mystified. 'What has he been telling you? Surely he didn't come to call, and somehow pretend that I had sent him here? That would be unforgiveable. I assure you Belle . . .'

Bella tossed her head and laughed. 'Of course he did nothing of the kind. He has more care for what is fitting, I should hope. But it was because of you he came here, all the same. He came here with a young woman from the village. They were looking for the doctor, who happened to be here attending me, because he was needed for some child who'd been badly burned.'

A child whose name was Olds, Victoria thought, and found herself turning an uncomfortable red.

Bella was babbling on. 'Of course, it was all very irregular, but he explained that it was an emergency. The girl had come to your papa for help, he said, and he'd offered to oblige. He'd already been over to St Just with her, but when they told him where the doctor was Mr Pencarrow brought her all the way back, although it was miles out of his way. I was sure you'd put him up to it.'

Victoria shook her head. 'As if I would!'

Bella laughed. 'Well, that's what he did. And for no reward at all! Wasn't that a kindly thing to do? Papa was most favourably impressed.'

'No doubt!' Victoria said ungraciously. 'And no doubt also Mr Pencarrow was so charming and apologetic that he was permitted to presume upon our acquaintanceship and make a claim on your hospitality?' This unlooked-for reminder of Daniel Olds had unsettled her, and besides she had an uncomfortable suspicion that Stephen Pencarrow, far from receiving no reward, had skilfully achieved the very thing he sought. She could see just how it would have been. He had clearly admired Bella from the start, and had seized the earliest opportunity to ingratiate himself with her family. 'Really, Belle, I am surprised at you.'

'Oh, Victoria, don't be such a grouch! I do declare, you begin to sound exactly like Miss Boff! Why on earth should Papa not invite him in? While the doctor took the girl back to the village, Mr Pencarrow had quite a long talk to Papa about his horse, and of course one thing led naturally to another. Now Petroc is hoping to buy one, and Stephen – Mr Pencarrow – knows a man who breeds. He volunteered to introduce the two, and that is where they've gone this afternoon.'

'I see,' Vicki said. 'How extraordinarily convenient.' Bella was right, she told herself, she was sounding like Miss Boff. After all she had no particular reason to dislike Pencarrow, except that he made her feel uncomfortable. Though so did the young man on the day of the umbrella incident, and she hadn't taken a dislike to *him*. She deliberately adopted a more teasing tone. 'So, Mr Pencarrow has become Stephen now, I see? I assume that didn't come from introducing Petroc to a horse?'

Bella turned scarlet, but she had the grace to laugh. 'Well, I suppose I have met him once or twice. Accidentally, you understand.' She glanced sideways at her friend from under her eyelashes. 'John, that's the groom I go riding with, has his eye on a girl from one of the seaside farms, so if I get tired and want to rest a little on a stile and admire the view, he is not averse to taking the horses down for a canter on the sands. Is it my fault that Mr Pencarrow sometimes walks that way?'

This was so outrageous that Victoria gasped. 'Bella, you didn't! But I thought as much! As soon as I heard that you'd caught that chill out on the St Just road. You went out there then on purpose to run into him. Well it serves you right. I shan't be sorry for you any more – sitting there, talking to a comparative stranger in the rain!'

'Oh, Vicki, of course it wasn't anything like that.'

But of course it was. Bella's guilty giggles told her that. 'So what about poor Petroc then? You do not think to marry him after all?'

Bella's face fell and she made a little moue. 'Honestly Vicki, I don't think I could, though I know Mama has set her heart on it. I can see the advantages, of course. He's a decent, honest sort of man: kindly and generous with money; background, all that sort of thing; you'd never want for anything, and he waltzes like an dream. But he is so very serious and dull. One would die of tedium in half an hour. And when you compare him to Stephen – well . . .! But wait until you see him for yourself.'

Victoria might have pressed her further, but at that moment Alice the maid reappeared with tea, and conversation turned to other things. The spread was every bit as excellent as Vicki had imagined it and she felt deliciously wicked, after ham, egg and beef sandwiches – in Lent! – and tucking into cream and jam and a piece of sinfully indulgent cake. 'Saved from the supper party,' Bella said, when the last morsel of the feast was gone, 'especially for you! But listen, I think I heard the carriage in the drive. That will be Petroc and Papa. Do you want to come down and be introduced?'

Victoria did, of course, although she had no wish to encounter Stephen Pencarrow again. But she need not have been concerned on that account. They went downstairs to find only the Colonel and Petroc Veryan in the hall.

'Delighted, Miss Flower, I am sure,' the latter said heartily, bowing over her hand, when the necessary introductions had been made. 'Isabella has told me such a lot about you.'

'And she has mentioned you, of course, Mr Veryan,' Victoria murmured, withdrawing her fingers. Though it would have been hard to recognize this broad-shouldered, athletic and fresh-faced young man from Bella's unflattering description. Far from the stolid bore she had been half-expecting, Victoria found herself face to face with a cheerful and animated man, with a square, plump open face, and a hearty laugh which boomed out when he talked. He was charming and courteous, but he had eyes for nobody but Bella, and as soon as he politely could he moved across to speak to her.

'I've managed to acquire a splendid horse,' Victoria heard him say, clearly delighted with the success of the afternoon's expedition. 'And that Pencarrow fellow's been immensely good – offered to stable for me till I leave, and even to ride her over when I go. Remarkably neighbourly of him, I must say. Really a sterling sort of chap.'

But when Bella said, 'Yes, isn't he?' and smiled back at him, Victoria didn't feel comfortable at all. She was almost glad that it was time for her to go and hurry back to Miss Boff and daily evensong. So few people came on Monday nights, that sometimes they were the only worshippers there.

*   *   *

70

There was little for anyone to smile about when Tuesday came. Gloom hung around the quarry like a cloud of smoke. Daniel could sense it as soon as he walked in through the gate.

'Here, what's to do?' he enquired of old Tom, as they made their way up towards the face, and out on to the horizontal bench of stone, to size up the boring angles for the next blast to be set. 'Everyone with faces like fiddles, and when I said good morning to Winker at the gate, he never even raised his eye to look.' Winker only had one eye to raise. Like a lot of other quarrymen he'd lost the other to a flying chip of granite years ago, though Mr Prowse had been good as usual and found a job for him at the gate.

'Haven't 'ee 'eard then?' old Tom said, drearily. 'Come to it, at last. Seems they clever folk up the Addlemernty've made up their stupid minds at last – and done the daft dratted thing, like they always belong to do. Buying the foreign stone they are, keep they Norwegian buggers in work instead of we. And all for the sake of a few shilling a ton. So you and me can go hang, Dan'l boy – or end up in the workhouse, for all they care.'

That was a long speech for old Tom, who was not given to many words as a rule, and Dan knew that it was a measure of how upset he was.

He tried to offer some comfort. 'All the same . . .'

Old Tom shook his head. 'Turning off a half a score o' men, come pay day.'

Dan felt himself pale. 'You sure of that?' No wonder Winker had been taciturn. If men were going, it was a ha'penny to a shilling that a one-eyed man would be among the first. And that went for Jamie Coombs as well.

His companion nodded grimly. 'Prowse come down 'ere last night, last thing – to tell the quarry captains, seemingly – and he's coming back again 'isself to tell the men today. And that won't be the finish of 'un, neither. Just you take a look down there, my 'andsome. See all they men? –' he gestured with one gnarled and blistered hand – 'be the end for 'alf of them before so long. Though you'd never think so, from the row they make, 'ark at them down there.'

You could hardly avoid 'harking at' it, Dan thought, as he gazed down on the scene. Prowse's was a only small quarry, compared to some, but it certainly made a lot of noise. He and Tom were having to half-shout to each other to make their comments heard.

He looked down at the scene. Men, in waistcoats, shirt-sleeves and bowler hats, down on the quarry floor were making the valley echo as they wielded picks, 'scappling' the large blocks roughly into shape. Their blows sent up little flakes of granite as they worked. There was the clear ringing peal of the 'jumping-rods'; each man liked to think his 'jumper' had a different tone, as they brought the iron down rhythmically to split the stone. From further off – down in the bankers, as they called the dressing yard, out near the gate, but still completely audible – came the softer tap of hammers and chisels as the masons worked, while overhead the cranes and derricks moaned and sang. Even the gang exposing the surface of the next stand of rock for quarrying, made a kind of peculiar music of their own; a swish and clatter as the clearers shovelled the unwanted soil, the overburthen as they called it, into empty trams, and then the grunt and rattle as the trammers toiled to push the loaded spoil away. And all this before the blasting teams like Dan's had even started yet.

'Music of industry, that is,' old Tom said, unexpectedly wax-ing lyrical. 'Leastways, that's what preacher said, years ago, and I never forgot 'un. Thought he were daft at the time, mind you, but now I think p'raps he was right, at that. Where'll us be without it, that's the thing. But it'll come to it, you mark my words.'

Dan tried to imagine the scene without the 'music of industry': the hammers silent, the yard empty, the great derricks stark and unused, skeletons against the sky, their chains hanging like cobwebs on their bones. It was a depressing vision. He gave a little shudder.

'Well,' he said, with a forced cheerfulness. 'Aren't helping any standing here gawping like a pair of pigs, are we? Let's have a look at these new setts they want for us to cut. This great piece of granite here will do it beautiful. Where're we going to have 'er, to blast 'er out?'

But even the interest of sizing up the job – a tricky one, since the block was lying toughwise, the worst way, to the bed – could not lighten Daniel's mood today. He would be all right himself, no doubt, and no doubt Dad would too. Men with skills would be the last to go. Even for lads like Zac there was a little hope; you couldn't run a quarry without 'boys'. Someone had to run the errands and do the thankless tasks, and because the youngsters were just starting out their wages didn't amount to very much. But for the likes of Jamie Coombs, things were looking bleak. Dan couldn't get his friend out of his thoughts.

Even the stone seemed to have 'turned cussed' today, as old Tom said; a block at that angle to the bedding joint was always the most difficult to bore, but this piece was particularly hard. Zac was kept busy all the morning, running to and from the smithy, taking the blunted borers down for sharpening. The ends seemed to be wearing blunt after only a few inches, when usually they would bore a foot or more. Progress was slow, and old Tom had lapsed back into his usual uncommunicative self, as if by that initial conversation he had exhausted his store of talking for the day.

Dan found his eyes straying more and more towards the site-office door, where the unfortunate ones would be summoned to hear their fate, if old Tom's rumour was to be believed. But there was no sign of Mr Prowse, and as the morning wore on, Dan was almost beginning to hope again.

When Prowse did arrive, much later on, Dan didn't see him after all. They'd struck another problem with the block, a false joint at an angle to the main seam of the rock. It was always a nightmare for a powder man, if the stone split along the secondary joint instead of coming clean, as not only could the whole block be ruined by the blast, but the granite could split in unpredictable ways. There had been more than one accident, over the years, when flying chips of rock had caused damage to unprotected eyes and limbs. It took all Dan's skill and old Tom's experience to place the blast hole to avoid the joint. It was absorbing work. And when Dan looked down towards the site office again, there was Mr Prowse just leaving it, with the pit captain hovering politely at his side.

It was impossible to tell anything at this distance, of course, but as Prowse walked slowly out towards the gate Dan saw one of the men from the dressing yard come out and shake his fist at the quarry owner's retreating back. He knew then, with a sickening lurch of the stomach, that all the tales were true.

'One thing you can say fer Prowse; he's man enough to do the thing 'isself.' He was startled by Tom's voice in his ear. 'And 'tisn't no use that daft bugger Johnson shaking his fist like that, 'tisnt Prowse's fault. Just as bad for 'im as 'tis for we. Any fool could see that, just looking at the man.'

And indeed Mr Prowse was walking like a man defeated, his shoulders stooped and with no sign of his usually sprightly step. Dan looked about for Jamie, but there was no sign of him, and he went back to his work with a heavy heart.

He didn't see his friend all day, but on the way home he caught sight of him.

'Hey, Jamie! Jamie Coombes!' he called, and made to hasten after him. 'All right?'

Jamie did pause and glance round then, but he didn't stop. Instead he shook his head and hurried off without a single word. But Dan had glimpsed his face, and his expression was eloquent enough.

Dan knew better than to follow him. Some burdens are better borne alone: a grown man doesn't want anyone to see him cry.

The Reverend Edward Flower permitted himself a moment of human vanity, and rubbed a little more pomade into his hair. The sharp smell of it pleased him, disguising the slight but definite aroma of mothballs that permeated his second-best clerical suit. He looked at his reflection in the long mirror of the dressing room and sighed. Foolish to worry so much about the visit of an old friend like Jonathan.

His own fault; he had allowed his enthusiasm to run away with him, and decided that it was necessary to reorganize the house – though he had only meant to catalogue the books, and rearrange the furniture in the spare rooms. But Mrs Roseworthy had somehow caught his mood, and thrown herself into such a frenzy of preparation that he'd wondered more than once if the invitation had been altogether wise. For weeks she had been making galantines and plotting what other delicacies could be entertained within the constraints of the Lenten observances which he himself imposed.

'Can't have 'im thinking that we don't know what's what,' she'd said, and insisted on dusting everything, including his study shelves, and shuffling his notes into more formal piles. He'd even let himself be talked into taking her niece on as a little bit of temporary help. 'You'll want someone to be serving at table, and that sort of thing, if this fellow does come 'ere to stay!'

Then Miss Boff had got herself into a flutter, and had been to ask his opinion several times about what it would be most appropriate for herself and Victoria to wear. In fact, if he was honest with himself, the frequency of her visits had begun to cause him some alarm. He had never quite forgotten what Victoria had said about the governess making eyes at him. Since then he'd been acutely aware of how often the governess came seeking his advice.

Even thinking about it made his collar tight. Just as well that there was no one here to see. He ran a loosening finger around inside the stiff ecclesiastical neckband, and tried to compose himself again.

What would Jonathan think of him, after all these years? A little old, a little bald, a little shabby, even, in his black broadcloth suit? That was pure vanity, of course, but a man could not help such thoughts. And what about this curate? It had been his own idea, but now that the moment had come, he was not convinced that was it such a clever one. Suppose

Victoria didn't like him, after all? Suppose he didn't care for him, himself?

Well, there was only one way to find out. The Reverend Flower straightened his shoulders, cleared his throat, and made his way determinedly downstairs.

The ladies were already in the drawing room. Victoria looked demurely pretty, as she always did, but Miss Boff had alarmingly 'got herself up' for the occasion in a gown of something stiff and purplish. She gave him a little knowing smile, and he was quite relieved, a moment later, to hear the sound of wheels in the lane. Mrs Roseworthy's niece, a small pink dumpling of a girl called Ruby, bobbed in shortly afterwards to announce: 'Excuse me, sir and ladies, but the Reverend Mr Stokes and 'is curate 'as arrived.'

Jonathan looked very much the same as ever (a little older, a little stouter, a little balder, Edward noted wryly) and had lost nothing of his cheerful ease of manner. He chatted to Victoria, managed to coax a smile from Miss Boff, and greeted Edward himself with such obvious affection that any awkwardness was dispelled at once.

'And may I present my curate,' Jonathan exclaimed, bringing the young man forward as he spoke.' He's an Oxford man, like yourself. Lionel Smallbone, this is my old friend Doctor Edward Flower.'

'Mr Smallbone? Delighted I am sure.' Edward found himself shaking a bony young hand, and looking up into a pale but pleasant face. He was surprised that he hadn't really taken in the young man earlier, because he was a very striking man. He looked like the painting of a saint – fair skin, a small unfashionable beard, something gentle and almost girlish in the features – but whatever else the visitor might turn out to be, well-named he certainly was not. There was nothing 'small-boned' about him; he towered head and shoulders over Jonathan; his hands and feet seemed somehow too big for him, and that – together with an embarrassed manner – added to the impression of his awkward height.

In that small room he seemed to take up a lot of space, so that Edward was moved to invite his guests to sit. They did so, but Lionel courteously selected the least comfortable chair, which was ridiculously low for him, where he sat with his knees almost higher than his ears, blushing to his hair roots whenever anyone addressed a word to him, until the dinner gong released him from his obvious misery.

Edward could feel a certain sympathy – he had been rather gauche himself when young – but he wondered why Jonathan had thought this lad a suitable curate for a parish such as this? That was likely to cause awkwardness as well, because to turn Mr Smallbone down now might seem disobliging. Yet this young man was not what he'd envisaged. He'd secretly hoped for someone intelligent, articulate and energetic, who could breathe new life into the parish, take some of the burden from his shoulders and sweep Vicki off her feet. It was hard to see the gawky Lionel in the role.

Nevertheless he went through the motions. After the meal – which was a moderate success – he took the young man to his study and asked him a good many questions. There was nothing that one could fault him on, in fact Edward had to admit that he was reluctantly impressed. He'd expected Jonathan's protégé to express Anglo-Catholic views, but Lionel was sound on liturgical matters – neither too popish nor, on the other hand, too anxious for reform.

But it was not until they rejoined the others that the die was cast. His old friend had desisted from his anecdotes (at which even Miss Boff had tittered once or twice, although she always frowned most disapprovingly at Edward's jokes), and suggested, almost casually, that Lionel should entertain them on the pianoforte.

'Edward, I think that you should hear him play before we go,' Jonathan said. 'He's a very musical fellow; very. A lot to offer in that department.' And Lionel got up, blushing, to comply.

He did play very well. In fact, he seemed to lose his embarrassment in the music. At first he performed entirely from memory, but then Jonathan suggested teasingly that he should play the Chopin piece which Victoria had been struggling with all week.

'She tells me that she has come to hate it, Lionel. Play it for her, and make her change her mind. She has the music book – she will turn the pages for you.' Jonathan sat back in his chair and smiled expansively.

It was then, as first she turned the music for their guest and then he returned the compliment – smiling encouragement while she wrestled with her party piece – that Edward began to change his mind. Shrewd old Jonathan! This was a much better suggestion than he'd thought.

Yes, he told himself, as the two young heads were bent earnestly together over the instrument, he would write to the Bishop straightaway. Mr Lionel Smallbone might suit the parish nicely after all. Very nicely indeed.

Two

Mayday before dawn was crisp and cold, but clear. Through the gap in the bedroom curtains Dan could see the stars. He eased himself out from under the blankets quietly, so as not to wake his brothers – not easy when all three shared a bed! – and groped his way downstairs to wash and dress.

He tried to be as silent as he could as he stirred up the fire and put the shaving water on to warm. Even so, before he had finished lighting up the lamp and lathering himself in the triangular piece of mirror over the sink, the door had opened and Jimmy Gannet had come tumbling in, still rubbing the sleep from his eyes.

'Off out to the horns are you?' Jimmy enquired eagerly. 'Wait a minute while I get some clothes. I'll come with you – always wanted to.'

Dan turned to him, soap suds still halfway to his ears. He was fond of his brother, but he hadn't set eyes on Mollie for a week. The last thing he wanted was Jimmy round his heels when he did. 'You can't do that, you haven't got a horn.'

'I have too,' Jimmy retorted, producing one from behind his back. It was a strange, misshapen looking thing, but unmistakably a horn. 'Tisn't a proper one like yourn, but Dad made it for me and it makes a noise. You listen . . .' And he would have tooted it, and woken everyone, if Dan hadn't quickly seized his arm.

Jimmy let out a howl that threatened to wake the neighbourhood. 'Let go of me!' he protested, as he tried to wriggle free. He looked up at Dan with a wicked grin, but it faded as he saw his brother's face. 'Oh, come on – don't be such a spoilsport, Dan. Reuben used to take you out to the horns, when you were young – and don't say why don't I ask Zac, 'cause he don't want to go, said he'd rather stay in bed for once. And don't tell me Mother wouldn't let me go – because she would, I asked her yesterday.'

'Child's right, Dan. So he did.' That was Ma now, disturbed by all the noise, come downstairs with a shawl wrapped around her shoulders over her flannel gown. 'You can take him with you, can't you, Dan?'

Dan sighed. Truth to tell he was a little bit concerned about today. There could be a little bit of awkwardness, and he didn't want Jimmy Gannet there to witness that – or to follow him and Mollie, come to that. He hadn't seen her since the day that Jamie left the pit.

In fact he was half afraid she'd been avoiding him. He could hardly blame her if she were. Couldn't be easy seeing another man still bringing home his pay, doing the job your brother couldn't do. Poor Jamie; rumour said that he was trying down the mines. Dan hadn't seen him, either, come to think. But Mollie's father still passed the time of day, and so did Stan Tregorran when they met, so Dan hoped that it would be all right. They'd not have spoken if there'd been hard feelings anywhere. Still, he was glad he hadn't said anything to his family about the tryst with Mollie.

He had no sooner framed the thought than Jimmy startled him. 'Danny's going out maying with a girl, that's what,' the Gannet said. 'That's how he doesn't want for me to go.'

Ma paused in the act of refilling the kettle from the pail. 'That so, Dan?' she asked him with a smile.

Drat! Dan was glad of the excuse to rinse his face and hide the scarlet rising to his cheeks. 'Well . . .' he said slowly. 'It's not exactly that . . .'

'Tis too then,' Jimmy chimed in at once. 'I heard Harry Varfell saying, up the blacksmith's shop. He wanted to take Mollie Coombs himself.'

If looks were daggers Jimmy would have been dead a dozen

times, but it was too late now, the damage was done, and after this everyone in the family would know. Dan knew exactly how it would be: they would pull his leg every time the name of Coombs was mentioned – and find a hundred reasons to mention it, as well, just as they teased Merelda about her fisherman.

Ma smiled sympathetically. 'I tell you what, Dan, you just take Jimmy up with you to the stile – there'll be no end of people once you're there, so it won't make any difference either way – and then when it's light and he's been out with the horns, Jimmy can come on home and leave you and Mollie to go picking may, or whatever 'tis you want to do.'

'I don't need taking, any road!' Jimmy protested, which was true. It wasn't all that far to the stile, even in the dark. But they both knew there was no point appealing to Ma; she wouldn't let the young ones out alone at night – ever since Reuben had been washed away.

'You hold your tongue, young feller, or I'll change my mind!' Mother said sharply. 'And mind you don't go making a pest of yourself to Dan. Then you can go with Merelda later on and watch the maypole dance, see the procession with the May queen and all. She'd go with you now, I s'pect, except she's been up half the night. Said she'd keep an eye on Lucy for a change, give me a chance to have a bit of rest.'

Dan felt guilty instantly. Of course it was the womenfolk who took the brunt of that. Lucy was coming on they said, but it was awfully slow, and Kitty still had to go next door to sleep. Sometimes the burnt child was tormented with the pain, and it always seemed to be worse at night. You could hear her sometimes through the wall, crying out, and someone always had to sit with her. Poor Ma was looking fair worn out with it.

Perhaps it was that, as much as anything, which made Dan grin reluctantly and say. 'All right then, pest, come on! Only as far as the stile, that's all. And mind you don't hang round us afterwards!'

Jimmy gave a whoop of delight which must have woken everyone for miles, and tied his boots on quicker than a wink.

They were outside and on their way, under a sky streaked with the first pale rays of dawn, almost before Jimmy had time to cram in his share of the bread and jam which Ma had insisted that they take.

Mollie was up and waiting on the step by the time the two Olds boys came into sight. Truth to tell she had been up for hours, trying on every one of her three skirts and 'tittivating her hair' as Eadie crossly said.

It was ages since she'd managed to run into Dan. Things were difficult with Jamie out of work, and she'd been glad to get a bit of scrubbing work down at the Worker's Educational Hall to bring in an extra shilling or two a week. Of course, it wasn't the kind of job she wanted for herself at all, but it was only while the regular woman was ill, so it wasn't going to last – unless the woman never came back to it at all, in which case Mollie would have to think again. Those few extra pence had helped to tide them over more than once. But the work was no good if you were courting: you were out all hours and when you did come back your hands were like cheese graters.

She glanced down at them now, ashamed to see them look so rough and chapped. Suppose Dan wanted to hold hands with her? She was still daydreaming of that possibility when she looked up and caught sight of him with his little brother by his side.

Drat Dan, she thought, what had possessed him to bring Jimmy along? She was almost ready to say something sharp, but there he was, bounding up to her with that lopsided grin, and snatching his cap off with an enthusiasm which could not be misinterpreted, and she found herself half-smiling after all.

'Morning Dan.'

''lo Mollie.' He didn't take her hand, but his grey eyes told her that he wanted to. 'Got your horn then?'

''Course I have,' she said, and off they went.

It was a silly business really, when you thought of it. Just a lot of folk with home-made horns, walking round the parish boundary as the sun came up, and tooting on their instruments with all their might. There was no tune or anything – the May horns weren't made for such luxury – just a loud hooting, then a wailing sound as the boys tried to outdo each other by holding their breath.

'Frighten the horses!' she laughed to Dan, and when he wasn't looking she tooted in his ear. But he got his revenge. Next time she was blowing, he filled his horn with petals and came up behind her and tipped it on her head. It was all ridiculous, and such good fun that by the time they'd worked their way around and come back to the stile once again, the sun was well and truly in the sky and everyone was breathless with tooting and laughter, to say nothing of the exertion of hurrying around for miles.

Jimmy Gannet, who had been plaguing them till then, giving them sideways glances and nudging everyone, suddenly lost interest in the game and, announcing that he was 'starved to rags', went off home in search of something else to eat. Other people, too, were drifting away in ones and twos, some to prepare for the maypole and parade, others to cut the traditional boughs of may to decorate their homes. Even Harry Varfell, who had lingered last of all, finally gave up and went, leaving the two of them alone.

'Well,' Daniel said, and suddenly there was an awkward pause.

Then Mollie said, 'How's Lucy getting on?' just as Dan said, 'How's Jamie, then?' and they both laughed.

'No, after you,' he said, and she told him her news, and then it wasn't a bit awkward any more. In fact, when a briskish little wind got up and Mollie rubbed her arms to keep them warm (foolish to wear her thin blouse, really, so early in the day, even if it was the prettiest one she had), Dan had his jacket off in a minute and draped it protectively around her shoulders.

He stood there then, holding her by his own lapels and looking down at her. He was so strong and handsome in his shirtsleeves that she found herself stretching upward till her lips met his. It was their first kiss; sweet and warm and tender.

Mollie opened her eyes and drew away, and there was Jimmy

Olds, standing by the hedge staring at them with eyes like saucepan lids.

'Forgot my horn,' he blurted. He snatched it from the hedge and scurried off.

Mollie bit her lip and coloured. She knew how quickly rumours spread. 'I'm some sorry, Dan . . .' But he had already seized her by the waist.

'Might as well do it proper then, since everybody knows,' he said, and this time he kissed her with so much fire that she was breathless and panting when he let her go.

He took her by the hand; if it was roughened he didn't seem to mind. 'Come on then,' he said, giving her a playful tug. 'Let's go round the fields and pick some may before that wretched child brings half the village up here to watch.'

So they went maying, although – as Jimmy pointed out when they returned, arms laden, to the maypole at the school – they hadn't really picked much considering how long it had taken them.

Victoria always went with Deedee to see the maypole dance and witness the crowning of the year's Queen of the May. This year, however, they had company. The new curate had been duly inducted into the temporalities of the parish and had taken up his post the week before, and – since he was living in the household – naturally he was invited to come too.

Vicki was still secretly surprised. First that Deedee had agreed to take a curate on at all, especially since she knew that he would have to pay for it out of his own pocket. But she was even more amazed that, once that decision had been taken, he'd selected Mr Smallbone for the post. When Dean Stokes had brought him round that night, she was sure that Deedee was not impressed. She was rarely wrong about these things – she could read Deedee's manner like a book – and she'd been quite convinced that evening that her father was sincerely wishing he'd never agreed to interview the man.

Yet something had clearly happened to make him change his

mind, because here was Mr Smallbone – Lionel, as she supposed that they should call him now – duly installed, and even larger than life.

She stole a sidelong look at the young man in question, as he walked along with Deedee now, deep in some earnest conversation. At least, Deedee was talking; Lionel's contribution seemed to be mainly nods.

He was quite good-looking, she supposed, in an ethereal sort of way, as he flapped along in his long black cassock like a kind of amiable bat.

Deedee was wearing a suit, as usual, but Lionel, with his High Church leanings, took his clerical image very seriously. In fact, he seemed to take everything in the same grave, solemn manner. No chance of his turning out to be the 'respectable company of your own age' which Deedee had once hinted at. One simply couldn't think of Lionel in a romantic light. Though she couldn't help a sneaking sort of liking and sympathy for him. He had been very kind to her over her musical attempts.

He caught her looking at him now, and flushed. Poor Lionel! She was convinced that underneath that sober, earnest mask he felt as awkward as he sometimes looked. He was sort of angular and shy, and his hands and feet seemed far too big for all the rest of him, as if he had tried them on in a shop and couldn't find a pair to fit.

She gave him an encouraging smile to signal her support.

This made him colour even more, but he did pluck up the courage to venture a remark to her: 'I was saying to your father, it's surprising that the church now sponsors things like this.' He seemed to realize that this sounded unfortunate, and he said hastily, 'I don't mean in St Evan, especially, but everywhere . . . It was firmly preached against at one time, as I expect you know. After all, it was once a pagan festival.'

It was hardly a scintillating opening, but Victoria did her best. 'Was it?' she said brightly, as if the pagan symbolism of the maypole was something which had caused her much concern. 'Really?'

'Oh yes,' Lionel said, and – as she had noticed once or twice before – his eyes took on an animation when he spoke. 'I believe it was a celebration of the goddess of the spring. Hence all these blossoms and the young girls as virgin queens. It was a kind of offering to her.'

Victoria felt her own cheeks glowing red. A gentleman didn't mention virgins in that way. She glanced at Deedee who was looking scandalized.

Lionel seemed unaware of it. 'The maypole may have been a kind of fertility symb—'

That was too much. Deedee 'hurrumphed' warningly and Lionel stopped, suddenly aware of the enormity of what he'd said.

'For the . . . for the fields and crops and things, that's all,' he finished weakly.

Vicki felt a unexpected burst of sympathy. There had been no intention to embarrass her, that wasn't Lionel's way. It was only his enthusiasm for the topic – or rather at finding something he could say – which had carried him away and led him into impropriety. But now he'd lapsed into embarrassed silence once again, and Deedee was frowning disapprovingly.

She said quickly, 'Yes, I understand one of the Methodist preachers spoke out against it, some years ago, and a lot of the chapel-goers wouldn't come. But everyone seems to have forgotten that. Look at them. I should think that everyone from miles around is here.'

Indeed, it seemed that everybody was. The school children were ready, all solemnly lined up in twos, the girls with flowers in their pinafores and hair, and the boys with brightly-coloured ribbons crossed over the chests of their best shirts. The brass band from the pit was there, warming up with little plomping sounds, while a team of women – some aged, some with infants on their hips – were spreading out an army of cups and saucers and trying to hold down a huge piece of paper (which was acting as a cloth) with plates of jam tarts and buttered splits. Groups of young people who had gone out with the horns were drifting back now in twos and threes as well, with bundles of may blossom in their arms.

There was a suggestive whistle from the direction of the schoolroom door as one pair came by. 'Been out maying, 'ave you, Dolly Jones? Make sure you 'aven't caught more than an armful of may!' one of the men shouted coarsely, and the others laughed.

She didn't recognize the man – a miner or quarry worker she supposed. There was a little gaggle of them lounging by the wall, trying to look as if they did not care for maypoles and pagan festivals. Everyone else – from wrinkled grandparents with sticks to children scarcely old enough to walk – was openly lining the route of the procession, or scrabbling for the best vantage point to see the maypole dance.

'Papa was asked to crown the May queen once,' Vicki went on. 'But, like you, he didn't think that it was quite the vicar's place.' She smiled, pleased to have found a clever way of making Deedee and Lionel seem to be on the same side of the argument.

She had succeeded. Deedee smiled. 'I forget who did it in the end. I see that Colonel Cardew's doing it this year.'

He nodded to where the Colonel and his wife were standing importantly beside the table where the blossom crowns were ready and waiting for this year's May queen. Bella was there too with Petroc still in attendance, Victoria noticed, and Stephen Pencarrow was not far away. He was chatting to the school mistress and pretending to make himself indispensable by fetching chairs. But like almost every other male, half of his attention was on Bella.

One could hardly blame them. Bella was looking stunning, as usual, in a beautiful cream dress, with hand-embroidered pale green daisies down the front, and a little cape and bonnet made to match.

Vicki gave a wry smile. The poor girl who was chosen to be queen looked a poor sight in comparison; a hefty young woman in her home-made muslin dress, who made her two attendant princesses look skinny and underfed. However, they were all three loudly clapped and cheered as they approached, and walked up to be duly crowned to the sound of a fanfare from the band. When they ascended to the floral thrones atop the decorated cart and led the procession round the route again, the onlookers began to cheer and shout as though it was a real queen they were looking at.

It all made Vicki herself feel invisible and drab, although her own dove-grey hat and dress were nicely cut and had been made brand new for Easter. So, when it was time for the maypole dancing to begin, and Deedee led Lionel away to introduce him to the Colonel (which of course meant the whole Cardew family), she felt quite unreasonably eclipsed.

She did not join the official party at once, as her father evidently expected. Instead, she lingered deliberately behind, looking at the dancers and the crowd, though immediately she wished that she had not. For there, walking slowly down the hill, their arms full of blossom and with eyes for no one but each other, were the Olds boy and that red-headed girl.

Of course, it was nothing to do with her at all. For some reason, though, her heart did an unpleasant little lurch. But she could not stand and stare; Miss Boff was right, it was not 'becoming'. So, when the young man looked in her direction and seemed as if he might have risked a smile, she turned away on purpose with her head held very high, and a moment later was engaging the Cardews in talk about the crowds, and flashing Lionel the most scintillating smile.

She rather hoped the Olds boy might have noticed, but when she looked around again, he'd gone.

Three

'But Vicki, you can't let me down. I'm quite relying on you over this.' Bella had walked over that afternoon to bring Victoria a book and now they were sitting together in the sun, in the little rustic arbour near the churchyard hedge. It was Victoria's favourite spot, though it was getting a little neglected now, like the rest of the garden, despite the attempts of old Sam Roseworthy to keep the lawn scythed and the weeds at bay. When the rhododendron hedge was fully out, in a week or two, this corner would become a wall of colour, full of the scent of flowers and the sound of birds.

But Bella was not looking at the view. She gazed at her friend and wailed in mock despair, 'In any case, you promised me you'd help!'

Victoria shifted on the wooden seat. Deedee had made it for Mother long ago, before Victoria was born – though no one but the two girls had sat upon it since. It was not really very comfortable, but it was out of sight of the house, and Victoria had made it a sort of hideaway for years. 'I'm sure I never agreed any such thing!' she replied.

'You did! You promised me the other day. I asked you – in private – at the maypole dance!'

Victoria said nothing but she had the grace to blush. It was possible. She had been so concerned with thinking about that Olds boy and his girl, she'd only half-listened to what her friend had said. But obviously she couldn't admit as much to Bella. Instead, she busied herself with pouring tea. Ruby had brought out a tray and – since Lent was safely over – a plate of home-made buns.

Bella, who had certainly never lifted a teapot in her life, watched her for a moment and then returned to her seemingly humorous attack. 'I thought then that you weren't really taking in what I was asking you! Of course, I'm not a bit surprised. I saw the way you patted down your hair and preened all afternoon. I knew your attention was on something else. Or someone else. I recognized the signs.' She giggled. 'So, Lionel is a big success? I'm pleased. It's time you had a little romance in your life.'

'Oh, Belle, don't be so absurd!' Victoria was startled into being impolite. 'Of course, it had nothing to do with Mr Smallbone. I've never thought of Lionel in that way.'

Bella had been Victoria's informant on many elements of life, and when she had explained some years ago what married people did to create babies, Victoria had refused to believe at first that anything so unlikely could occur. But Bella had been right about a lot of things – that tiresome monthly bleeding for example – and Vicki had been reluctantly convinced. 'If you had a mother, Vicki, she would tell you all these things,' Bella had murmured sympathetically. 'But of course you can't ask your papa, and I doubt if Miss Boff tells you very much.' And Vicki, who knew that Miss Boff would prefer death in boiling oil to mentioning anything so unsavoury, had been obliged to accept Bella's version of events. Even now, she found it difficult to do. Why, that would mean that Deedee and Mamma . . .? She shook her head.

She handed Bella a teacup, and added, 'In any case, I was listening perfectly.'

'You're blushing,' Bella teased her, as she sipped her tea.

'Well, are you surprised?' Victoria parried. 'Now I know what you're asking me to do: help you to meet Stephen Pencarrow privately? Of course I can't encourage you in this. You know perfectly well how much your papa would disapprove – and, besides, you intend to marry Petroc; you told me so yourself. How can you even think of such a thing?'

'Only listen to yourself, Miss Victoria Boff!' Bella said, helping herself to a bun with a defiant laugh. 'It is hardly meeting privately to see him on the road. How very straight-laced you've suddenly become! Is this the influence of your Lionel? I can see that he's a very sober soul.'

'He's not my Lionel!' Victoria said, with energy.

'Well, even if he's not, I'm sure he'd like to be!' Bella said. 'I saw the attention that he paid to you.' Victoria was about to protest again, but her friend said with sudden earnestness, 'But, of course, you're right. He's not your beau – not yet at any rate.' She put down her cup and turned to Victoria, 'And I'm not promised to Petroc, either – yet. So what's the difference? You would not feel that it was improper for you to smile, or talk a little to another man. Why should it be inappropriate for me? And where's the harm? I only want to talk to him, that's all. Stephen is such a charming, entertaining man. And he's acquainted with my family, now – Papa thinks him a most obliging fellow.'

'Then talk to him while your family is there. That seems to solve your problem perfectly.'

'Oh, Vicki, don't be such a goose. You know quite well that wouldn't be the same at all. In any case, if my family's there, we're scarcely able to exchange a word. Petroc has found every excuse to prolong his stay, and now has appointed himself my guardian, and won't allow another man within ten yards of me.'

'And quite right, too. After all, you are to marry him.'

'Vic, for the hundredth time, it isn't settled yet! I'm just not sure about all that, you know.'

Victoria turned scarlet. She knew what Bella meant.

Bella was still talking animatedly. 'The whole purpose of Petroc coming here was for me to see what I thought of him, and then make up my mind. How am I to do that, if I am never to speak a word to anyone else? Am I expected to become a sort of Egyptian princess, shut up in a hareem?'

'Now you're being silly, Belle!' Victoria spoke impatiently, and then regretted it. This was as close as they had come to quarrelling. She added, more gently, 'If you really do not want to marry him, surely it would be kind to tell him so?'

Bella looked at her, her big eyes open wide. 'But, Vic, that's just the trouble. I don't know what I want. Petroc is nice, he's rich, he's fond of me, he dances very well . . .'

Vicki laughed. 'A very desirable attribute in a husband, I'm sure!'

'Don't be so beastly, Vic, you know very well what I mean. It would be suitable. And my father hopes for it.'

'Well, there you are,' Victoria said. 'Perhaps, if you don't know what you want yourself, you should let your father's wishes guide you? I'm sure he has your happiness at heart.' She looked around for some way to change the subject, and her eyes lighted on the parcel Bella had brought. 'Now, if you have finished with your tea do let me see that book you promised: *Ann Veronica* by Mr H.G. Wells! I hear it's quite deliciously scandalous.' She stretched out her hand to pick it up.

Bella snatched the packet away. 'No, Vicki, listen. This is serious. This is my whole life we're talking of. Would that be enough for you, if you were me? Will you be content to marry Lionel, without even considering anybody else, just because your father hopes you will?'

Victoria laughed. 'Fortunately he doesn't, so the question won't arise.' She made another little playful snatch towards the novel.

Bella held it away from her and looked at her, surprised. 'But Vic, of course he hopes you'll make a match of it. Surely even you must realize that? Why else would he have bothered with a curate suddenly? He's never felt the need of one till now.'

It was not a comfortable thought. 'You think so?'

'Naturally I do, and so does everybody else. Mother was saying at breakfast yesterday what a good idea it was, your father bringing a curate to the parish, and giving you the chance to meet a suitable young man.'

Of your own class, she meant, but Victoria was too preoccupied to mind. She found that her playfulness had vanished. Could this be true? Deedee had employed Lionel for her sake? He couldn't have! But of course he could! She recalled, with an uncomfortable twinge, her own words to Deedee not so long ago: 'I'll never find anyone to marry me'.

'But . . . Lionel?' she said the words aloud.

Bella gave her arm a friendly squeeze. 'I know. It's far too soon to even think of it. But now you understand the way I feel. I've nothing against Petroc – he's very nice. Perhaps in the end, I'll even marry him. But oh, Vicki, haven't you ever looked at anyone and wondered . . .?'

Victoria said nothing for a moment, and then she replied slowly, 'Very well, Belle. I think I understand. What exactly are you wanting me to do?'

Bella laughed. 'I don't know. I wanted you to think of something. I can't use Jack the groom to go out riding any more. He got such a wigging last time – after I got wet and caught that chill – that he refuses to let me leave his sight. So what am I to do? I can't go out walking over to St Just alone – all the tongues in west Penwith would wag.'

Victoria put down her cup and saucer with a sigh. 'Stephen comes here nearly every week to see Papa,' she said slowly. 'If you simply said that you were coming to see me, perhaps you could contrive to meet him on the way.'

Bella jumped to her feet. 'Oh, Vic, you are a trump. I knew you'd find a way. You always were so good at organizing things.' Bella was so genuinely pleased that Victoria couldn't help but smile. After all, as Bella said, what harm was there in this? A little innocent adventure, that's all. This was the twentieth century, after all. And it would give Bella a chance to make up her mind properly. No girl should be bustled into marrying a man, just because her father thought she should.

She was about to venture something else, when an urchin in a ragged shirt and cap suddenly put his head around the hedge. He turned scarlet when he saw the girls, but he snatched off his grubby headgear and approached them timidly.

''Scuse me, Misses, I'm some sorry to disturb your tea, but is Dr Flower here? I've been 'ammering at the door for minutes, but I can't make anybody hear.'

'I believe my father and the curate have gone over to the church.' Victoria got to her feet, conscious of Bella's disbelieving eyes. One of the problems of living in a vicarage, however, was the constant possibility of visits from the poor. She put on her vicar's daughter voice and said, 'What is it that you want him for?'

The boy turned more crimson than ever, but he blurted out. 'Thing is, Miss, they want him down the quarry. Been a bad accident, there has. Don't know yet how many people hurt. Pit capt'n sent me up here at once, to fetch the Reverend quick.'

Bella said, 'More sensible, surely, to send for the doctor? If it is serious, that is.'

Victoria knew better. If they wanted Deedee, it was bad. Doctors cost money and there was no point in calling to tend the dead. 'I'll fetch my father for you.'

She went over to the church at once, half-running to disguise her thumping heart. As long as it wasn't the Olds boy who was dead, she murmured to herself. Oh dear heaven, don't let it be that.

She'd quite forgotten Bella and her plans.

The accident had happened from a clear blue sky.

Dan was sauntering over to the face with Tom. They'd had a good morning, and a fine block of granite was waiting for them to blast it free. The day was warm and they'd worked through without a pause and had only taken a few minutes to snatch a bit of crowst (a half a pasty and a cup of tea), down in the shade of the powderhouse, out of the dust and grit.

His father was working over by the pile, with another member of his team preparing a huge block of trimmed granite for the crane, ready to be lifted on to a cart. It was hot work and Dad was sweating in the heat. He called out to Dan and Tom as they went by, teasing them for their lack of haste.

'All right for some, innit? Bore a few 'oles and then go sit and eat your pasties in the sun. Like as if tomorrow's soon enough.' He stood back and signalled that the pair of iron spikes had been driven into place and securely clamped, so that the crane could start to take the weight. Once he was satisfied he turned back to his son, grinning all over his face. 'Mind you two don't burst something, hurrying like that!'

They were the last words Dan ever heard him say.

There was an almighty crack and one of the overhead steel ropes gave way. Dan looked up and saw it snaking towards him through the air, like a gigantic whip.

'Get down!' he shouted, and flung himself on Tom, hurling the old man to the to the ground and throwing himself on top of him. Only just in time: the wicked lash of steel bounced off the rock face opposite, instead of slicing off Tom's head as it would almost certainly have done. But as it bounced back, it caught Dan a glancing blow across the legs. He felt a searing pain along his calf, and just had time to register that the bone and sinew were exposed, before he closed his eyes and a red mist enveloped him.

He did not learn the rest till afterwards, though he was to see it a thousand times, later in his dreams.

When the rope snapped the lifting harness sagged. The granite lurched sideways, still clamped firmly in its jaws, and hurtled downwards to the limit of its scope. It dangled drunkenly for a tantalizing second before the other rope gave way and the whole contraption came crashing to the ground. Daniel's father and his partner were still under it, though those who witnessed it and moved the shattered block of stone away, always said privately that in that bloodstained mess it was impossible to work out which bits of who were which.

Even that wasn't the end of it. When the other end of rope snapped back it took the craneman's left hand with it, clean as a whistle at the wrist. Meanwhile, all the crashing and screaming panicked the horses at the gate, and poor old Winker took a hoof across the face and lost the sight in his remaining eye. It didn't kill him, but it might as well have done. He bore the scars of it for life, and never worked again.

But Dan didn't know that at the time. He knew nothing at all until he woke up on a makeshift stretcher, being carried home, with his head throbbing and his leg on fire. Even then he couldn't remember what had happened (the painful memories did not come till later). He tried to struggle up and ask them, but a voice he did not recognize said, 'Shush, you rest. Time enough later for all that.'

Somehow he had no energy to argue. He slid into unconsciousness again.

It was Harry who brought the word to Mollie Coombs. She had come home late from her scrubbing job as usual – the regular woman still had not come back – and had just sat down to a supper of last night's potato pie, which Eadie had grumblingly warmed up for her, when there was a timid tapping at the door.

'Come in if you're good-looking,' Eadie bawled, reluctant to get up from her seat beside the fire, where she was rocking little Stanley in her arms. She'd taken him to see his grandmother that day, and they were both tired after his first visit out. 'Door's on the latch.'

The knocking came again.

'I'll get it,' Mollie pushed aside her plate.

Eadie called after her, 'One of the men come for Fayther and them boys, I expect. There's some big meeting down the quarry pit again.' She laughed. 'If that's what they're after, it's a waste of time – all three of ours have stayed down there for it, and haven't bothered to come home between. Waste of time me hurrying back from up St Just! And their supper's getting cold, and all.'

Mollie wiped her greasy lips before she opened the door, half-expecting to find Dan Olds standing there. Instead, it was Harry Varfell on the step, twisting his cap in his strong, plump hands and blushing painfully. His face was screwed into such an anguished frown that Mollie's first thought was to comfort him.

'Hello then, Harry,' she said heartily. Truth to tell, she felt a bit badly about Harry. She hadn't seen him much since maypole day, and she hadn't been very kind to him even then; ignored him once or twice when Dan Olds was about, she recognized guiltily. But he looked so tragic standing there that she put on her most jollying laugh to say, 'Don't look so cast about, my handsome. Mightn't ever happen, whatever 'tis.'

He stopped fidgeting then and looked at her, and as he did she looked into his eyes and what she saw there made her catch her breath. 'Harry! What?'

And he said, as the whole world seemed to slow down suddenly, 'It's already happened, Moll, my handsome. I'm some sorry to bring you news like this, but better hear it from me than some stranger, anyroad.'

'Is it Fayther?' she managed, a hundred awful pictures floating before her eyes. But he was shaking his head. 'Not Jamie? Or Stan? We should have guessed. They've none of them come home. But never heard the hooter, and with this meeting down the quarrypit tonight, I thought—'

'Hooter went though, Moll,' he said quietly. 'While you were out working, I suppose. It's bad. Two men killed and others hurt. The Oldses took the worst of it. Father's killed dead, and Daniel's hurt bad, too. Proper hero 'e was too, from what I hear. Saved Old Tom's life, by all accounts, but he's in a bad way hisself. They've had the doctor to him, but he's still unconscious, seemingly, and it's touch and go if his leg will ever be right again . . .' He paused, then added awkwardly, 'I thought you ought to know, being as how you're sweet on him, I know.'

But Mollie was hardly listening. 'Dan? Hurt? Dan?' She was repeating the words idiotically. 'I must go down there. See him – anything.'

She made to rush past Harry, but he put out a restraining hand. 'Mollie, you can't do that, my handsome. There's a man lying dead down there. Tisn't as if you were a friend of Mrs Olds.'

He was right, of course. If Mother was here, she could have gone – all the older women would be there – but it wasn't for young people the likes of her to go bursting in and demanding to see Dan.

97

'Anyway,' Harry said, 'there's nothing you could you do. Not tonight, at any rate. In a day or two, maybe. When Dan's come round a bit – supposing that he does.'

Suddenly she felt her own legs were giving way, and she was grateful for the support of Harry's arm. For a moment she stood there, but then she allowed him to lead her gently back into the house. Harry whispered to Eadie what was going on, and even stayed a little while, but Mollie sat silently, staring into space, until Fayther and the boys came back at last and she was obliged to hear the full horror of the tale.

'Good thing they dead men both belonged to the Workers' Friendly,' Fayther said. 'Leastways the funeral'll be sorted out, and there'll be a bit of something for the wives. Though I 'spect there'll be a whip-round by and by, and all. Mind, I feel sorry for the families. Especially that Mrs Olds, poor soul. What she must be going through – lost a husband and frightened for her son. And with that child still not recovered yet.' He pushed away his empty plate and picked up Mollie's, which she had hardly touched. ''Ere, want this do you, Mollie girl? Only, I'll have it if you don't. No point in wasting a tasty bit of pie. Famished, I am, with all this.' He'd stayed behind with Jamie and Stan to clear the site and help to move the dead.

She nodded dumbly. She didn't care.

'One thing about it,' Stan said, leaning back on his chair and loosening his braces in the way that Mollie couldn't stand, 'that's five men gone today from down the quarry pit. Prowse needed to get rid of ten, he said. Could be good news for some folk, in the end.'

Mollie gave a little gasp, and Jamie – at whom this 'comfort' had been aimed – got up at once and left the house, slamming the door behind him.

'Stanley Tregorran, can't you hold your tongue!' Eadie said, frowning at her husband warningly. 'If you can't talk better sense, don't talk at all. That's Jamie's friend you're talking about, down there lying hurt. And can't you see our Mollie's had a dreadful shock? You know she was half-walking out with Daniel Olds. Surprised you haven't made her cry.'

But it wasn't until she'd gone to bed that Mollie's tears began. Not for herself, but for Daniel, and for poor Mr Olds, who would never come home to eat leftover pie again.

Four

'So, the funeral of the quarry workers is arranged?' It was supper-time the day after the accident and Victoria pretended to be casual. But she asked the question as soon as Deedee had finished saying grace.

She'd been wanting to prompt her father for more news ever since he'd come back from the pit, but up to now she hadn't had a chance. He was so worn out when he first came home that he had merely said, 'Only a few men affected, mercifully, though bad enough. Two poor fellows killed.' And then he'd gone to bed. And today he had been busy all day with Mr Prowse who, as one of the churchwardens, naturally had a call upon his time.

Vicki tried to reassure herself that, with a small-scale accident, it was unlikely to involve anyone she knew but it was impossible to be absolutely sure. She wanted to ask outright about the names, but she felt Miss Boff's eyes upon her and desisted. It would be very hard to explain her interest, and her governess would certainly have asked. She contented herself with enquiring, 'Is the funeral to be a big affair?'

'Big by their standards, anyway,' Deedee answered, allowing Ruby to serve him with the soup. The girl had been taken on permanently in the house since Lionel arrived. 'There is some providential fund which pays the funeral expenses.'

Lionel murmured, 'Shall we be called on to officiate?'

Deedee shook his head. 'Both of the dead men were chapel-goers, if they were anything,' he said. Victoria knew what that meant. The chapel people had their own non-conformist graveyard and their own traditions: brass bands and hymn-singing and painted iron carts.

Lionel seemed reluctant to accept this view. 'The men were a bit gruff, but they were glad enough to see us when we went down to the scene. Some of them were positively welcoming.'

'Of course they were,' Deedee said simply. 'In distress people always turn to God. Nevertheless, they are entitled to do things their own way. The church cannot seek to trespass on their grief.'

Lionel looked so discomfited that Victoria was hard put not to grin, and she hid her amusement by crumbling her bread.

Her father obviously felt that he had been too harsh. 'But your instincts do you credit, Lionel. We are not instructed to show Christian charity only to our own. I think that we might call on the families, perhaps, to see if there is anything wanted – that sort of thing.' Lionel looked up in surprise and Deedee went on with a smile. 'In fact, you may find they're expecting it. It has always been our custom to take something to the sick.'

Miss Boff nodded sententiously. 'Mrs Roseworthy makes an excellent nourishing jelly from our chicken bones, for instance, and the Christian Ladies' League has a scheme for distributing their outgrown baby clothes. Much the most satisfactory way to help. If you give them money, men of that class are inclined to squander it on drink.'

Deedee maintained his smile, but his voice was a little sharper as he said, 'People also have their pride, Miss Boff. It is sometimes easier for them to accept our help if it doesn't come in monetary form.'

Miss Boff turned scarlet up to her ears and sprinkled pepper into her soup with unnecessary force.

Ruby had finished serving soup by now, and Deedee allowed her to leave the room before he added, 'Besides, there is obviously a limit to what anyone can do. If one began making cash donations in that way, one would soon have the whole parish at the door. Although there are sure to be some pitiful cases here. That poor woman with the husband that was killed . . . What was her name? Her eldest boy was injured too, it seems, and she already has a sick child at home. It's hard to see how she will keep out of the workhouse, after this.'

Victoria stared at him. 'You're not talking about the Olds, are you?' She could feel a cold shiver running up her back.

Deedee smiled at her. 'Olds, yes, of course, that was the name. Well done, Victoria.' Then the oddness seemed to strike him, and he added with a little frown, 'I didn't know that you were acquainted with the family?'

For a moment Victoria did not know what to say – her mind was busy with imagined pictures of the injured boy – but she was rescued, ironically, by Miss Boff.

'Surely you remember, Dr Flower, that rather impertinent young woman with red hair, who turned up here asking to borrow your bicycle?' Miss Boff offered the information instantly, as if by doing so she could redeem herself a little in her employer's estimation. 'It was the Olds family she called about, as I recall. An infant had fallen in the fire, or something of the kind. I believe Victoria has called since with a pot of jelly for the child.'

Deedee cocked an eye at his daughter over his spoonful of soup. 'Is that so, Victoria?'

It was certainly true. She had taken an opportunity to go, although it had been an unfulfilling visit. She had been met at the door by a skinny child, who had taken her offering gratefully enough, but hadn't asked her in. There'd been no sign of the older boy at all – not, of course, that she'd really hoped to run into him, or anything.

She was about to stumble an answer, but her father went on unexpectedly, 'In that case perhaps you could call round there again with Lionel. The family may find it easier to accept help from somebody they've met.'

Victoria's heart gave a little leap of painful embarrassment. She nodded and moved the conversation on to other things, before any more awkward questions could be asked. She could never have disguised her blushes under Miss Boff's relentless gaze. Ever since Deedee's earlier rebuke the governess had been watching Victoria, waiting for her own excuse to chide.

Sure enough, it came a little later, when the meal was over and the ladies had moved to sit down in the other room.

'I'm sorry to have to speak to you like this, Victoria,' Miss Boff began, not sounding sorry in the least, 'but a young lady should take much smaller portions on her spoon. It looks most unbecoming, especially in Mr Smallbone's company.' She broke off as there was a movement at the door.

Victoria looked up, and saw that Lionel had come into the room. He must have heard her being scolded like a child. She turned an embarrassed shade of red, and so did he, but he proved an unexpected ally all the same.

'I'm sure Miss Flower could not be unbecoming, if she tried,' he muttered, giving Miss Boff an uncomfortable smile. He moved to the piano and opened it, adding rather awkwardly, 'Your father would like a little Chopin, Victoria. Would you care to play?'

And the governess could only sniff and flounce.

That night before she went to bed, Victoria said her prayers as usual, first and most earnestly for Daniel Olds, and then for his family and her own, and then more dutifully for Miss Boff too. Miss Boff! Imagine Lionel standing up to her like that. Vicki gave herself a little shake. It was not proper to let trivial things intrude on your devotions, but she couldn't prevent herself remembering what he'd said.

'And bless Mr Smallbone, too. Amen,' she whispered to the dark. She was still smiling as she blew out the light.

Lionel tried to look at himself critically in the small mirror over the tallboy in his room. His face and shoulders looked all right, as usual. The wispy blondish beard and hair against his robes gave him an almost apostolic air, but he knew that the whole picture was not so flattering. If only his hands and feet were not so large! He wasn't even sure about the beard these days: it was no longer fashionable, but it hid his receding chin. And was that a pimple beginning on his neck? He gave it a little prod and made it worse.

Well, it could not be helped. There was not the slightest point in being vain. It was unlikely that Miss Flower would even look at him. He had never been a success with girls. Not like his hero Hugh Grandison at school: tall, blond, athletic, bronzed and beautiful.

Lionel ran a finger round the starched band around his neck, as though it were too tight. It always made him uncomfortable to think of Hugh, whose effortless talent at everything and air of careless charm had always had girls swooning at his feet and all the junior boys queuing up to carry his cricket pads. He'd always made Lionel feel inadequate – a mixture of admiration and despair.

He sighed. If Hugh had been walking to the village with a girl – even if it *was* only to take comfort to the sick and the bereaved – he would have known exactly how to handle it. Lionel could just imagine him – confident, handsome, elegant – chatting to Miss Flower unselfconsciously and helping her courteously over stiles.

Why couldn't he himself be more like that? This was a rare opportunity. He'd never walked anywhere with a girl alone, but he knew he would be awkward and ill at ease. Even his long black curate's robe, far from lending him dignity, only made him feel more conspicuous and gauche. Well, it was no good standing here; he would keep Miss Flower waiting if he didn't go down soon. He went out quietly, closed the door, and began to make his way downstairs.

There was a longer mirror on the shadowy half landing, and he stopped there to inspect himself again. Did he look too much of a fool? He glanced around. There was nobody about.

He stretched out a hand towards his reflection in the mirror and rehearsed: 'Can I assist you?' No, too grave. He tried a smile. 'Can I assist you?' he intoned again, displaying far too many teeth.

He modified the idiotic grin. 'Can I . . .?' he tailed off in consternation, aware that Victoria was already at the bottom of stairs and was looking up at him with undisguised amusement. Drat, drat and double drat! Now she would laugh at him and think he was a fool. That had really put the icing on the cake!

He was aware that he was blushing like an idiot. He wished the ground would open up and swallow him, but there was nothing for it but to go down to meet her. He did so, trying not to meet her eyes.

She surprised him by saying, sympathetically, 'Practising what you are going to say? Poor Lionel. I know just how that feels. Miss Boff used to make me do it all the time.'

He was so astonished that he forgot his discomfiture. 'Did she?'

Victoria grinned. 'Oh yes! If ever I so much as went out to tea, I had to practise everything, from how to hold a knife to "good-bye and thank you so much for having me".' She laughed. 'I still associate having a new dress with walking three times around the room with a book balanced on my head, just to make sure that I was straight and the back was "hanging properly". You know what she's like. You heard her the other night. Thank you for standing up for me, by the way. It was most gallant.'

He looked at her, but she was serious.

'She reminded me of Matron, when I was at school,' he said, as if that explained everything, and this comment made Victoria laugh.

Suddenly embarrassment was gone; it was all right. This was not a 'girl', the silly, flirty, giggly kind he knew, nor a 'young lady' giving herself airs, making polite conversation and standing on social ceremony. This was just a person, like himself. She might as easily have been a boy. He wanted to tell her so, but that might have sounded uncomplimentary.

He was still thinking about how to reply, when she said, 'Well, if I am to take you to the village, shall we go?' And he didn't have to say anything at all.

It wasn't all plain sailing. There were times when Lionel still found himself at a loss for words, but the walk down to Polvidden was not really difficult at all, and when they came to the stile he offered her a hand as naturally as he would have done so to his mother – although Victoria was up and over the stone bars more lightly than he could manage himself, encumbered as he was by heavy robes.

As they neared the house, however, Lionel began to feel uncomfortable again. The last time he had visited like this, his vicar had been with him – and he had been expert at dealing with the real, raw grief within. It was something quite different to face it with this inexperienced young girl.

He glanced at her, but she was knocking at the door. She looked a little anxious, too. In fact, he was rather surprised that she had come. Her father had half-suggested it, of course, but she had seized upon it with a surprising enthusiasm. Almost as if she actively welcomed the opportunity. It couldn't – could it – have been for his company? That was a disconcerting thought, if not an entirely unpleasant one.

She looked across at him and smiled, just as the door opened and they were ushered in.

The house was even worse than he'd imagined it: small and cramped and squalid, full of damp washing and the smell of fish, and the close unwashed proximity of what seemed like hordes of Oldses, big and small. A thin boy with legs like a stork's had shown them in, though he should almost certainly have been at school. Perhaps the family did not have the penny fee.

By the fire a small girl swathed in bandages was propped up in a chair. Lionel counted two other children too, not including the one who was lying ill upstairs. He was not good with children – never quite at ease with them – and he was actively relieved to follow the elder girl, who said, 'You'd better come into the best room, then. Mother's in there with the coffin, now.'

Not only Mrs Olds but half the village too! The musty little parlour seemed crammed and overstuffed, though in fact there were only half a dozen women there. A coffin took up so much of the room that the furniture had been moved back to make space for it, and the visitors were huddled awkwardly, perched upon the arms of horsehair chairs, or standing behind the potted plant, trying to find a clear square foot of floor. The place smelt of damp and polish, and there was a general atmosphere of chilly airlessness.

Lionel was about to say something conventional when the widow, who had been sitting white-faced in a chair, recognized important visitors and got to her feet.

'Why it's Miss Flower and Mr Whatsisname,' she said, rubbing her hands in the clean apron which she still wore over her mourning black. Her eyes were red-rimmed, and her face was like a kind of tragic mask, strained with the effort of not giving way to tears. 'Come to see him, have you? That's some good of you, but I'm afraid they've already screwed him down. Did it before they ever brought him home.'

One of the women clucked protectively, 'Just as well too, for your own sake, you poor lamb.' She nodded at Lionel. 'Better off not seeing, if you ask me. Great lump of stone like that can make a proper mess of a man.'

Lionel had seen the bloodstained quarry yesterday and he could imagine, with a lurch of the stomach, the sight that might otherwise have met their eyes. He glanced at Victoria to see how she was taking it, but she was already murmuring something comforting to the widow, and producing her little jar of jelly as though it were some kind of magic cure.

'I brought some more of this for Lucy,' he heard her say, and the woman took it mechanically. 'Perhaps you should have some of it yourself. And perhaps your son, when he is well enough. How is he, by the way?'

She sounded genuinely concerned, and Lionel was impressed. However, it was too much for the widow's self-control and she broke down immediately in tears.

'Do the poor soul good, to 'ave a bit of cry,' the clucking woman leaned over to whisper to Lionel in an undertone. She had bad breath and smelt of onions and he had to check himself from stepping back. 'Doesn't do your 'ealth no good, bottling it up like she's been doing. Mind, it'll be a poor lookout for 'er, losing two wage earners at once like this. Folks round 'ere will do what they can, of course, but we got our own to see to, that's the truth. Even 'alfpennies don't grow on trees, you know.'

'I'm sure the parish will do everything it can,' Lionel said, rather formally. His words were greeted with a dreadful hush.

Too late, he realized what that sounded like. The 'parish' only meant the 'workhouse' to the poor. And he had spoken too loudly: the widow had overheard.

'It's very good of you, I'm sure,' she said, with defiant tear-stained dignity. 'But I got two children still bringing in a wage. We aren't ready to throw ourselves on the workhouse yet. Won't do neither, while I've got an ounce of strength left in my bones.'

Lionel tried to mutter something, but the harm was done. The room was filled with animosity. Victoria was looking daggers at him, too, and he was very glad when a little later they were able to excuse themselves and leave.

Mollie hurried quickly down the lane. She had judged her moment for this visit thoughtfully. Not too soon – that would have been impertinent as she wasn't a friend of Mr Olds, when all was said and done, and there wasn't anything formal between herself and Dan – but not so late that it looked as if she didn't care.

Pity she didn't have something a bit more suitable to wear, but apart from this she only had her black, and you couldn't go looking like a funeral. So, the plain blue skirt would have to do, with a clean blouse and her chapel hat. She'd even taken a clump of grass to shine up her working boots.

The door was standing open as she approached, but she was not surprised. Some of the older village woman would be there paying their respects. Only to be expected, that was. But there was Miss Flower, of all people, coming out of the house, with that pink-faced new curate gangling at her side. What on earth were those two doing there, talking to Jimmy on the step? Mollie felt unreasonably put out.

Of course, she realized a moment later, they were calling officially on Dr Flower's behalf, but somehow it didn't make it any easier. All very well for them, she thought resentfully, dressed to go anywhere. Just look at Miss Flower's dove-grey costume, hat and gloves! And no worry about waiting for the proper time to call. She could just visit any time she pleased.

Mollie had half a mind to turn tail and walk away till they were gone, but she realized that Miss Flower had noticed her and – worse – was whispering something to the curate at her side. And now, horror of horrors, she was coming over with a determined smile.

'Miss . . . Coombs, isn't it?'

Of course it was, silly heifer, Mollie thought. Who did she think she was, with her patronising ways? But of course, you couldn't say that sort of thing aloud, not to the vicar's daughter anyroad.

''Sright,' Mollie forced her own face into a grin, but there wasn't any warmth behind the smile. Nor in Miss Flower's either. Like when she went up to the vicarage that time. For no very good reason that she could explain, there was something that crackled between them like wet sherbet on a dab. Well, she wouldn't be outfaced. She found her voice. 'You been visiting the sick?'

Miss Flower turned pink-faced, but she said, in a throbbing voice that reminded Mollie of Aunt Annie talking about the clock, 'Yes, it is so unutterably sad. A husband dead, and that poor boy injured there. We came to see if there was anything we could do.'

Mollie said nothing, and after a moment the curate added earnestly, 'We brought a little pot of jelly for the child.'

Mollie gave a bitter little laugh. She didn't mean to sound derisive, but really it would be comical, if it was not so sad. 'A pot of jelly?' she said. 'How's that going to help? Don't you know anything at all? Tisn't pots of jelly they want, it's hope – and the good Lord alone knows where that's coming from. Two wage earners taken at a single stroke! Even if poor Dan gets back on his feet, how's he ever going to find work again? Quarry's in trouble as it is, who's going to want a half-lame powder man?

And it's not only now, it's all his life. Suppose he was walking out with somebody? How will he ever support a wife and family now? Think of that, did you, with your jelly pots?'

She had hardly allowed herself to think about it all till now and she found her voice catching with tears and fury as she spoke.

It must have had some effect. She saw Miss Flower flinch.

Good! she thought, goaded by some inner devil. Passion made her cruel; she went on: 'And they've had the doctor to and fro, besides. How do you think they're going to pay for that? So, no, Miss Flower, unless you've got a job of honest work hidden in that pretty reticule of yours, I don't think there is anything you can do for them.'

Miss Flower stepped back, ashen-faced. 'I'm sorry. We only hoped to help.'

Mollie almost felt ashamed. 'Well, I'm sorry to be blunt, but that's the truth. So, if you'll excuse me?' And with her head held high she swept past Miss Flower and into Daniel's house.

He was conscious again, and she sat with him for an hour; he was pathetically glad to see her.

Five

Victoria walked home in a sort of daze. It had been dreadful, just dreadful, visiting that house. First of all, there was the place itself. How could decent people live all crammed up like that?

Of course, she had seen it all before, a hundred times, but that had been different. Those were just Deedee's parishioners, not real people that she'd stopped to think about. But this was Dan!

Lionel was saying something, but she shook her head. She scarcely took it in. Her mind was still full of that red-headed girl, attacking her so fiercely in the street.

But Lionel was repeating what he'd said. 'Miss Flower, surely . . .' he insisted, 'isn't that your friend that I can see?'

It was, of course. Bella was sitting waiting on a tree stump by the stile, immaculately dressed as usual, but switching at the grasses with a stick and generally wearing an air of fidgety impatience.

Victoria gulped. Of course! She had completely forgotten Bella and her affairs. This was Thursday, Penzance market day, and the day when Mr Stephen Pencarrow had been due to call.

'Oh dear!' she said to Lionel. 'I quite forgot. Isabella said that she might call by with a book for me today.' She gave him an apologetic smile, and without waiting for him to catch up with her, hurried to the stile and went to meet her friend, who stood up to greet her as she came. 'I am most truly sorry, Belle. There has been an accident at the quarry and Lionel and I have been visiting the families.'

'Oh, it doesn't signify,' Belle said, in a martyred tone of voice, which signalled quite clearly that it did. 'At least, not now that

111

you've arrived. Though I was so afraid you wouldn't come at all. I came to call on you as you proposed, but Miss Boff said that you were out. She did say you weren't likely to be long, so I thought I'd loiter here a little while and wait. Ah, Mr Smallbone, there you are, good afternoon. How fortunate that I should meet you here. I have just come from the vicarage. Dr Flower has a visitor. I think they are expecting you. Something about some music you were hoping for?'

This was an obvious hint for him to leave, and Victoria was rather hurt on his account, but Lionel took his dismissal in good part. He simply said, 'Then I'll bid you ladies a good afternoon.' And hurried to the house.

'You succeeded in running into Mr Pencarrow then?' Victoria said, turning her back on Lionel's retreating form. 'Don't look so surprised, Bella. You must have done, to know what he had come about today. Though it was a little indiscreet, perhaps, to make that so clear to Lionel.'

Bella made a little face. 'In fact, Miss Clever, it was Miss Boff who told me that – grumbling that you were out with Lionel, when he was wanted here about some music manuscripts!' She grinned. 'But you are quite right, Vic, I did run into Stephen. Your little plan worked wonderfully well, though I'm very glad you came home when you did. It could have been confoundedly difficult, if we hadn't met, you know! Petroc would have wanted me to tell him all about my afternoon and I shouldn't have in the least known what to say.'

This was all rather scandalous, and Victoria was surprised into a laugh. 'But now you will?'

'Oh yes. I can tell him what you were wearing, what we talked about, that sort of thing . . .' She broke off with a giggle. 'Well, not all of it, of course. I was going to ask you what you thought of *Ann Veronica*, but now I can tell him about this accident. It's quite lucky really, it makes something interesting to tell.' She sighed. 'He's turned into quite an inquisitor about me when I am out, and I'm a perfect fool when it comes to inventing anything. I don't have your wit for imagining things.'

The suggestion that she was an accomplished story teller did not seem altogether a compliment, and Victoria found herself saying rather bitterly, 'I shouldn't have thought you would have had any difficulty imagining my clothes! You might have said that they were grey or brown and been quite certain that you were correct!'

Bella gave her a limpid look. 'That's just it, Vicki. You would have known at once how to reply. I should have blushed and stammered and made it obvious that I hadn't seen you in the least. But now, you see, it's all worked perfectly.' She slipped her hand into Victoria's arm, and began to walk back towards the house. 'But don't go out next time and abandon me, will you Victoria? Promise me?'

Vicki stopped and freed her arm with energy. 'Next time! Now, look here, Belle, this has got to stop! I've helped you this once, that's enough. You cannot really expect me to condone the fact that you are sauntering through country lanes alone with a young man you do not even have an understanding with!' She was too distressed to be grammatical.

Bella put her head on one side and looked at her. 'But Vic, you've just done that very thing yourself.'

Victoria coloured. That was literally true, of course, though she hadn't thought of it like that. 'But that wasn't the same thing at all!' she cried. 'We were on parish business. And anyway, Deedee himself suggested it!'

Bella bestowed a pitying smile. 'Of course he did. Didn't I tell you he was hoping for a match?'

And to that Victoria found – as she turned and marched furiously back towards the house, with her mind spinning and her cheeks aflame – she could find no sensible reply at all.

'Then, Mr Smallbone . . . Lionel . . . it is quite arranged!' The visitor in Edward's study seemed a pleasant sort of chap – extremely helpful and obliging, though perhaps a little confident and loud. He was wringing Lionel's hand now in both his own with almost uncomfortable force, and saying heartily, 'I shall

take you out to visit Ralph. You will be impressed with him I
know – he is quite an artist in his way – and this collection of
sheet music is remarkable. It belonged to a friend of his who died
– tragic business – only recently, and he has left everything to
Ralph. I am sure you will find something to interest you there,
and Ralph would be delighted to see it go to someone who would
value it.'

Lionel smiled. 'That's very good of you, Mr Pencarrow.' And
disengaged his hand.

Pencarrow relinquished it with a parting squeeze that made its
owner wince. 'Think nothing of it, my dear fellow. Any friend of
Edward's is a friend of mine. You'll like the cottage too –
beautiful views from there along the cliffs. Perhaps we could
take Miss Flower and her friend and make a day of it? I'll speak
to Ralph about it sometime soon, and let you know. I shall be
calling to see Dr Flower again – with that illustrated Spenser, if
possible, eh Edward?'

The vicar gave a little rueful laugh, and put down the old
volume he'd been looking at. 'Stephen, you know my weaknesses too well. This is really splendid Blake. But yes, perhaps
the Spenser if you can. And really then I shall have to call a
halt. I have a curate to support these days, after all.' He showed
Pencarrow out towards the stairs. 'Till Thursday fortnight,
then.'

'Till then!' Pencarrow said. 'Don't trouble to come down. I
know you're longing to enjoy your Blake. Miss Boff is downstairs – she will see me out.'

Edward hesitated, and Lionel said, as he knew he was expected
to, 'Allow me!' He led the way down into the hall, waited while
Pencarrow pulled on hat and gloves, and opened the door to let
the caller out. At that same moment Victoria and her friend
emerged from the morning room.

Miss Cardew led the way, laughing and talking animatedly.
'Yes, really, Victoria dear, I must be going. I've already been
longer than I meant. I'm very pleased that you enjoyed the book.'
She turned, as if surprised, and said in a more gentle tone, 'Why

Mr Pencarrow, I declare! Are you leaving too? I was just about to go myself.'

Pencarrow bowed slightly. 'Then perhaps you will permit me to offer you a lift? I have the trap outside.'

'Delighted!' she replied. 'If you will give me a moment to put my bonnet on?' She moved to the mirror as she spoke, and her eyes caught Lionel's briefly in the glass. She raised her eyebrows at him, and smiled . . . coquettishly, that was the word for it.

He felt himself turn crimson instantly. Thank goodness Victoria didn't do that sort of thing. It was exactly the sort of behaviour that made him uncomfortable. Not that Miss Cardew wasn't pretty . . . He supposed she was, in a raven shepherdessy sort of way. But all that simpering and dimpling and fluttering her eyes – that wasn't attractive in the least! Whereas, Victoria . . .

He glanced in her direction She was looking disapproving too, saying gently, 'Really, Belle . . .!' Almost as if she'd read his thoughts.

But Isabella Cardew only tossed her head and said, 'Thank you, Stephen, I am ready now. Why, here's Miss Boff! Goodbye, everyone. Goodbye, Miss Boff. Mr Pencarrow has consented to drive me home – isn't that just too kind of him?'

Miss Boff gave Pencarrow an approving smile, but as the visitors departed, Lionel heard Victoria mutter quietly, for some reason which he didn't understand, 'Too kind? Yes, Mr Pencarrow, I think it is – very much too kind, indeed.'

Daniel was sitting up on Mother's bed. She'd made it over to him, since the accident, saying that she couldn't sleep in any case and would rather spend the night down in the chair, or keeping watch on Lucy in the other room.

He knew what that really meant, of course. She couldn't bear to be in Dad's bed, now Dad wasn't there. It would have to be faced, eventually, but in the meantime Dan wasn't complaining. He couldn't have slept in the same bed as Zac and Gannet, anyway. His leg was splinted – a great wooden slat on either side held on with bandages to keep it straight – and it seemed to take up all the room there was, even in this empty double bed.

It throbbed, too, something terrible, though Mother and Melda brought him soothing drinks, and home-made comfrey tea to 'bring the fever down' and help the bones to knit. But it wasn't fever keeping him awake at night. It was seeing, over and over, that snaking line and knowing that the stone was going to fall.

He shifted his weight a little, lifting himself an inch. His leg felt like a block of stone, itself. Mollie, who had been sitting on a stool beside his feet, stood up at once to help, but there wasn't anything that she could do.

'You all right, Dan?' she said anxiously. She'd been very good. Stayed for an hour, and was content to sit without wanting him to talk, or trying to jolly him as some of Mother's other visitors had done.

He nodded wearily, although 'all right' didn't really describe the way he felt. 'They weren't going to tell me about Dad, at first,' he said, following his own train of thought.

She nodded. 'Thought they'd save you from the news, I 'spect.' She didn't sound surprised. 'Must have been an awful shock for you.'

'Yes,' he agreed, but it wasn't really true. He'd seen what was going to happen at the time. His last memory was of a sickening certainty, and almost as soon as he'd come round one look at Mother's face had told him everything. He'd put them out of their misery in the end by asking them outright, 'How many dead?' They'd told him then but – though it still left him with a hollow ache – the truth had not really come as a surprise.

He took another sip of comfrey tea. It tasted disgusting, but reassuring too: the flavour of childhood illnesses.

'Worst thing for you will be not being able to go to the funeral,' Mollie remarked.

He nodded. 'Wanted to,' he said. His voice was weak. 'But doctor says I'm not even to go downstairs for another week or two. Give the bones a chance to mend, he said, and of course, there's other damage, too.' He'd had one glimpse of that, the day of the accident when the doctor first came to set and splint the leg, but the sight of his own mangled flesh, combined with the pain, had sent him into merciful unconsciousness again.

Mollie said, with forced cheerfulness, 'You go on like you're going, Dan Olds, you'll soon be on your feet. The new King's to be crowned next month, and there's to be no end of goings-on. Street parties, races, tug of wars – all sorts; and a big beacon bonfire up St Evan hill. Can't have you missing that.' She could not meet his gaze, however, and as she looked away he realized that there were tears trembling in her eyes.

'Oh Moll!' he said miserably. 'No use pretending! You can see as well as I can how things are – though I daresay King George will manage to get crowned without my being there! But, when it comes to more important things . . .' He sighed. 'Hopeless, it is, isn't it? What're we going to do? 'Course, it will be better when I can get up and work, but even then . . . Dunno as Prowse will ever have me back. Not that you need all that much strength in your legs being a powder man, but all the same you've got to nip about. No good just hobbling about. Once a charge is laid and you've lit the fuse . . .' He tailed off.

'What does the doctor say?'

Doctor! That was another thing. Mother would have to pay the doctor's bills somehow. Of course the St Just man was very good – never pressed for what you didn't have – but the money would have to come from somewhere in the end. And they owed him no end for Lucy as it was.

Dan had spoken to Mother about it, but she wouldn't heed. 'Don't be so daft, Dan. It's your whole future 'ere. You end up with twisted legs, you'll never walk again. End up pulling yourself round by your arms, in a 'and cart like Josiah Smith, trying to sell a bit of rag and bone. What kind of life is that for anyone? Bad enough your father gone without seeing you reduced to that. No, if we can do anything to help, we will, and worry about the money afterwards.' And that was all that she would say.

But Dan was worrying about the money now.

He said something of the sort to Moll. She astonished him when she came very close and took his hands in hers.

'I know, Dan,' she said, softly. 'I was thinking about that before on the way here to see you this afternoon. Won't be easy for you, I can see. Have to make a new start somewhere, more than like. But –' she met his gaze and her eyes weren't laughing now – 'I don't know how to say this to you quite . . . and we'd only just started walking out . . .' She sighed and looked away.

He braced himself for the expected blow. He didn't blame her. He was a cripple now, or was like to be. Who would be interested in him?

'Thing is, Dan, if you still wanted to, I'd be prepared to . . . well, to wait a bit – if you were thinking about . . . you know what I mean . . . something more serious, by and by.' He must have looked startled. She withdrew her hands and started to backtrack hastily. 'I mean, I aren't pressing you or anything, and 'course, we'd have to see how we got on. Courtin' and all – that's if you wanted to. And whether you could find a job somewhere. But I thought, p'raps, with you lying 'ere like this . . . well, it might cheer you up a bit to know . . . 'tisn't the end of everything, so far as I'm concerned.'

Dan shifted on the bed uncomfortably. He hadn't been prepared for this, at all. If he understood aright, Mollie had just half-proposed to him. Out of pity, probably, he was aware of that. But it touched him to know that she still thought so much of him. It couldn't have been easy to say that. He stretched out his hand and captured hers again.

'Mollie, you don't know what that means to me. I can't hold you to it, 'course – nobody could expect you to be tied like that, when 'tisn't even sure how well I'll do. But you're some sweet to think of it . . .' He pulled her closer, and she bent over him, waiting to be kissed.

But it was not to be. He was stretching upward to her lips, when they were interrupted by the thundering sound of Jimmy's footsteps on the stairs. He galloped up them like a cavalry

charge, and burst into the room, almost before Mollie had time
to jump away.

He wasted no time delivering his news. 'Ere. Dan! You've
never guess what I just seen!' He stopped, realizing that the girl
was in the room.

'Well, tell us,' his brother prompted, with a laugh.

Jimmy grinned. 'That Miss Cardew from down St Evan
House. Canoodling in the lane she was, as bold as brass – sitting
with some fellow in a trap. Tried to pretend they weren't, of
course, but I know what I seen. And that chap knew it too. Look
here!' He opened his grubby fist and revealed a silver sixpenny
bit. 'Gave me that, he did, to hold my tongue. A whole sixpence
of me own, just think of that!'

'Give it to Mother, that's what you should do!' Daniel said.
Sixpence would buy a meal for all of them.

Jimmy laughed. 'She'd want to know where I got it then.
Though I s'pose I could say I found it by the stile.' He looked at
Dan and Mollie thoughtfully. 'Course, there might be other folk
who'd pay me to keep quiet. You two were mighty guilty-looking
when I came in. Worth a penny, is it, not to mention that?'

Mollie looked ready to retort indignantly, but Daniel only
laughed. 'And a fat lot of good that'd be! First thing you'd do is
go and blab it out, it seems, even if I had a penny to give you,
which I don't. You'll never make your fortune blackmailing, my
old son, unless you keep a secret better'n that.'

Jimmy looked crestfallen and went downstairs. Mollie looked
at Dan, but the moment was over, and after a few minutes she left
too. Jimmy must have given Mother the coin, because there were
sausages for tea.

Part Three

June – August 1911

One

So there was to be a summer outing to visit Mr Ralph Mills, the artist, in his 'enchanting' house out on the cliffs! Miss Boff was looking forward to it more than she'd admit. More that was quite seemly, in a woman of her age. It was to be quite a party, it appeared.

Stephen Pencarrow was arranging it. He was a friend of Mr Mills, who was anxious to meet Lionel about some rare music manuscripts left behind when the musician friend he'd shared the cottage with had died some years before. So, really it was Lionel's occasion, although Mr Mills had generously asked everyone to tea, and invited Victoria to bring a friend for company. Miss Boff was going along as chaperone, and even Doctor Flower had consented to cycle over and join them later on.

Victoria was as excited as a child – indeed she had been a child when she had been there once before, visiting with her father years ago. Miss Boff recalled the occasion very well. Mr Mills' musician friend had been ill, even then, and the vicar had made a pastoral visit to the house. Victoria had talked of nothing else for weeks – the magic artist's garden on the cliffs.

The day appointed for the excursion was fine. Pencarrow was driving, of course, but it was a tight squeeze for all four of the others to squash into the trap, and there was a lot of untoward hilarity. Miss Boff should have chided them, perhaps, but even she felt in a holiday mood. She had put on her new heliotrope-coloured dress today in homage to the sun, and a huge purple straw bonnet to protect her skin, and she found that she was predisposed to smile. So she said nothing, except to observe quite mildly that Victoria and Bella were chattering like a pair of birds.

They even looked rather like a pair of birds, she thought. Victoria was a decent muted wood pigeon, safe in her tawny brown, while Bella glittered unbecomingly in that bright budgerigar blue – she even had a feather in her hat! Miss Boff smiled at her own fancy. And it wasn't just the girls. Lionel Smallbone, all in black, looked like a lanky crow and Mr Pencarrow, though he was dressed soberly enough in a smart houndstooth jacket and bowler hat, somehow reminded her of a peacock, strutting and preening and showing off.

It was worse when they set off down the lane. Admittedly he drove very well, but there was no doubt whom he was trying to impress; he was succeeding, too: from time to time Bella Cardew was casting little looks at him.

Miss Boff began to purse her lips. After a little while they met a farmer in a cart, and Mr Pencarrow refused point-blank to reverse the trap. He made the other driver get down from his seat, unhitch the horse, and walk his equipage all the way back to a gateway in the hedge to let them pass. A most ungentlemanly thing to do, and the farmer wasn't best pleased, you could see – muttering and grumbling underneath his breath. But Miss Cardew seemed particularly pleased.

It was not at all proper, under the circumstances, and Miss Boff knew how to put a stop to it. She looked at the young woman rather sharply and enquired, 'So, Miss Cardew, your cousin has gone home again? He has been with you for some time, I understand. He mentioned as much when he called in at the vicarage last week. No doubt you and your family will miss him very much? But Victoria says that you are going to London soon, for Coronation week, and I imagine that he has pressing business awaiting him at home.' She gave her archest little smile. 'Especially now.'

Bella Cardew, who had been exchanging admiring glances with the driver, flushed and murmured vaguely that this was true.

She looked uncomfortably around as if seeking some way of changing the subject.

But Miss Boff was not so easily deterred. She had been the only one at home when Petroc Veryan had called a day or two before, much to that young gentleman's dismay. 'I particularly wished to see the vicar,' he had said, 'about obtaining a licence and arranging the reading of the banns. Miss Cardew has consented to make me a happy man, though of course that's confidential until the announcement's made.' And Miss Boff had kept the secret – until now.

But now it was time to let Miss Cardew know she knew. 'Oh come, Miss Cardew, you must not be shy. You are among friends here.' She saw Victoria's look of astonishment and went on, 'I understand that we may hope . . . that you may have news?'

Her words had a remarkable effect. Victoria was speechless with confusion. Lionel looked embarrassed, too, and Stephen Pencarrow, glancing over his shoulder to stare at her, seemed thunderstruck.

Only Miss Cardew maintained her presence of mind. She turned, two bright spots of colour in her cheeks. 'News?' she said stiffly. 'I am very much afraid, Miss Boff, that I have no idea at all what it is that you might be alluding to.'

It was Miss Boff's turn to look abashed. She felt her face turn the same purple as her ribbons and she sat very bolt upright, compressing her lips as if to prevent any more unfortunate words from escaping them. 'I'm sorry, Miss Cardew, very sorry indeed, if I've spoken out of turn,' she said at last, in a voice strangled by embarrassment. 'But I understood . . . from Mr Veryan himself . . .'

'Be that as it may, Miss Boff, let me assure you that there is no question of anything of the kind. Whatever Mr Veryan may have said to you, there is no understanding at present between himself and me. Be assured that, if and when there is, your household will be among the first to know.'

Miss Boff said simply, 'Oh!' and slumped back in the seat. She felt eclipsed, as if someone had burst her like a bubble.

After that an uncomfortable silence fell until Lionel, to everyone's relief, took sudden inspiration from the gulls and began to talk about the nesting habits of seabirds and the disappearance of the Cornish chough.

All the same, when the cottage came in sight at last, and Stephen suddenly proposed, 'I wonder if the young ladies would care to get down and walk a little?', Victoria was only too happy to agree, and Miss Cardew said, 'What an excellent notion,' in a tone which showed she was just as anxious as her friend to get down from the trap and escape the atmosphere.

'I'll take Lionel down to meet Ralph Mills, and we can get the business part of the afternoon over, while you stroll down to meet us,' Pencarrow said. 'It shouldn't take more than a few minutes, but I'm afraid it would be tedious for you. Miss Boff, would you care to join the walkers, or to ride with us?'

It really wasn't a question. A dozen demons couldn't have kept Miss Boff from driving directly to the cottage now.

Stephen helped the two girls down, then climbed aboard again and raised his whip. The little trap went trotting on, leaving the friends together on the path.

Lionel shifted uncomfortably on his seat. He would have given much to have been able to get out and accompany the girls. Conversation in these circumstances had become impossible: Pencarrow was concentrating on the lane, Miss Boff was still looking like a basilisk, and in any case he had exhausted his knowledge about choughs, so he was very pleased when the trap drew up outside the cottage gate, and an ageing servant hobbled out to take charge of the pony and unhitch the trap.

His greeting was hardly welcoming: 'Mr Mills'll be expecting you by this. He'd 've seen you comin' from the 'ouse, same as me,' the fellow grunted with a scowl and led the animal away.

Lionel's heart sank to his polished boots. He'd had such high hopes of this afternoon: Victoria had enthused about the house, and the collection of music and manuscripts had promised to be an intellectual treat, but now he was suddenly less sure. The governess had caused embarrassment to everyone, though there had clearly been some terrible mistake. It was surely clear to everyone that Miss Cardew had no loyalties elsewhere: she was blatantly interested in Pencarrow; it showed in her every gesture, every look. She held her head on one side and smirked whenever Stephen spoke to her, and pretended to hang on his every word. And Pencarrow hadn't discouraged her.

Lionel shook his head. He had never cared for that kind of twittering femininity. Thank heavens Victoria didn't behave like that.

He glanced back along the stony track, where the two girls could still be seen deep in conversation as they walked along. Laughing, too, by the look of it. That was a good omen, at least.

He turned to offer to escort Miss Boff, but Pencarrow already had her on his arm and was leading her firmly but politely through the gate. Lionel followed. The cottage was as charming as Victoria had said: a little lime-washed cottage, huddled behind high walls, but looking out at the front across the sea. Inside the shelter of the walls someone had built a garden out of stone: rocks of all colours and every shape had been turned into a kind a wandering maze between the gate and door, interspersed with clumps of the cliff-top flowers. Through an inner arch, a further courtyard garden could be seen, this time an enchantment of honeysuckle and wild rose. There seemed to be even a few vegetables and herbs, though the top of a solitary tree, which had grown higher than the protecting wall, had bent dramatically sideways in the wind.

It was a delightful place, and here, away from the sea breeze, the air was still and warm with the faint perfume of the flowers. Lionel had taken two steps down the path when the front door opened and a man came out.

Lionel would remember that first impression of Ralph Mills for the whole of the remainder of his life. Not a big man, though his presence seemed to overflow the doorway and flow out to meet them like a tide. Not a young man, either, the thick, neat hair was tinged with grey, and he was slightly plump under the exquisite cut of his nonchalant silk shirt and flannels, but his stride was energetic as he came towards them, hands outstretched.

'Pencarrow, my dear chap, welcome. How marvellous to see you. And this charming lady –' he took Miss Boff's hand and bent over it, making her flush that purple hue again – 'this must be Miss Boff.' He had a light, pleasant, modulated voice.

A fine tenor, Lionel thought, without meaning to, and was reminded instantly of Hugh at school. Not that this man was remotely like him really, but there was something athletic and attractive about him, and the same clean male smell of talcum and bay rum.

Ralph Mills turned to him. 'And you? You are the music lover, Lionel?' He smiled, and Lionel felt as if the artist had somehow seen into his mind and read his thoughts. 'Ralph Mills. I am delighted to meet you. Stephen has spoken about you such a lot.' He took Lionel's right hand firmly in his own and closed his other hand around the wrist with as much genuine warmth as if the two men had been friends for years. 'I'm sure we two shall be splendid friends.'

Lionel was too taken aback to do more than stammer, 'A beautiful place you have here. This garden – planned with a real artist's eye.'

Ralph's smile grew warmer still, if that were possible. 'I am glad it pleases you. My late friend Matthew Mackintosh designed it – it is his music collection you have come to see.'

'We might do that at once, with your permission, Ralph,' Pencarrow said. 'Get the business part of the afternoon over before the young ladies arrive. They stayed behind on purpose, and to stretch their legs a bit. It is a long drive here from St Evan.'

'With pleasure.' Ralph Mills really looked as if it was. 'And Miss Boff, would you care to see the house, or will you take refreshment in the nook? That's what Matt used to call the inner garden, and it's a good name, as I expect you'll see.' He was leading the way through the arch as he spoke, and Lionel could see exactly what he meant. A picnic table had been laid for seven, though it was not a picnic as Lionel understood them: there was a linen tablecloth; fine china; gleaming glass; wooden bowls full of salad leaves; nectarines; strawberries and a huge picnic hamper to one side, its lid decorously ajar, hinting at further legs of ham, fresh bread and cheese and all kinds of other delicacies. A pitcher of something sparkling stood under a muslin cloth, while a hint of rusticity was added by the wide shallow baskets filled with lavender. The table was a composition in itself.

Miss Boff seemed oblivious of this. 'Please don't worry about me, Mr Mills,' she said. 'I'm sure it's very pleasant in the front, with the sea and everything. And I notice there's a seat out by the gate. I'll just sit and wait there for the girls.' And I can keep an eye on them from there; she didn't say the words but all three men understood.

Ralph Mills exchanged glances with Pencarrow, and said, 'Then I'll have Young bring you out a tray. You must be thirsty after your long drive.'

'I'll keep Miss Boff company,' Pencarrow said. 'The young ladies won't be very long, and I'm sure you two don't need me to help.' And so it was arranged.

Pencarrow was right, it did not take very long. From the moment Lionel set eyes on the music room – 'I haven't changed anything. I haven't wanted to,' Ralph Mills told him, soberly – he knew that what Matthew Mackenzie had collected – in this as in everything else – would please him very much. And so it proved; the pieces that he had been looking for, and much, much more – some of which were quite unknown to him – all delighted him as soon as he began to hum the notes.

'There's Matt's pianoforte over there,' Ralph said. 'Please, help yourself. It would a pleasure for me to hear it played again.' He smiled ruefully. 'Matt was the musician, I'm afraid. I'm far too lazy ever to have learned.' He went across and opened the lid of the instrument. 'Please.'

Lionel sat down unwillingly; it was strange being in this room with Ralph. It was less a room than a shrine, he felt, everything – papers, books, music, even a pipe – had been left exactly as it was the last time Mackenzie had sat where he was sitting now. He felt uncomfortable trespassing on that. And yet there was something domestic about it all, oddly familiar as if he were a ghost revisiting a place that he should know; perhaps because the dead man's taste was so close to his own. He strummed a few notes of the manuscript. The instrument was slightly out of tune, but – predictably – it was a delightful thing, the tone, as well as the inlaid ebony.

He glanced up. Ralph Mills was looking at him, half-smiling, half with pain. 'Please, go on – it is like having Matt with me again.'

The voice was so wistful that, for some reason, Lionel felt disturbed. He closed the instrument quickly and stood up. 'Thank you, no, that's quite enough. There is no decision to be made. I should like to buy the whole collection, if you will part with it.' He had spoken without thinking, and he added, mortified, 'As much of it as I can afford, that is.'

Ralph Mills crossed the room and came to stand close to him. For a moment Lionel thought the man was going to touch his arm. He could feel his heart thumping and his throat was dry. Ralph said in a very quiet voice, 'Don't worry about that. I'm quite sure we can come to some arrangement.'

Lionel looked at him in despair. Was the man reading his thoughts again? 'We can?' he enquired stupidly. He meant the money. Of course he meant the money. What else could he mean?

Mills said, 'I am more concerned that Matt's things should go to a sympathetic home than getting the highest price. In any case, if this copyright bill goes through parliament, these old pieces will be reproduced commercially – quite cheaply, I should think.'

Lionel gulped. He was being quite absurd. He found a smile and forced himself to say, 'That is very kind of you, Mr Mills. The vicar would like a Coronation concert in a week or two. Some of this would be most appropriate. But, of course, I can only take what I can pay for now.'

Ralph Mills flashed him another smile. 'If you prefer. There's no need for a final decision, anyway. Take what you're sure of, and come back another day.'

The invitation vaguely troubled Lionel. He put down half the bundle he was carrying, almost at random, and showed Ralph the rest. 'How much would you ask for these?'

'For those?' The sum Ralph named was so derisory that even Lionel was taken by surprise. 'But only to you, Lionel, because I know that you'll appreciate them. I know Matt would have liked that. But, as I say, no need to pay me now. Come and look at this again, and please play the piano for me once more. I would love to hear it played properly again.'

Lionel, who was wondering in confusion how to answer this, was saved the necessity of saying anything by an imperious knocking at the door. It proved to be the grumpy ancient he had seen before, now metamorphosed into indoor staff by the addition of a rather worn black coat.

'Ah! Young!' Ralph Mills cried, apparently unmoved by the striking inappropriateness of the name. 'What is it?'

'Them young ladies 'ave arrived, sir,' Young announced, and they went down to join the others.

As soon as the trap had trotted out of earshot, Victoria turned to her friend accusingly. 'Bella, what was that all about? What do you suppose that Petroc said? I suppose he did say something as it seems a strange thing for Miss Boff to invent.'

Bella swished at a clump of sea pinks with her shoe. Her face had turned pinker than the flowers. 'Well, since it has all come out anyway, it is true! He went to the vicarage to ask about the banns.'

Victoria gasped. 'Bella! He's proposed? And you are to be married soon?' Suddenly she felt let down and betrayed. 'Why ever didn't you tell me? You must have known that I'd find out very soon.'

Bella pouted. 'Except that there's nothing whatever to find out. Oh, yes, Petroc did speak to Papa and propose. Down on one knee and all that sort of thing. "Belle you know how I feel, old girl, will you marry me?" Well, I'd tried to avoid it long enough, but then I had to make up my mind.'

'So you said "yes".' Victoria tried to put her hurt aside. 'Oh Belle, I'm really very glad. I'm sure he'll make a lovely husband – and you'll be a lovely bride, just think of that.'

'Vicki, do pay attention!' Bella said. 'It's not like that a bit.'

'But you *have* accepted him?'

'Well, no. Or rather, yes. It's true I did accept him, at the time. He gave me a ring and everything. But then I changed my mind and gave it back. Oh Vic, it's such a mess. I should have told you earlier, but I knew you'd just put on your Miss Boff face and chide. I told Petroc I thought that I was far too young – so close to my birthday and everything – and asked him to give me time to think. I didn't know he'd gone to see about the banns, meanwhile, and told that wretched Miss Boff everything.'

'So you turned him down!' Vicki was slightly scandalized, not least with herself. To think that she'd once complained that life was dull.

'Well, not exactly, no. I did promise him that he could hope, and said I'd give him my answer properly at Christmas time.' She looked at Vicki helplessly and shrugged. 'That's why he went home so suddenly – and of course, our trip to London gave him the excuse. Papa was inclined to be furious, but Mama said that I was right to take my time. I had only just come out in society she said, and if I was spoken for at once I wouldn't have any fun at all, with all the summer balls and everything, but if it was announced at Christmas we could have an Easter wedding, and that is always prettiest. Trust Mama to think of things like that.'

'So, she's convinced that you'll accept him then.'

Bella made a woeful face. 'Well, perhaps I will do, when it comes to it. After all, I very nearly did. And Petroc was so perfectly sweet about it, when I asked him to take back the ring. Said he would save it for me until I was sure, and he would always love me whatever I decided. Then I almost changed my mind again and said I'd have him on the spot.' She looked at Victoria slyly, and began to laugh. 'But I did restrain myself in time. Oh, Vicki, am I the most awful tease? Truly, I don't mean to be. It's just, it's nice to be grown-up and young, without having a house and a husband to see to.'

'And with Stephen Pencarrow to make eyes at you?' Victoria found that she was laughing too.

'Well, that's better than lectures about seagulls' eggs,' Bella retorted, and she capered down the tussocky path, doing a sing-song imitation of a preacher's voice and declaiming to the air, 'The lesser spotted murglestrop is an unfortunate bird. It lays its eggs upon the wing, and drops them in the sea. What lesson, brethren, can we learn from this . . .?'

'Oh, do be quiet, Belle!' Victoria laughed, half-running after her and almost losing her bonnet in the wind. 'Lionel is all right.' She caught up with her friend and they walked for a long time in companionable silence, watching a little fishing boat far out to sea, its brown sails bellying in the wind, accompanied by a trail of swooping birds.

But as they neared the house, she plucked up the courage to mention it again. 'Seriously though, Belle, if you really prefer Stephen Pencarrow, why don't you marry *him*? I know your Papa would disapprove at first – Pencarrow owning only a farm or two, and that sort of thing – but he is a gentleman. And your family wouldn't want you to be unhappy all your life. I'm sure that you could bring them round, in time, and I don't imagine Pencarrow would be averse to it.'

Bella looked grave. 'Well, we have talked about it – once, but it's not as easy as you'd think. For one thing, Stephen has an old entanglement, a lady in Penzance . . .'

'Not now, surely?' Victoria was sincerely shocked. 'Not when he's also seeing you?'

Belle looked pained. 'She is a widow lady, I believe, and it would cause her pain to break it off. He was willing to do it, if I would consent, but obviously I couldn't ask him to.' She gave Victoria that arch look again. 'To tell the truth, Vicki, I am not sure that I could ever marry him. Have you seen his house? It's so small and inconvenient – five or six big rooms at most – and so far away from everything. And that's what it would mean. St Evan House will go to my brother Horry, naturally.'

Vicki was staring at her. 'Bella, you don't mean to say you've been? To Mr Pencarrow's house, without a chaperone?'

But Isabella Cardew cut her off. 'Shh! Not a word! Here's Stephen coming now. And I can see your father too, behind us, pedalling up the track.'

Stephen Pencarrow reached them first. 'May I offer you two charming ladies an arm, and have the pleasure of escorting you to tea?' he enquired, with his most ingratiating smile.

Victoria was on the point of refusing angrily, when it occurred to her that he might be hoping for just that. So she replied, 'Of course,' charmingly, and allowed him to walk back to the house like that, one girl on either side.

The house was as charming as she had remembered it, and she had the same feeling as she had done as a child, sure that if she'd turned her head a minute earlier she would have done the impossible and seen the wind – instead of only the ripple where it had passed, just out of sight, across the grasses and the dancing waves.

Deedee joined them as they reached the gate. Lionel and their host came down shortly afterwards, and they all went into the arched garden to have tea.

Two

D an was getting better, so everybody said. At least his leg was, he thought bitterly, though when he looked down at himself he hardly recognized the poor mangled thing. The shattered bones had knitted together after a fashion, and he could begin to hobble about a bit again, so long as he was leaning on a stick like an old man.

He had been glad enough of even that at first. Such a relief to drag himself downstairs and sit in the kitchen for a change, instead of lying there in Mother's bed and staring at the same walls all the time. Lucy was making progress too by now, not waking up at night, so Ma was looking a bit more rested than she had been – so that had pleased him too, though he noticed she was getting thinner; worrying about money, almost certainly.

Things were a little better than he'd feared. Old Tom's family had been very generous – sending every bit of food they could afford ('We'd have lost him, if it hadn't been for you'). And the doctor had agreed that they could pay him back at sixpence a week, but it couldn't go on for ever. Even sixpences didn't grow on trees, with only Zac and Melda's wages coming in. Together those two didn't make what Dan had earned, let alone replacing Dad's wage packet as well. There'd been a whip-round at the quarry, of course, and the Friendly had paid out for the funeral, which helped, but it was clear that the few pounds in the sock under the bed weren't going to last for much longer.

If only this new Insurance Bill of Lloyd George's had come in, there would have been a bit of money then, even if he was sick. (And to think that he'd been one of those who'd murmured against the idea of four pence a week out of his pay-packet!) But the promised national insurance hadn't happened – yet, at any rate – so it was no good dreaming. The grim fact was, now that he was 'on his feet' again, he had to find some work fairly soon or it'd be the workhouse for them all.

But what? It was all he could do to hobble to the door, let alone hold down any kind of job. He said so bitterly to Ma one day, when she was making bread. She had set him to sharpening the knives with emery, over a piece of paper on the table top, so he was doing something useful for a change.

He murmured savagely, 'Wish there was something proper I could do. Fat lot of help I am, stuck here like a tree – and you scraping round for 'apennies to make ends meet, and all.'

She looked at him. 'Well, I was thinking, Dan, there is something, if you're sure you're up to it. Now that you're able to get downstairs again.'

He stared at her, crazy hope stirring in his heart. 'What's that then? 'Course I'll do anything, if I can.'

She sighed. 'Only because you mentioned it yourself, mind you. I shouldn't 'a liked to ask you otherwise. It's just that I was speaking to Mollie Olds the other day and they aren't making out so well theirselves, you know. Poor Jamie's been put off at the pit again, and her fayther is afraid that he'll be next. It's some poor lookout down the quarry now.'

Dan felt his spirits sink. He could see now how Jamie Olds must feel – with able-bodied men after any work there was, what chance was there for anyone like him? 'And?' he prompted, concentrating fiercely on his knife.

'Well, the up and down of it is, she had a scrubbing job – only a few hours a week, but it brought in a bit – but now she's thinking to go up the new co-operative dairy factory instead – they're looking for strong girls. Save her miles of walking every day, and better pay as well – though of course it's longer hours by far. Thing is, Dan, she'd put in a word for me where she is now, if only I had somebody to keep a bit of eye on Lucy in the day. Wouldn't be for long, o' course – Mollie was only filling in, in

any case. But it would be something. With a shilling or two extra
we could have our Kitty home. They've been some good to her
next door, but we can't go on like this for evermore.' She looked
at him. 'I'm some sorry, Dan, I know it's not a man's place doing
things like that, but you could do it mostly sitting down, and I'm
blest if I know how we shall manage else.'

She looked as if she might burst into tears. It was harder on her
than on anyone, all this, and he was not fit for anything else.
What could he say but 'yes'?

So, for weeks mother set off before anyone was up, and came
home again exhausted at midday, while Dan sat at home like a
girl washing pots and shelling beans and rolling ironing and
trying to stop Lucy crawling into things. That wasn't as easy as it
sounded, either, now she was on the mend. She seemed to be
more of a handful every day. Sometimes, when he looked at the
pair of them – poor Lucy's awful puckered skin, and himself with
one useless leg that never would be right – a dreadful blackness
seemed to come over him, and for two pins he would have
dragged himself to the cliff and thrown the both of them to
kingdom come.

Even Mollie didn't come to see him like she used to – couldn't
do, now she was working all hours at the dairy factory. She did
look in of an evening sometimes, but of course then everyone was
home, and you couldn't get a bit of privacy anywhere. He had
tried, at her suggestion, going for a short walk – or rather, a short
limp – along the lane but the effort had defeated him and he'd
been glad to hobble home again. Mollie had gone on chattering
about the factory; how they had uniforms to wear and everything
had to be scrubbed through every day, and how the churns were
tipped by a machine; and she tried to pretend that she didn't
mind his ugly, twisted, useless leg at all, but he saw the pity on her
face – when she thought he wasn't looking – and he hadn't
repeated the experiment.

There had been other visitors: men from the quarry dropped
by once or twice to see how he was doing, but Dan didn't ask
them in – too ashamed to have the village know that he was

reduced to keeping house – and after that they didn't come again. Except for Tom, of course – he came quite a lot – but that was different.

Jamie Coombs called too, one last time, but only to announce that he was giving up and going up country to look for work. You'd have thought that he, of all people, would understand how Dan was feeling, but the reversal in their roles embarrassed him, and he couldn't meet Dan's eyes. He hopped from foot to foot the whole time he was there, until it was quite a relief to both of them when it was time to go.

The curate from St Evan church had looked in twice, with that good-looking Miss Flower from the vicarage; the same girl who'd turned her umbrella inside-out that time. Dan made a little face. Might be an announcement there, one day, but if so, Dan didn't rate it much. She was nice enough, but Dan simply couldn't take to him at all: such a girlish-looking sort of fellow and with such preachy ways! Last time he'd called with Miss Flower, he'd stood there on the step (Dan hadn't let them in, of course), and lectured Dan about the virtues of 'patiently bearing vicissitude' or some such thing, till Dan could cheerfully have throttled him.

No, Miss Flower deserved someone better'n that, from what he'd seen of her. A real nice young lady, he'd always thought she was – not a bit stuck up or anything. Mind, Mollie thought otherwise.

'So, Miss Lah-di-dah's been here again, has she?' she said, when Dan mentioned it to her. 'I don't know whatever good she thinks it does. Gave you a pot of jelly, I suppose – like as if it was a pot of gold. If she wants to be a bit of use, I don't know why she can't find something a bit more sensible to do. Told her so, too, to her face, once when I met her in the lane! Her and 'er blooming jelly pots. I don't suppose she even makes the stuff herself!'

'Well, I've been glad of it for Lucy,' Ma put in, mildly. 'I will say that. Did her a power of good. And it isn't like taking charity, like it was coins she was doling out.'

'Got a coin, anyway, didn't we?' Jimmy Gannet piped up from the stool. 'Took the jars down to Penvarris shop and they gave us a penny for them all. That's how we had those stale buns last night. Lovely they were too, toasted, weren't they, Dan?'

Dan didn't want to have an argument, so he just smiled and turned the conversation round to Mollie's job again. She had been telling them how many churns of milk the factory could process in a day. 'It'll all come to that, one day, you see if it doesn't,' she said, triumphantly. 'People'll stop buying from the farms direct, and have their milk and cheese and things from us. Or shops will do, which will come to the same thing. Much more hygenical, that's what.'

This was such a ridiculous idea that everyone wanted to have their say, and Miss Flower and her jelly were forgotten. Only, a little later when Mollie went to leave, she paused a moment on the step to say, 'Another time if you have stale buns for your tea, make sure you let me know. I b'lieve I know how I can get you a drop of cream to go with it. Then we'll see who helps to put a bit of flesh on Lucy's bones.'

Almost, Dan thought as she softly closed the door, as if there was some sort of competition about it.

Mollie was humming as she sauntered down the lane a few days later, enjoying the warmth of sunshine on her shoulders for a change. It might be 'hygenical' up at the dairy factory, and she did like working with the other girls, but she missed the fresh air something terrible.

That's why she'd seized the opportunity this afternoon, her precious fortnightly half-day, to come out here to Crowdie's for the milk. Bizarre really, when she worked up at The Hill, but the jug that she carried in the basket on her arm belonged to Auntie Anne (who didn't hold with factory milk) and Eadie wanted a dozen eggs as well.

She dawdled a moment at the bend, glorying in the sunshine glinting on the sea – you could just see it if you stood up on the stile – and the warm sweet smell of buttercups and grass. A nosy cow came ambling up to stare at her and Mollie reached out and scratched its warm, dappled flank.

'You making lots of work for us, are you?' she said. Crowdie, like every other farm for miles around, put out his churns for the dairy every day. 'Keeping us girls busy up The Hill?' The cow looked back at her reproachfully, chomping on a straggle of grass and buttercups. Mollie laughed. 'Here, don't look at me like that,' she said. 'I got the afternoon off – more'n you've got, I suppose!'

That reminded her of Eadie, who was slaving back at home, and she jumped down from the stile rather guiltily. If it wasn't for Eadie doing most of the household chores again, she wouldn't be here at all; the job up at The Hill would not be possible. What would happen when the Tregorrans left number nine and moved into a place of their own? No, she wouldn't dwell on that. Time enough to worry about it when it happened. Mightn't come to it, in any case.

She walked on slowly up the lane, patches of stickleback clutching at her skirt. Never mind. She'd have a new one from the tallyman; she could afford it now. She was bringing home five and three a week – good wages for a girl, Polvidden way – and she got a canteen lunch and uniform, though they had to be paid for at so much a week. All the same, she was making a contribution to the family, and still had a few pence a week to put aside for a new green skirt if she wanted one.

For her bottom drawer, she would once have said, but now she didn't know. Dan seemed so different these days, all inward-looking and glum, as if that stone had fallen on his soul instead of just his leg, and crushed his spirit too. He never laughed these days, the way he used to do, and he was looking terrible. She shook her head. Of course, what else could you expect? Anyone'd look terrible if they knew they'd always have a limp like that, even if the pain stopped in the end – and she knew that hadn't really happened yet. You could see the torment in his face sometimes, though if you asked he only snapped your head off and said that he was perfectly all right. So, it was early days . . .

Anyway, she thought, stopping to pick a piece of meadow-sweet and bury her nose in its soft summer scent, what kind of existence was it for a man, stuck there in the house with a small child like that? Dan'd be himself again soon as ever he found himself a job – though what that job would be, with this leg like that, it was hard to think. Suppose he never did get proper work again, what then? She shook her head again, firmly. She was being morbid, she told herself. Dan was still Dan and she'd promised him she'd wait. Things would turn out somehow, and if not . . .? No point in worrying about it now, and meeting trouble before it came. She was wasting a lovely afternoon by letting herself dwell on gloomy thoughts.

She picked up her skirts and hurried up the rise to the five-barred gate, where the short cut led across the fields. It was a bit steep and slippery in places, but she loved the walk and if there was nobody about she could abandon herself to running like a child. She put down her basket and was about to unlatch the heavy gate when she heard someone call her name.

'Mollie! Mollie! 'Ere, wait for me!' Harry Varfell was hurrying towards her up the lane, his big face pink with exertion.

She wasn't sure that she wanted company, but she waited for him to reach her and he came puffing up.

'My life, Moll,' he panted as he reached her side. 'You don't half go some speed when you've a mind. I've been chasing after you for 'alf a mile – saw you standing on that stile – but bless me, it's worse than trying to catch that blessed colt of Mrs Mill-bury's.' He smiled down at her from his enormous height. 'What you doing here then, Mollie girl? Thought you was working up the dairy factory now?'

'Got a 'alf-day off,' she said, brandishing the basket playfully. 'Off down to Crowdie's, get some eggs, and collect some milk for Auntie Anne.'

'Well, now there's a lucky thing,' he said, his amiable moon face lighting up in a smile. 'I'm going that way myself. I'll come with 'ee, if 'ee like.'

He looked so pleased and hopeful that she couldn't turn him

down, and they ambled the rest of the way together. Whatever Harry's business out that way was that afternoon, it couldn't have been very pressing, because when she came out of Crowdie's gate there he was again, ready to carry her jug and basket all the way back to the St Evan road.

When they did get to the signpost, though, he stopped. He didn't meet her eyes, but blurted out, 'Something I wanted to ask 'ee, by the by. You know there's going to be a beacon bonfire on the hill, come Coronation Day? Don't look as if your Dan'll make it, now, I mean, with his bad leg and all. But it's a pity if you have to miss it too. I was wondering if – in that case – you'd come along 'a me?'

'I couldn't do that, Harry, that would hurt him something cruel. Anyway, I'm going with Eadie and the folks.' He looked so crestfallen that she had to add, 'Though, there's a whole host of us going together, come to think – friends of Stan and Fayther's from the pit. Prowse is giving them the whole day off. Suppose there's no reason you shouldn't come with us as well.'

This time his face lit up like a Coronation beacon on its own.

Then he did say goodbye reluctantly, and when she looked back a moment later she saw him hurrying away in the opposite direction as if all the hounds of hell were after him. She had to smile. Poor Harry! He must have gone miles out of his way just to walk with her, and now he'd be behind with his errands all the afternoon. Old Man Varfell would have his guts for gaiters later on!

She was still smiling when she got to Auntie Anne's.

Victoria looked back at the retreating figures with a frown. Surely she couldn't have been mistaken after all? But no, there was no mistaking that red hair and orange skirt – it was that Coombs girl from Polvidden all right, walking with that young giant of a man, so deep in cheerful conversation that neither of them had even noticed her as she approached the stile.

She stood, brushing the grass seeds from her hems, and watched them go. She was conscious of a rather wicked sensation of satisfied surprise. She had always thought of Mollie Coombs as somehow belonging to that nice Olds boy, yet here she was, walking along with someone else entirely, looking as comfortable together as a pair of old shoes. A good thing, too, Victoria said to herself unkindly, that brazen hoyden wasn't nearly good enough for Daniel.

She picked the last of the sticky buds from her skirt – one couldn't turn up at Lower St Evan House trailing pieces of meadow grass – and started to walk up along the lane. Poor Daniel, and that dreadful house. She had persuaded Lionel to accompany her back there once or twice – somehow she didn't like to go alone – but now that Daniel was on his feet again, there really wasn't very much that one could do. The thought reminded her uncomfortably of Mollie Coombs and of that uncalled-for outburst in the street.

She found herself flushing, although there was nobody to see. Anyway, she thought grimly, as she came to the entrance of Bella's house, and turned into the carriage drive between the curved granite walls, Mollie was hardly helping Daniel, walking about the countryside like this, enjoying the company of another man. Daniel probably didn't even know, and the poor boy still had that awful injury. Victoria felt quite indignant on his behalf. Any heroine worth her salt would have known where her romantic duty lay.

She rounded the corner and there was Bella on the lawn, sitting under a parasol with a book, and with a little table at her side. She got up at once when Victoria appeared.

'Dear Vic!' She offered one cheek to be kissed. 'I thought, after our picnic on the cliffs, it would be fun to take tea out here on the lawn. Besides, no one can hear us here, and there's so much to tell! Such plans! You know Papa has taken a house on the Coronation route, and we shall able to see it from the balcony.'

So Victoria sat and sipped elderflower tea, while Bella prattled on about the trip, and about her latest 'accidental' rendez-vous; how Stephen had admired her dress, and how extremely dashing he had been. Victoria knew she ought to disapprove, but somehow these exploits were so deliciously daring, that just hearing about them added a little excitement to the day.

'Go on,' she breathed, knowing her eyes were wider than the saucers on the tray. 'Then what did he say?'

She didn't think of Daniel Olds again that afternoon.

Three

Inspiration came to Victoria quite suddenly. She was sitting in the arbour, reading *The Life of Wilberforce*, since Miss Boff had recently embarked on a programme of 'Improving Biographies'. Secretly, though, she was itching to start on the new novel which Bella had left her, and which was discreetly concealed under the cushion at her side.

Not that she much feared to be disturbed today: Bella was gone to London; Deedee was busy with the verger over at the church; Lionel had gone out visiting the sick; and even Miss Boff had taken the coach and gone into Penzance for once, in search of new trimming for her Sunday hat.

Victoria had just reached the end of the appointed chapter, and was preparing to put Wilberforce away and indulge herself with Mr Galsworthy instead, when a grizzled head poked itself around the hedge. It was an unprepossessing sight: straggling grey eyebrows, rheumy eyes, and a face tanned to a deep berry – brown, where it could be seen above the thick grey beard.

'Af'noon, Miss,' the apparition said, then – apparently realizing that she was alone – the owner of the head appeared in glorious entirety.

He was not tall – no taller than she was herself – but at first sight he appeared immensely plump; until Victoria realized that he was wearing two separate coats buttoned up over what seemed, from the ragged remnants of the sleeves, at least half a dozen shirts and pullovers. His filthy trousers were held up at the waist with string, and his boots (the ones he wore) looked far too big for him, though the ones around his neck looked bigger still. He clutched a greasy old felt hat politely in one hand, while the other held a bundle tied up in a grimy cloth. Even from where he stood he gave off a rich aroma, like a farmyard pile. Clearly this was a 'gentleman of the road'.

Victoria sighed, and slid her novel guiltily away. She knew what to expect. Such tramps were frequent summer visitors, the more so as Deedee never turned anyone away. Miss Boff declared they had a secret code, telling each other this was a useful house to try, and Victoria believed it, she had seen tell-tale symbols scratched outside on the gate. She'd tried to tell Deedee about it, but he'd only laughed and said that it didn't alter one's duty to the poor.

All the same, he never gave them money outright – they 'would only drink it' as Miss Boff would say, but instead offered the tramps an opportunity to work in exchange for food and cups of tea or – especially if the weather was bad – a blanket and a place to bed down in one of the stone outbuildings behind the house. Deedee kept a little pile of blankets specially, hand-knitted by the ladies of the parish and carefully purchased at the spring bazaar, though he never told the earnest knitters what he bought them for! The tramp was always given the blanket that he used – it was no use for anything else afterwards.

Miss Boff didn't like having them about. 'Why don't you send them to the workhouse, vicar?' she always said. 'There's a bed and food provided for them there. And a bath, if they had a mind to it – but of course they don't. These people always carry lice and fleas.' But even she had to admit that the men worked hard (if you kept an eye on them) and would trim the hedge or cut the grass with shears quite tidily – though you couldn't trust them with the flower beds.

'Spare a few coppers for an old man, Miss?' the tramp enquired.

'You'll have to work for it,' Victoria said, as she had been taught to do. 'But I daresay something can be found for you. You wait here. The vicar's in the church. I'll go and speak to him about it now.'

The old man nodded, 'Thank 'ee, Miss.' He set down his bundle and produced, from a pocket in his inner coat, a large coloured pocket-handkerchief of great antiquity. He carefully spread this on the grass beside the rhododendron hedge before lowering himself on to it and sitting back with all the satisfaction of a king upon his throne.

Victoria was secretly amused. She couldn't help wondering whether the handkerchief was supposed to protect his clothes from the lawn or the other way about. She kept a straight face, however, and with a cheerful 'I shan't be long' she set off across the back path towards the church.

It did occur to her to glance behind her once – she would never hear the last of it from Miss Boff if the tramp should take it into his head to wander into the house and pocket anything – but he showed no signs of it. Ruby and Mrs Roseworthy were there and would soon have put a stop to that.

She chided herself for uncharitable thoughts, and hurried on, mentally preparing a possible list of gardening chores that the visitor might usefully perform. It was a long list by the time she reached the church. Old Mr Roseworthy did his best, but the garden was far too much for him these days. Pruning, weeding, clipping back – there was enough work in those tasks alone to keep a dozen tramps busy for a week – to say nothing of the digging and replanting that really needed doing.

And there was to be a vicarage tea here on the lawn, in honour of the coronation too, with half the parish coming here to see. She sighed, remembering that lovely garden on the cliffs. If only they had something like that here. She'd have to speak to Deedee; he really should think about letting old Mr Roseworthy go, or finding a younger man to help, at least, or this whole garden would get completely out of hand. Deedee would grumble about the cost of course, but . . .

She stopped, transfixed by a sudden thought. Of course! Why hadn't she thought of it before? It was the perfect solution. The vicarage needed a gardener, the Olds boy needed work.

The idea struck her with such force that she was obliged to put out a hand and steady herself against a gravestone, while she thought. It would have to be light work at first because Daniel was still on a stick, but he was getting better now, and he needn't do any real digging for a while. It wouldn't pay a great deal, of course, only a few shillings a week, but it would be something, and under the circumstances no doubt Deedee could be persuaded to be generous. And it would be secure employment, too, not like quarrying, where men were still being put off every week, so Lionel said. If Daniel could be certain of his job, think what a relief that would be to his whole family.

Yes, the more she thought of it, the more she was delighted with her plan. The fact that it would mean that Daniel was here, where she could see him every day, was not at all a reason for her scheme, she told herself, merely a pleasing additional circumstance. That would show Miss Mollie Coombs a thing or two. Victoria could offer somebody 'real help' – as that appalling girl had said – and give a young man back his self-esteem. Even Miss Boff and Deedee would approve; this was real Christian charity.

She tried to imagine Daniel's face when he heard the news. It gave her a little pleasurable glow.

And she was still there, leaning dreamily against 'Gypsy Jamieson, widow of this parish' a few minutes later, when her father came around the corner of the church with the verger at his side.

'Victoria?' his voice disturbed her reverie.

'Oh, Deedee!' she exclaimed, straightening up and hurrying to meet him. 'I was looking for you. I have something to ask you.' As she spoke she realized guiltily that she had completely forgotten about the tramp, who must still be waiting in the garden. 'Two things, in fact.' She outlined her ideas.

Deedee heard her out, and agreed at once that the tramp should be found a task. 'Get him to chop that pile of wood up for the fire and ask Mrs Roseworthy to give him bread and cheese.' But he did not, as she had rather expected, leap at her other idea with the same enthusiasm. 'Let me think about that, Victoria. It may not be as easy as you think. Oh, it's an interesting idea and there is much to recommend it, but they are proud young men, you know, these Cornish quarrymen. They don't take kindly to what they see as charity. Besides, this lad has valuable skills and he was the leader of a team. It might be harsh for him to become a labourer under old Roseworthy's command.'

Victoria was disappointed. She had been secretly hoping to take the glad news to Daniel herself, at once. The idea that he might not warmly welcome it had not occurred to her.

She must have looked as crestfallen as she felt, because her father smiled and reached out to pat her on the arm. 'Don't look so cast down, my dear. It is a kindly thought, and there may be a way. Leave it with me, I'll see what I can do. Now, if you'll excuse me, I've not finished here. We've got these special coronation services, and the verger is concerned about our yews.'

And with that, for the moment, she had to be content.

It was Mr Prowse himself who mentioned it to Dan. He called round one afternoon in person, like the gentleman he was, to ask after Dan's health.

As Ma said to Daniel, afterwards, 'How many quarry owners would do a thing like that? Lucky thing he called round when he did; if I hadn't been back home from scrubbing, and in the kitchen ironing by then, you'd've been too embarrassed, like, to show him in. And then see what would have happened? You'd have missed your chance!'

Dan said nothing. They both knew that if Prowse'd been an hour or two earlier, he'd have caught Dan stringing beans – or rather he wouldn't, because Ma was right, Dan would never have answered the door to him.

'Good of him, though, wasn't it?' Ma persisted. 'Thinking of you at once like that.' She turned to Kitty who had just come in from school. 'Hear that, did you? Vicar's looking for someone to help him in the garden, and happened to mention it to Mr Prowse. 'Course he's a churchwarden, always was, and he thought of our Daniel straightaway.' She was rolling ironing as she spoke. 'Only think of that! Kitty, don't come traipsing indoors in those dusty boots. Take them off and put your socks on properly. And Jimmy Gannet, get yourself a 'andkerchief. Can't go round like heathens, the pair of you, when you've got a brother working up the vicarage.'

Daniel protested, uncomfortably, 'Oh, don't go on so, Ma. Tisn't settled yet. Mr Prowse only said he'd mention me. Anyhow, I'm not so sure it's such a good idea. How you going to manage Lucy, if I'm not here to keep an eye on her? Tisn't as if I'd get a proper wage – hardly much more'n Zac and he's just a kettle boy.' He didn't dare admit, even to himself, how much even those few bob a week would mean. A chance to get out and be a man again – not a proper job, down the quarry or the mine – but work, real work, and earning a little bit again, instead of sitting home like a useless wreck. (He would have said 'like a woman' once, but experience had taught him better sense; he couldn't do half the work his mother did, even now.)

Ma beamed at him. 'Don't you worry about that, Dan'l lad. Mrs Next-Door'll have her willingly, and be glad of a few pence a week to do it. And if you're earning, we'll still be better off. I hear they're generous up the vicarage, too. They b'long to send Old Man Roseworthy home with all sorts of bits. Half a cake they gave him once, just on account of it had gone a little stale. And bits and pieces left over, dinner time. You do a good job up there, and I shouldn't be surprised if they did the same for you.'

'I told you,' Dan said irritably, 'tisn't settled yet!'

But it wasn't long before it was. Zac came back from the quarry earlier than usual. 'Message for you from Mr Prowse,' he said, grinning cheekily from ear to ear. He sat down on the back step and unlaced his boots, taking his time deliberately.

'Well?' Daniel demanded, almost shouting with impatience. He could have shaken Zac, but the news was good. He was to present himself up at the vicarage next day, and if he suited, then the job was his.

Lionel was making progress with the choir. It had been very difficult at first. The congregation had become used to mumbling through the hymns while Miss Boff manfully droned out the tunes on the harmonium. She played the notes accurately enough, but rhythm and expression were not her strongest points, and given that the instrument was prone to unexpected squeals and gasps if not pumped with sufficient regularity, there was a distinct lack of musicality about all aspects of the hymns.

Yet the church boasted a proper little organ, only a few decades old, and there had once been the tradition of a choir. So, there had been talent in the parish once. It could not all have been buried with the organist, and Lionel had been entrusted with finding it again.

He'd started with the Sunday school, which turned out to be a splendid place to start. Seven or eight children attended every Sunday – largely, Victoria maintained, to collect their attendance stamps, which depicted lurid Bible scenes, and the lives – and sometimes the gory martyrdoms – of the more famous saints. These children were easily coaxed into practising, and soon another four or five older ones appeared, seduced by the promise of a surplice and a coloured band to wear, volunteering to 'give 'un a try' and join the choir.

They were inclined to equate volume with effectiveness at first, but most young children can be taught to sing, and some of these had music in their blood. Their first anthem, at the Eucharist the previous week, had been a great success, and Lionel was working on the coronation concert now – though their accents still gave him some concern.

They had been struggling this evening with ''Oly, 'oly, 'oly, Lord God A'mighty!' until Lionel hit upon the strategy of promising that whoever made the best 'H' should carry the cross on Sunday morning and lead the choir's procession into church. That worked like magic – though he now had cross-carriers lined up for months ahead – and afterwards Lionel had been further cheered to discover three adults waiting for him: 'Come to see if you was wantin' voices for the singing, now that there's a proper choir again.'

Lionel made a pretence of auditioning them (though truth to

tell, he would have welcomed anyone who was not actually tone-deaf), and the choir had three new members as a result.

That should improve the singing next week, he told himself, as he folded up his music and prepared to leave the church. A few more recruits like that and he could begin to work on one of the more demanding works that he had acquired from Matthew Mackenzie's collection.

It would be rather nice, he thought, to take up Ralph Mill's invitation and call back to see the rest, but there was something about the notion which obscurely troubled him. Not that he would be intruding, he was sure that Ralph would welcome him, but there was something not quite comfortable about the whole idea. Perhaps it was simply that he longed to go, and that was a selfish and ungracious thought, when so many parish matters pressed. Yes, perhaps it was that.

In any case, he told himself severely, there was no point in thinking about extra music yet. It would be months before they could manage what they had. Longer, if he could not somehow find a way to wean Miss Boff off that harmonium without offending her.

He sighed, and genuflected to the altar, before blowing out the lamps and walking out into the soft Cornish evening air. He pulled the church door closed behind him, and when he turned he was surprised to see Victoria scurrying across the churchyard from the lane, her hair dishevelled and her skirts awry. Her pretty face was furrowed in a frown.

'Miss Flower?' he said, and she stopped, confused. Obviously she had been so wrapped up in her thoughts that she hadn't noticed he was there. 'Are you . . .? Is everything all right? You seem a little bit . . . preoccupied.'

She recovered herself in an instant. 'Oh, Lionel! How you startled me. Yes, I am quite all right, thank you. Just that I had a little scheme – a little good deed that I hoped to bring about – and I haven't been able to persuade Deedee of it yet. So, I have been out walking in the lane, and now I've been rather longer than I meant. I fear I shall be late for supper, and Miss Boff will fuss.' She smiled, and gestured to the music in his hand. 'But you have been engaged on more useful business, I observe. Your little choir has been practising. How is it coming on?'

As usual, she made him feel at ease. She had shared a confidence with him, and that inspired him to say in turn, 'Like you, I fear my problem is Miss Boff.' He outlined the question of the harmonium.

Victoria laughed. 'Well, why don't you invite her to join the choir? I'm sure she'd be delighted to be asked – especially if you flatter her a little, and make it seem that she's been singled out. She has a reasonable voice, you know, though one never hears it in the hymns – she's too busy concentrating on the playing.'

Lionel looked at her admiringly. 'I say! What an intelligent idea. That's very clever of you, Miss Flower.'

Victoria made a little face. 'I only wish Deedee thought as much of my ideas. Come on, or we shall both be late for supper.'

Miss Boff was waiting for them when they got inside, but Lionel did not give her time to fuss. He turned to her immediately, and said warmly, 'Ah Miss Boff. We have just come from practising the choir. I was just mentioning our difficulties to Miss Flower, and she has emboldened me to ask you something . . . Could you, do you think, consent to join as? I had three other adults come to us tonight, but we need someone who really knows the tunes – someone to hold the group together, as it were. I know it is presumptuous of me, but if you could see your way . . .?'

Victoria had been right. Miss Boff positively glowed. 'Well, I should be glad to help, of course . . . if you could spare me from the harmonium.'

Victoria caught his eye and smiled. And she smiled even more broadly, a little later on, when the Reverend Flower turned to her and said, 'Oh, by the way, Victoria my dear. That little kindness you suggested yesterday; I think I've found a way to bring it off. I had a word to Prowse today – I thought the suggestion would be better if it seemed to come from him – and I'm glad to say our little plan has worked. I've had a word to Roseworthy as well –

he grumbled and insisted that he managed perfectly, but he saw the sense of having assistance in the end. Of course, I'm not making any permanent commitment, but the boy is coming here tomorrow, and we'll try it out.'

This news seemed to please Victoria immensely. What a kind-hearted girl she was, Lionel thought. It gave her genuine pleasure to do good. In fact, after that announcement she was so light-hearted that she at last consented to his own – oft-repeated – suggestion that they should try playing a duet.

Four

When Dan set off next morning he felt a proper fool. He didn't know what to wear for one thing; his old quarry clothes didn't seem right, somehow, nor did his Sunday best, so in the end at Ma's insistence he'd put on Dad's best coat and shirt, which were rather short and wide for him, and his own good trousers, which had been 'bought to grow' and were consequently just a little bit too long. Ma'd insisted that he wear a cap. And, of course, he still had to have his stick for walking distances.

'Done up like a circus monkey,' he complained to Mollie, when he met her on his way, coming the other way along the road.

'My life!' Mollie said, in genuine surprise. 'Imagine runnin' into you, this time of the morning, too!'

'Yes!' Dan pretended to agree, but of course it was no accident. He wasn't sure what time exactly he was wanted at the vicarage, so he had timed his journey on purpose so his path would cross with Mollie's. It was rather early, really, to be setting off – Mollie had to be at work by eight o'clock and certainly no one would be expecting him till nine – but he'd persuaded Ma and everyone that he walked so slowly now, he needed plenty of time to get there and rest his leg before he started work. If Ma guessed the real reason for his early start, she hadn't said a word.

'Starting work up the vicarage today,' he added. He hadn't seen Mollie since he'd got the job.

She nodded. 'So I heard. Stan came home full of it last night – he heard it down the quarry yesterday.'

155

Dan sighed. 'Almost knew it before I did, then!' he said.

Mollie glanced at him. 'I'm some sorry, Dan, if I spoiled your news, but Mr Prowse was talking to your Zac about it, and of course then it was all around the pit before you could say knife.' She grinned. 'Would have come down last night, to say how pleased I was, only Jamie would have taken it that 'ard, if he ever heard – Prowse never went out of his way to find a job for *him* – and you can't trust Stan to keep his great trap shut. And looks like Jamie might be coming home. Hasn't found anything sensible, even up to Hayle. Without he takes a job in the explosive works, and I aren't very keen on that. Looks like we'll have to pawn our Eadie's ring, and pay his ticket to America. Still, I'm some glad for you, Dan, I truly am. Better one man with work than two without.'

He looked at her anxiously. There was something not quite happy in her tone. 'You sure, now, Moll? You aren't just saying that? I know how it is, when it's your own family wanting, and other people seem to have the luck.'

'My dear life, Dan! What do you think we are? As if anyone round here would grudge you anything, after what you did. And with your Da killed and all. No, I really meant it, course I did. Anyhow –' she gave him a sly dig – 'I'd be some fool not to be pleased for you.'

It took him a moment to work out what she meant. When he did, it made him think. He said slowly, 'Well, it's a start, Moll, certainly, but that's all it is. I'll be earning like a junior at the pit. And then there's Ma and the little ones to think about. I'm sorry, Mollie, if this got your hopes up again, but I can't see how I can think of settling down, not for a long time yet.'

She went on smiling determinedly, but she couldn't meet his eyes. 'Said I'd wait for you, didn't I?' she said, with a pretence at gaiety. 'Only I can't go on this minute waiting here! I'll be late for work, and then where shall we be?' She glanced at him. 'It's the same thing for me, too, you see. I got people relying on me at home, glad of the few pennies I bring in. Unless of course, we two got together . . . later on, of course, when things have settled down.'

Daniel didn't say what they both knew about bosses at places like The Hill not liking married women working there. Too likely to get in the family way and give their notice in – or even if that didn't happen, wives were still apt to have to stay at home if anyone in the family was ill, or else they worked so hard that they got ill themselves. He just said, 'Well then. Better go. Wish me good luck at the vicarage.'

Mollie pulled a mocking face. 'Won't need good luck, will you, there? Not with Miss Good Fairy Flower looking after you. Be in her element, she will, with you to fuss over all day long. Give you so much chicken jelly, if you don't look out you'll start to look like one.'

'Here!' Dan said, half-laughing, 'What's got into you? Proper wet blanket you've turned out to be! Here am I starting a new job, and all you can do is find fault with it. Thought you were supposed to be pleased on my account!'

Mollie had the grace to look abashed. 'Well, so I am. Only it's that Miss Flower – makes me sick. Her and her fancy nimby-pimby ways. I know you think she's very nice and all, but I can't care for her myself. I don't know what it is about her, but I wish you were working anywhere but there, and that's a fact.' She looked him in the eyes and gave a rueful grin. 'Now, I'm being silly, and I'm getting late. See you one evening in the week, perhaps? Then you can tell me all about the job!'

'And you can tell me how you're getting on with yours,' Dan shouted after her, but she'd already gone.

So, that was what had been biting her! Miss Flower! Yet Miss Flower'd never been anything but kind, as far as he could see. He shook his head. Girls could be very odd like that sometimes. He walked on thoughtfully to the vicarage.

When he got there he found to his surprise that he had to sit on the wall and rest his leg awhile before he felt well enough to go and knock the door.

Now that Daniel had actually come – and she could see him this minute from the window of the room, weeding and pruning in the rose garden as though trying to make up in one morning for ten years of neglect – Victoria was suddenly overcome with self-consciousness. She had envisaged herself, several times, sweeping out to meet him with a gracious smile and making encouraging remarks about his efforts, but now that he was physically here she found it wasn't as easy as she'd thought.

Normally, on a lovely day like this, she would have taken her book into the garden and sat under the arbour in the shade. But that would have meant walking past Daniel, and having to find something appropriate to say, and she was overcome with ridiculous confusion at the thought.

His presence was so physical for one thing. Old Man Rose-worthy pottered around the garden in the same faded jacket and cap whatever the weather, but Daniel had stripped down to his shirt and rolled up his sleeves, so that – even from her vantage point in the window of the morning room, where she had retired under the pretence of studying – she was acutely aware of his strong tanned arms. Would the skin on that muscular back be as tanned and smooth, she found herself wondering dreamily.

She brought herself up short, ashamed.

Whatever could she have been thinking of? Bad enough to be sitting here, surreptitiously watching him at work, instead of getting on with *The Life of Wilberforce*. As for forgetting herself to the extent of imagining what he looked like underneath his shirt . . .! She picked up her book resolutely, and was about to find her page, when Daniel glanced towards the house.

He must have seen her. He was smiling; a pleased, delighted smile. In fact, he had put down his garden shears and straightened up, and took a step or two towards the window where she was.

She felt a little flutter of excitement, but she remembered who she was. She didn't fling the casement open and call out to him, as she was half-tempted to; she must retain her dignity. How should she behave? A little wave and smile, perhaps, and then she'd turn away? Yes, that would fit the situation, perfectly: not too forward, but at the same time showing friendliness. She moved the drape a little more aside and raised her hand in greeting, then realized too late that Daniel's smile was not for her at all.

Old Roseworthy had found a little stool from somewhere, and was bringing it, so that Daniel could sit down to his task. Obviously his leg was hurting him. This was what the smile was about.

But her movement at the window had attracted his attention, and now he *was* looking directly at her. Her hand was still frozen in mid-wave, and he had noticed it. He gave her a deferential smile and doffed his cap, bowing his head in her direction as any gardener might.

She nodded rather frostily in return, then turned deliberately away, but not before she'd seen his look of puzzlement. She bit her lip. How could she have been such a fool? She was still frowning when a voice disturbed her thoughts.

'My dear Victoria . . . Miss Flower . . . are you quite well? You look a little pale.' Lionel had come into the room.

She forced herself to look at him and smile. 'Perfectly all right, thank you, Lionel. I have a little headache, that is all. Nothing that a brisk walk in the sea air won't blow away. Were you looking for me?'

He hesitated. 'Indeed I was. I have been thinking for several days of driving over to call upon Ralph Mills, and he has written me this very morning inviting me again. He has an acquaintance staying there this week – a cousin of the friend he shared the cottage with, who has come down to Cornwall for his health. He might be interested in those manuscripts, if I am not, but Ralph felt that he had promised me. I shall have first refusal, he insists.'

'I see,' Victoria murmured, wondering what all this had to do with her.

The question must have been written in her face. Lionel smiled. 'I mentioned it to your father earlier, and he suggested that I use the pony trap for once, and take a turn out there this afternoon. But for that I'll need to have it harnessed up. A local farmer keeps it for you, I believe? You father thought that you might care to come and introduce me to the man, and I can ask if it's convenient?'

Vicki put down her book at once. 'Of course. Give me a moment while I get my hat and gloves.' It had occurred to her that, to go down to the farm, they would have to walk past Daniel on the way. And for some reason, which she could not at all explain – just as on the morning of the maypole dance – it pleased her to be seen in Lionel's company. That would show Daniel that she was a young woman to be taken seriously, and not the fool that he must think she was! She seemed fated to make herself ridiculous in his eyes: first turning her umbrella inside out, then being caught in mid-wave like that! And of course he couldn't know that he owed his new job to her, though she would have given a good deal to have Lionel tell him so.

She led the way into the hall and tied on her prettiest bonnet.

Lionel followed her, saying earnestly, 'This may turn out to be a very useful call. Ralph thinks this visitor might consent to come and play the organ here. Ours is a nice little instrument, if only it were used. This man built organs at one time, by all accounts, and would be glad to find an instrument to play. He intends to settle in St Buryan, and of course it is a long way of a Sunday, but the fellow has a bicycle, and he might be persuaded, till the weather turns at least.'

It was hard to resist his enthusiasm. She dragged her thoughts away from Dan and found herself saying, 'It would make a great difference to the church.'

Lionel nodded. 'Your esteemed father thinks so too.' He looked at her, flushed, and went on with a rush, 'I suppose you would not care to accompany me? I would appreciate the company, and you could blow the cobwebs away from that head of yours at the same time.'

She hesitated. Certainly the cottage had been a charming place, and there would be something to be said for getting away from the vicarage for the day. She sighed.

He misinterpreted. 'You need not be alarmed. I promise you will not be overset. I'm not unfamiliar with managing a trap.'

The idea that the aged Bluebell might need managing made Victoria laugh. 'I see you have not met our pony, Lionel. The poor thing's so ancient that the difficulty is to make her go at all! That's why we use the trap so rarely nowadays. But yes, if I can be spared this afternoon, I'll drive out with you willingly.' She grinned at him. 'You might be glad of my company if Bluebell turns frisky suddenly.'

It was wicked of her to tease him in that way. She saw him flush. He said, awkwardly, 'I should be glad of company in any case. I should feel a little uncomfortable calling there alone. I am not an intimate of Mr Mills'.'

He said it so humbly that Victoria was instantly contrite. 'Come on, we'll walk down to the farm. I'll introduce you to the farmer, and to Bluebell, too.' She took his arm, and set down the path, trying not to look at Daniel on the way.

Lionel, though, glanced towards the rose patch, murmuring, 'Your new protégé is working hard. I was very touched by that idea, you know. And a vicarage should tend its gardens properly – it seems only appropriate, somehow.'

Daniel had looked up by now to watch them pass, and Victoria could feel his eyes on her. She coloured. She wanted to seem charming, educated, feminine, but she didn't quite know how to begin. She looked at Daniel, gave a little artificial laugh and quoted lightly in a consciously Bella sort of way, ' "Christ hath a garden walled around . . .".'

She meant it for Lionel, but it was Daniel's voice that took up the verse: ' "A Paradise of fruitful ground, Chosen by love and fenced by grace, From out the world's wide wilderness.".'

She was too astonished to be self-conscious any more. She stared at Daniel. 'You know the work of Isaac Watts? You read poetry?' It was an impertinent question, rudely asked, though she had not intended it to be.

He interpreted it as a rebuke. He coloured, seizing off his cap and holding it in front of him in both his hands. 'Not really, Miss. I'm some sorry if I spoke out of turn, only they learned us that piece of verse at school once when the school inspection came. Had to say it off by heart, I did, in front of the visitors and all, and when you started reciting it . . . well, I couldn't seem to help me'self.'

Victoria could not resist a smile, especially when Lionel said, sounding like a school visitor himself, 'You seem to have recalled it very well. The inspectors must have been impressed with you.'

'Not really, sir.' Daniel had been gazing at the ground, but he raised his eyes at that. 'Said that we murdered English poetry, pronouncing how we did.' He had such laughing, mischievous grey eyes. She hadn't remembered that they were so grey. She grinned at him, and – reassured – he went on cheerfully, 'Teacher gave us elocution lessons after, for a week, but didn't do no good. Didn't stick to us no more than limewash to a fish.'

This time Vicki laughed aloud, and Lionel said, 'One should pay attention to one's teacher,' exactly as though he were Miss Boff.

'I daresay you're right, Reverence, but where's the good? She wanted me to sit a scholarship. Couldn't have taken it, in any case. There isn't time or money in our 'ouse for that sort of thing.' He seemed to recollect himself. 'But there, no good crying for spilt milk. Doing all right down at the pit, I was, till this happened to my damty leg, saving your pardon, Reverence.'

Lionel caught Victoria's eye and smiled. 'Never mind, my good man, carry on!' he said, and they carried on themselves, leaving Daniel to his work.

When they were out of earshot, Lionel said, 'A pity his schoolteacher didn't have more sense. Putting ideas like that into his head. It only leads to discontent.'

She looked at him. 'You mean about the scholarship? But surely she was right? Don't you think that with a bit more education . . .?' She trailed off. Already a thousand schemes were rushing through her head. She would teach him, rescue him, become his doorway to a better life.

Lionel smiled indulgently. 'He might have made something more than a quarry man of himself? Perhaps. The boy is clearly bright, or he wouldn't have been team leader at the pit. But of course he's right. You've seen the house he lives in. It's always the same in these poor families: no money for the education that might help them rise – there's always another mouth to feed, another bill to pay. The church does its best of course, but . . . in any case, you heard him, he was happy as he was. So there you are.' He shrugged. 'Well, you and I won't set the world to rights. Is this the house?'

It was, and the pony trap was soon arranged.

Victoria did accompany Lionel that afternoon, but though Ralph Mills was very welcoming and the organist did agree to come, somehow it was not altogether a success. Not for Victoria, at least. Lionel seemed distinctly ill at ease with everyone and she couldn't help feeling that she was obscurely in the way.

Dan pushed his cap back further on his head and picked up his garden shears again, but he watched Miss Flower and the gentleman till they were out of sight.

He nodded to himself approvingly. Proper lady, that one was, and no mistake; too good for that wretched curate chap, though he didn't half think himself clever and above you, you could see. Always spoke to you, he did, as if he was the Angel Gabriel, doing you a favour by addressing you at all. And him wandering about in that parson's dress of his, all black and gawky like a wounded crow.

Dan grinned. Well, he'd given him something to think about today! 'You read poetry?' She'd sounded quite impressed. Bit of good fortune, really, seeing it was the one poem that Dan really knew! That and the one about the king. How did it go? 'To seek, to find, to strive and not to yield'? Something like that. He liked the sound of it. He piled his clippings into the wooden wheelbarrow, lifted the heavy handles and set off down the path, chanting the line over and over to himself and matching his uneven footsteps to the beat.

It irritated him, that limping tread of his, but he couldn't conquer it, however hard he tried. Dratted thing would seem all right, and then it let him down the moment he forgot and put his full weight on it. All very well for the doctor to shake his head, and say the recovery was quite remarkable – it wasn't near remarkable enough. Silly thing, really; when he was stuck at home, he'd been delighted at the chance of work. Now he was earning a little bit again, the horror of the thing came home to him. He couldn't stop here, playing at gardening, for evermore. Once he'd got things back to rights there wasn't work here for more than half a man, and come the winter there wouldn't even be that.

But what else was he to do? He was beginning to despair of ever getting back to quarry work again. Things at the pit were getting worse and worse. Zac had come home only yesterday, saying more men were going to be turned off next week. Trouble on the railways, it seemed, and no way for Prowse to shift the stone they cut, even supposing he could find a buyer for it.

Dan sighed. Perhaps his teacher had been right. 'You're a bright pupil, Olds. You could get a scholarship and go to county school. You could make something of yourself,' she'd said; only of course, he hadn't paid her any heed. Who from Polvidden way had ever gone to school past Standard Six – if that? Out earning money, instead, soon as they were big enough to wield a pick. He was the odd one as it was, traipsing in to evening classes at the Institute, to learn geometry and algebra. Cost Dad enough, that had, at the time, though it had paid off handsome in the end. A black powder man needed good reckoning these days too, if only to calculate the powder charge. It was a proper scientific art, none of the old 'tip it in and see' that used to be the way of it. And now all that studying was wasted, after all.

'To strive, to seek, to find, and not to yield.' He tipped his heavy barrowload on the pile – it was almost as high as his head by now – and he went off to find a match to light it with. Old Roseworthy had put some in the shed to light his pipe, but he'd used the last of them and Dan had to go begging in the kitchen for a candle and some spills. Proper performance it was too, to get the pile to light, and when it did it filled the place with smoke, so Daniel's clean shirt looked a picnic in no time at all. And then, of course, Old Roseworthy turned up.

''Ere, what you doing setting fire to they? Want to let the green dry out a bit – and some of they leaves would compost anyway. Don't you know the first thing about gardenin' at all?' That was the trouble, Dan thought to himself, he didn't know anything but quarrying.

'Well, too late now!' Old Roseworthy went on. 'Fire's caught now and no mistake. Better you stay here and keep an eye on her – we'll have the whole hedge up to blazes else. Here, use your shovel, like this, keep 'er down, and when she's finished, shovel earth on her – make sure she's well and truly out. You have the furze catch fire, round here, it'll spread underground and burn for weeks.' He saw Dan's chagrined face. 'Well, no harm done this time, I suppose, but if you want a bonfire again, young Olds, make sure you ask me first!' And he went off grumbling.

Dan felt a proper idiot again, standing there prodding at the fire. He'd meant to be a help, that's all, but when it came to gardening, he'd really no idea. So much for 'To strive, and not to yield'! He was muttering despondently to himself when someone came towards him through the smoke.

'Oh, Daniel! It's you. It's just a bonfire, I see. Thank goodness for that! I thought at first the garden was on fire! Oh, this smoke – however can you bear to stand so close?' It was Miss Flower, coughing and waving at the smoke. She looked at him. 'Oh, poor boy! You're smuts from head to foot!'

Dan dragged a grimy hand across his brow. 'My fault, Miss,' he said, unhappily. 'I lit a fire when I didn't ought. And mind your pretty dress or you'll get black as well.' He shook his head. 'Bad enough for me. Just look at the state I've made of my good shirt! Ma'll have my hide for hangings – and all because I'm just plain ignorant. Don't know a seedling from a weed without Old Roseworthy points it out to me. I'm afraid I'm a disappointment in this job. I'm that stupid, I could kick myself.'

He bashed at an errant spark with bitterness, but when he looked up she was smiling at him. 'Poor Daniel. You mustn't blame yourself. Of course you don't know anything about gardening. But you can learn. I'm sure I have a book somewhere, with plates of garden plants, *A Girl's Guide to Nature*, or something of the kind. Miss Boff gave it to me when I was young. When you come inside to wash, I'll look it out for you.'

He wasn't sure about going home with *A Girl's Guide to Nature* underneath his arm – Jimmy Gannet would never let him hear the end of it – but she meant it well.

He said, 'Would you, Miss? I'd take that very kind. I dearly love to have a bit of a read, but there isn't a right lot in our house, 'cept an attendance prize that Melda won one time at Sunday school. I've read that, scores of times.'

She had taken off her bonnet and was standing there, fanning away the smoke with it, as if it was the most natural thing in the world. She looked at him. 'Well, I've got lots of other books as well – a whole box of them. I was going to give them to the Mission sale, but if you would care to borrow some of them. . . ?'

He shook his head. 'I haven't got time, Miss – not with everything . . '

'Oh, Daniel!' she laughed reproachfully at him. 'Of course you have. Miss Boff says that you have time for anything, if you only want it hard enough. It would be another chance at education, in a way – and I would help you, if you wanted it.' She'd turned a delightful shade of pink.

He found himself smiling back at her. 'Well, if you're sure?'

'Of course I'm sure,' she said. 'And now I'd better go and change before this smoke gets too deeply into my clothes! I've lingered here too long as it is. Lionel went down to return the trap, but he'll have got back to the house by now and everyone will be wondering where I am.'

She turned and left without another word, but when he went into the wash house to rinse off the black, he found an old shirt folded on the bench, and on it two books and a scribbled note:

'For Daniel. You can borrow these.'

So he took them home.

166

Five

M ollie meant to look in at the Olds's house several times that week, but somehow she couldn't seem to manage it. It was difficult enough, her being up the factory first thing, and him working at the vicarage all hours, but then there was this trouble up the quarry pit. The Union was getting restive, with so many men put off, and even Stan and Fayther had got involved. Off to meetings nearly every night, which meant nobody to fetch coals or water or to chop the wood, so what with that and little Stanley getting teeth again, Mollie had been proper rushed off her feet.

Then, one evening when she did contrive to call – by spending all her free afternoon chopping sticks and helping Eadie with the ironing – she had a surprise: Kitty and Mrs Olds were sitting darning socks, while Lucy played with spills beside the fire, but otherwise the kitchen was empty. No sign of Dan, or any of the others, come to that.

'Hello!' Mollie put her head around the door. 'Where's everybody got to?'

Mrs Olds got up at once to set the kettle back on the hob beside the fire. 'Zac's gone off with Jimmy Gannet somewhere, picking whelks, and Melda's out with that young man of hers.' She grinned. 'Get a bit of fish for tea tomorrow, anyhow.' She swilled the teapot with a bit of hot water, then picked up a handful of the tea leaves which had been drying on the sill and dropped them in.

She looked tired, poor woman, Mollie thought. No wonder, with things the way they were.

'And Dan?' she asked.

Kitty made a little snorting sound. 'Upstairs in the bedroom like Lord Muck! Reading, if you ever heard the like! Better go up quick, if you want to speak to 'im. He'll be too gentrified directly for the likes of us.'

Mollie looked enquiringly at Mrs Olds.

''S true,' she said. 'He's up there with a book. That Miss Flower lent it to him, seemingly. Said he should improve himself, now his leg is bad, maybe even get a clerk's job somewhere in the end.'

Kitty stabbed at her darning ferociously. 'As if they townfolk would even look at Dan. He don't even speak like they b'long to do!'

Mrs Olds was fetching cups and saucers from the shelf. 'I can't see it myself, either, Kitty girl, but there! Kind of Miss Flower to take an interest, I suppose, and Dan's that thrilled, you'd think he'd won a hundred pounds. And it does take his mind off things. You go on up, Moll – tell him there's a cup of tea. Perhaps he'll take a bit of notice, since it's you. No good me shouting up to him, it's a waste of breath. He's that deep in his reading he doesn't hear a word.'

Mollie smiled thinly and made her way upstairs, but she was fuming inwardly. Drat that Miss Flower and her interfering ways. What did she think she was up to now? You might have known that something like this would happen, the minute Dan went up the vicarage!

She flung open the bedroom door, but Dan didn't even stir. He was lying face downwards on the bed, with a big fat book propped up in front of him. Mollie sat down on the edge of the bed and leaned her head over against his.

'My life!' she said. 'You got a job on there. All those long words, and little tiny print, and no pictures anywhere. Where you up to? Page sixteen? Take you all year to read it at that rate.'

Dan put the bookmark in the page and closed the book. She could read the title on the cover now, *The Adventures of Oliver Twist*. Dan rolled over on his side and looked at her. 'It isn't easy,' he confessed. 'Lots of words I never heard before. But I can fathom it. Good story too – about a boy sent to a workhouse when his mother died.'

Mollie tossed her head, more impatient with all this than ever. 'My lor!' she said. 'Can't she give you something a bit more cheerful to read than that?'

'I think it comes out all right in the end,' he laughed. 'Look! There are some pictures, see. There's him holding a picture of a pretty girl. Looks like he comes to be a gentleman.'

Mollie snatched the book away and dropped it on the floor. 'And what do you suppose? You're going to do the same? Don't be so daft. All very well for Miss Flower to give you fairy tales, but I've got a bit of real life waiting here for you. If you can tear yourself away, that is?' She reached out a hand and stroked his hair.

'Have you now?' he said, and took her in his arms, but he didn't kiss her as she'd hoped he would. Instead, he struggled up on one elbow and gazed towards the door. Mollie sat up again, and did the same. Jimmy was standing there, a broad smile on his face.

'Ma says the tea is waiting, and are you coming down?' he said. 'Zac and me're back. And I saw what you were doing – 'alfpenny or I'll tell.'

Mollie threw caution to the winds. 'Nothing to tell!' she snapped back, saucily. 'Dan and I are walking out, and fixing to be wed.' She glanced at his face. 'One of these days. Isn't that right, Dan?'

'One of these days,' Dan said, getting to his feet, and giving his brother a halfpenny all the same. 'Now, you get off downstairs, Jimmy Gannet, tell Ma we're on our way.'

So there it was; easy as that! She'd spent weeks dreaming how she'd get him to propose. And now the thing was done.

'Don't I get a kiss, then?' Mollie said, brazen to the end, and felt his lips close warmly on her own. 'Better'n any old book, this, isn't it?' she added.

He laughed. 'You're a caution, you! Have to watch out for you when we get wed. Come on! Ma's waiting with the tea.'

Jimmy had blabbed it all out straightaway, halfpenny or not, as Mollie knew he would. Everyone clapped and whistled as they came in. Ma was so delighted at the news that she insisted on boiling up the whelks the boys had brought, and having extra supper there and then.

It was round the village in a flash, as well, and when they went to the Polvidden coronation tea, they went together, hand in hand. And, as Mollie said to Daniel afterwards, there seemed to be more celebration for the pair of them than for the King himself. They didn't go up to see the beacon lit, because of Daniel's leg, but everybody understood – except for Harry Varfell, who looked sour as milk.

Mollie felt a little guilty about that.

Edward Flower, Vicar of St Evan, cycled slowly down the lane, aware of a sensation of contentment which was rare with him. He sent up a little prayer of thanks. Perhaps there really was a God, and Jonathan was right, as usual. All this aridity of soul had merely been a test, and things were working to a Higher Plan. One could believe it, on a day like this.

It was a fine clear late-summer afternoon, the hedges full of flowers and the lazy buzz of bees, the distant sea dazzling in the sun. Of course, there were many troubles in the world, and a pastor was bound to remember them in prayer, but this was a day to glory in creation, especially when a man was on the way out to St Just to have tea with a friend, knowing another rare edition was awaiting him.

And things were working out so beautifully at home. That new lad, Daniel, for instance. He had been with them only for a month or two, and already that had proved to be a great success. The coronation tea and concert had been a triumph for the church, and the garden had looked splendid on the day.

Victoria was blossoming as well. Pleased with her little project, obviously, and with reason, too – appointing that boy had been an inspired idea. He smiled. Wonderful to see her taking a real initiative in caring for the poor and unfortunate, like this. Perhaps he should consult her more on parish work.

He had reached a steep portion of the road, and for a moment he was obliged to concentrate on his pedalling. Indeed when a smart little wagonette and pair came trotting down the hill towards him, he was glad to draw into the hedge and stop. A hand drew down the window as the carriage passed, and a cheerful voice called out to him, 'Dr Flower! Good afternoon to you! You've chosen a nice day for a ride!'

He had just time to recognize Miss Cardew's smiling face and to raise his hat, before the vehicle swept out of sight around the bend. Of course, he remembered, Bella was returned from London now, and Victoria had invited her friend to the vicarage for tea. No doubt that's where Isabella was going, electing – in this weather – to take the coastal road, and use the carriage rather than to walk. Sensible girl! It was too hot for exertion. His own face was streaming in a most un-vicarly way. He took out his handkerchief and mopped his brow, before he jammed his hat back on his head and mounted his bicycle again.

He smiled. A toiling clergyman, perspiring in the heat. How poor Miss Boff would disapprove! Although, even she had been more sunny recently – instead of finding Lionel tiresome, as she had always done before, she'd suddenly become a convert to his cause. More than that, she positively beamed at him, and hummed little tunes whenever he appeared. Edward was too much of a gentleman to wish Miss Boff's attentions on poor Lionel, but he found the situation gratifying, all the same.

It was all to do with the choir, apparently, or so Victoria maintained. Miss Boff had been elevated to soprano lead, a masterstroke of musical diplomacy. That was another blessing – thanks to Jonathan, again – Lionel was doing wonders with the choir. The anthem was a treat to listen to last week, and the standard of congregational singing had improved dramatically. Not least because Lionel's new organist had settled in, and there was now no need for the harmonium at all. A lapsed Presbyterian, unfortunately, and therefore not a communicant, but he played the organ particularly well.

Yes, Edward thought, things were falling into place quite splendidly. He had a good deal to be thankful for.

He had reached the brow of the little hill by now, and – since he was in good spirits and there was nobody about – he allowed himself a small unwonted liberty, he took his feet off the pedals and freewheeled down the hill with his legs outstretched, revelling like a child in the freedom and the speed. Of course, it was courting a divine rebuke. As he neared the steepest slope a playful gust of wind snatched at his hat and bowled it clean across the hedge, like a round black clerical pie dish sailing through the air.

He watched it in dismay, but it was some moments before he could safely steer on to the grass verge and bump uncomfortably to a stop.

Serve yourself right! he told himself, unrepentantly, as he left the bicycle propped against the hedge and retraced his path back up the hill on foot, but, he found when he got to where he thought he'd lost the hat, at first he couldn't see where it had gone.

This was the spot, surely, just opposite that gate? Yes, he remembered that big clump of lady's smock. The wind had been blowing off the sea, so it hadn't gone to seaward, mercifully. Presumably it was somewhere in the field. He climbed on to a milestone beside the wall and peered. Yes, there it was, right over there, caught in a clump of furze beside the bottom hedge.

There was a stile a little further on, and he climbed over it. There were no animals in the field that he could see, but there had been cows there sometime recently, and he had to be careful where he put his feet. He picked his way across, and with a stick managed to retrieve his hat without too much ado, though he did catch himself on the prickles doing so. It took him a few minutes to unhook himself and longer still to brush down his battered headgear and coax it back into something resembling its familiar shape.

He took out his pocket watch and looked at it. Good grief! If he wasn't careful he'd be discourteously late arriving at Pencarrow's house for tea. That would teach him to play infantile games! He looked around. There was a small path leading back the way he'd come, cutting off the corner of the hill. That would be a great deal quicker than the road! He made his way across to it and, holding his hat firmly on his head, began to stride out purposefully down the track.

It was pleasant walking, sheltered from the wind and road, especially as the next field was full of uncut hay. He followed the path dutifully around the edge, enjoying the sweet smell, though someone before him had been more careless of the crop. There was a wide area in the corner where some thoughtless soul had lain, enjoying the warmth of the afternoon, and flattening the grasses under him.

Or her? There was a scrap of lacy cloth beside the wall. A lady's handkerchief, still folded carefully. He picked it up.

It was a pretty thing, made of fine cloth, obviously of the highest quality. It was embroidered, too, with three intertwined initials worked into the threads, C.T.L.? C.L.J? Something of the kind. And totally unused. Someone would be sorry to have left that lying here. But he could think of no one with a name with those initials. Someone from St Just perhaps? That wasn't very far away. Best to ask Pencarrow, he might know. Edward slipped the dainty thing into the pocket of his coat, and hurried on.

He got back on his bicycle, and pedalled – decorously now – the remaining mile or two to where Pencarrow lived. He rode so energetically that he arrived only a little late, and Stephen poohpoohed any apologies. He'd been delayed himself, he said, returning from Penzance, and had hardly been inside the house an hour.

Edward did show him the handkerchief, but he shook his head. 'Can't be any help there, I'm afraid. Now, come into the garden, do. I found the most delightful book of coloured plates for you. I'll show it to you when we've had some tea. Not quite the one you wanted, I'm afraid, but I'm thinking of going up to London in a month or so and I'll keep an eye out for that one while I'm there.'

Edward spent an enchanted afternoon. He even succumbed to temptation and agreed to buy the book, though the extravagance gave him the usual pang of guilt. He didn't give the handkerchief another thought until he came across it, much later on, emptying his pockets when he went to bed. He opened the top drawer of his bedroom desk and put it carefully away.

Bella alighted from her perch by leaning lightly on the coachman's arm, and hurried over to her friend, who had come out to meet her at the gate. 'Oh, Victoria, how wonderful to see you! I seem to have been in London such an age! And there's so much to tell!' She made a little kissing motion in the air, two or three inches from Victoria's cheek. 'Heavens, it's so hot! And in September too – I simply had to bring the wagonette.'

Victoria smiled. 'Would the driver care to come in for a drink? We have a little elderflower, I think.'

Bella shook her head. 'I think not, Vicki, though it's kind of you. John has other errands to perform. Very well, John, that will do. You may call for me at five.' She watched the wagonette trot out of sight, before she added, 'Poor John, he used to be my groom. I told you about him before, I think.'

'The one who had an assignation with a girl, and left you unattended in the rain?'

Bella laughed. 'Don't sound so disapproving, Vic. It suited both of us. Just as it suited us to bring the wagonette today. One must have a little excitement in one's life – it's so dull here after London, otherwise. Speaking of which, you'll never guess who I saw on the way. Your poor father, pedalling up the hill towards St Just. Pink as a peony, poor man.'

Victoria frowned. 'Belle! Don't tell me you have been out there yourself? Visiting Mr Pencarrow, no doubt? And with my father expected at the house!'

Belle laughed, that little tinkling laugh she reserved for her more outrageous doings. 'Oh, I didn't visit at the house, of course. I simply chanced to meet him on the way. I'd sent John off with the wagonette – he was only too anxious to go, of course – while I got out to take the air, so Stephen and I had a little stroll around the lanes until John brought it back again. What could be more innocuous on such a lovely afternoon?' She took off her bonnet and shook out her hair. 'And certainly it's rather warm. What about this elderflower drink that you were promising?' She made to move towards the house.

But Victoria refused to be beguiled. 'Belle, honestly!' she cried. 'Suppose someone had seen you? Think what a scandal for your family! Mr Pencarrow knew my father was to call this afternoon – it was most uncivil of him not to be at home. And don't pretend that you were simply walking down the lanes – you know quite well there are hay-stalks in your hair!'

Isabella plucked at the offending straws, but she did not look the slightest bit contrite. 'Well,' she said, looking roguishly up under her eyelashes, 'in any case it doesn't matter now. Oh Vicki, can you keep a secret? Swear you will? I can't keep it to myself another minute.' She seized her friend's hands urgently, and went on in a excited undertone, without waiting for Victoria's reply. 'You see, I've quite made up my mind. I simply can't think of marrying Petroc any longer.'

Vicki had been half-fearing this for weeks, but all the same she was appalled. 'But Belle,' she stammered, 'I thought you hoped to wed him in the end. You can't have expectations of Mr Pencarrow, after all. He is promised to that lady in Penzance. You told me so yourself.' She sighed. 'This is my fault as much as yours. I encouraged you! I should have known that it would lead to trouble in the end!'

'Hush! It is still a secret as yet, but Stephen feels as I do. We spoke of it this very afternoon. The arrangement with the widow was a duty, that is all, and of course he is an honourable man.'

Victoria had always had her private opinions about that, but she nodded doubtfully. 'So he will disengage himself? It is to be hoped she does not sue for breach of promise, then.'

Bella made a face. 'It will take a little time of course – it must be handled tactfully, but Stephen promises he'll do so when he can. I shall convince him to move to London afterwards – it will minimise ill-feeling, and I could not face living in that dreadful house of his, and of course I can expect very little from Papa. The house and contents go to my brother, Horry, naturally – or to my cousin Petroc, if Horry dies without an heir.'

'Have you told Stephen that?'

Bella coloured. 'Oh yes. He was a little shocked, at first, that I had no expectations of my own, but he said he felt no differently. And after today . . .' Her colour deepened, but she met Victoria's eyes.

'And what is so particular about today?' Vicki demanded, and then worked out the solution for herself. She was so shocked and astonished that she sat down hard on the wall, staring at her friend with startled eyes. 'Bella! You didn't? I don't believe it. You can't have allowed him to . . . what you told me once? I can't believe it of you, Belle,' she said.

'Well, of course we didn't – at least, not properly,' Bella backtracked hastily. 'Just enough to make it quite impossible for Stephen honourably to do anything but marry me.'

'So you led him on to trap him,' Vicki said, indignantly. 'I think that's very nearly as reprehensible.' But inwardly she was a little bit in awe.

Bella seemed to be aware of this. She dimpled. 'Just enough to make sure of him, at least. And if we are to be betrothed, what difference will it make? Just think, in just a month or two I shall be formally engaged. Perhaps we can announce it at the Christmas Ball – though I suppose I'll have to work hard to convince Papa.'

And Stephen will have to disentangle himself from the widow first, Victoria thought. But aloud she said, 'And what about Petroc? Isn't he coming back around that time? To have your final answer, I recall.'

'Oh, don't scold, Vicki. I shall write to him at once. Will that satisfy your feelings of propriety?' She smiled that dimpling little girl smile that people found so irresistible.

For once Vicki found it slightly irritating. 'Well,' she said, 'there's no point standing here. What's done is done, I suppose – though I'm still surprised that you could be so . . . unladylike! And I hope you're right about Mr Pencarrow's plans, that's all.' She led the way along the path towards the house.

Bella reached out and gently touched her arm. 'Oh, you didn't hear him, Vic. He adores the ground I walk on, that's what he said. And he promised faithfully that if I let him . . . you know . . . touch me in that way, he'd disengage himself and marry me.'

'Oh, very well, then!' Victoria was terse. 'No doubt you're right, as usual, and it will work out in the end. But understand this, Belle, I refuse – absolutely refuse – to be involved in any part of this again. If you intend to see Mr Pencarrow you can't pretend that you are meeting me. You must find some other excuse, though I suppose, once you are engaged, there will be no need for further subterfuge.'

They had reached the house by this time, and Ruby let them in. 'Mrs Roseworthy says there's elderflower cordial and scones.'

'We'll have it in the drawing room,' Victoria said, and then – as Ruby disappeared – she added to Bella, hurriedly, 'Let us talk about something a little more decorous. How are your family?'

Bella did that little dimpling smile again. 'My family is well, thank you. And yours? How's Lionel?' She settled herself on one of the small armchairs in the bay, while Vicki sat down in the other, opposite.

It was an unfortunate vantage point, perhaps, because at that moment Daniel came into view, pushing a wheelbarrow towards the shed. The day was so extremely warm, that – evidently thinking himself unobserved – he'd stripped down his undershirt, revealing a back so rippling and smooth that Victoria found herself watching him, transfixed.

She smiled, remembering the day before. She'd gone out into the arbour while he was having lunch – a horrid lump of bread and shrivelled cheese – and helped him with his reading, as she'd been doing recently. He was a quick scholar, and he loved to learn. They had been bending earnestly over his list of words – the ones he hadn't really understood – and his hand had accidentally grazed

177

her wrist. She could still recall the unexpected tingle on her skin, and from the way he flushed she knew he'd felt it too. And now, seeing that expanse of handsome back . . . It almost made one understand why Bella could behave the way she had.

'Vic?' Bella's voice recalled her to herself.

'Oh, Lionel's very well,' she said. Too late. Bella had twisted in her seat to see what had attracted her attention so.

'That's the young quarry man that you took pity on? He seems to be doing very well. I see that now he hardly limps at all. All that fresh air and exercise, I expect – an outdoor life suits people of that type. Good-looking fellow, isn't he! No wonder you can't keep your eyes off him.'

Despite herself, Victoria felt the colour flood her cheeks. Bella saw, and pounced upon it instantly, saying with a triumphant little laugh, 'My dearest, Vic, you're smitten with the man. And you have the audacity to lecture me! Oh, don't protest! Of course, I know it's quite impossible, a vulgar, uneducated fellow of that common sort. But certainly he's a pleasure to the eyes. Poor Lionel! He must feel the contrast terribly! He is so very weak and pale by comparison.'

'I assure you,' Victoria attempted to sound dignified, 'contrast does not enter into it. This is a charitable concern of mine. I'm helping the young man with his education, encouraging him to read, and helping him to refine his speech.' Even to her own ears she sounded prim.

Bella was giggling uncontrollably by now.

'No, Belle, I mean it. There is nothing untoward. And I'll say it once again: there is nothing between Mr Smallbone and myself. Even if there were, Lionel is too much of a gentleman to condescend to petty jealousies. Such comparisons would not occur to him.' All this was perfectly true, she told herself, although certainly she did find Lionel rather humourless and ineffectual beside Daniel's effortless, cheerful masculinity.

'Of course,' Bella said. She was still smirking, but just then Ruby came in with the tray, and conversation turned to coronations, hats, and suffragettes, and other wonders of the capital.

Part Four

November – Christmas 1911

One

It was unseasonably cold. The church bell had not long since struck five, but already there was a sharp nip in the air and the churchyard grasses crunched beneath her feet. It would be jolly chilly in the church for choir practice tonight, and she had promised Lionel she would go and practise with the choir, since they were short of a soprano for the week – poor Mrs Prowse was in bed with a chill.

Victoria regretted now that she undertaken this. It meant she had to look in before tea and run over the anthem before the others came. And it had turned so cold. It was to be hoped it didn't take too long! There would be a hard frost later on, she thought, huddling herself under her new pale-blue woollen fitted coat.

It was a little victory, that coat. A present from Deedee for her birthday yesterday, together with her smart new two-piece costume and matching blue kid gloves. All thanks to the influence of the new queen. Her Majesty always dressed so beautifully – you could see it in the pictures on the tins of coronation jam, and Bella had talked of little else since she came home from the capital. Heavy capes and ostrich-feathered hats were quite out of fashion nowadays, and if Queen Mary thought that pale blue was decorous, even Miss Boff could hardly disagree.

It was true that the new outfit was nothing like as warm as last year's ugly brown (which in any case was suddenly too tight around the chest), though Victoria would have perished rather than admit as much. It would be a pity to spoil it all by dirtying her hems, and there were little muddy puddles everywhere. She lifted her skirts carefully to avoid the frosted dew and watched with great precision where she put her feet. Miss Boff had scolded that pale blue would soil, and Victoria didn't want to prove her right.

She was so engrossed in guarding her dresses and looking where she trod that she almost blundered into Daniel Olds who was busy with a trowel at the stile.

'Hello, Daniel!' she said with a smile. They were enormous friends by now. 'How are you? How is the reading getting on?'

He snatched off his cap and grinned at her. 'Halfway through that second book, I am. The one about David Copperfield. And I'm doing grand, now, thanks to you. Not half so slow deciphering as I used to be.' He gave her a wicked sideways glance. 'I've been reading it to Kitty – and Jimmy too, though he's too much of a fidget to listen half the time – but she do love it, just as much as me. Shan't know what to do, shall we, when I finish it.'

She was about to correct him: 'You should say "she loves it", Daniel, and forget the "do",' but she stopped herself in time. It was just enthusiasm which made him slip into old ways. Most of the time he was careful of his speech and had been working really hard to lose the worst mistakes. She had often stopped to help him, while he ate his lunch (she had persuaded him not to call it 'crowst'), and now he could say 'good afternoon' and 'how are you?' like any gentleman. But he was still apt to be, in his own words, 'all ends up like Porthscowen ducks' if he got excited about anything. She smiled. Phrases like that were so picturesque, it was almost a pity to school it out of him.

She found that he was smiling back at her. The twinkling grey eyes charmed her, as they always did. She looked away. 'Well, we shall have to find you something else!' she said, with a briskness modelled on Miss Boff.

He fiddled with his cap suddenly and stared at his boots. His ears, she noticed, had turned red with cold. 'Don't know if I'll be here much longer to lend it to, Miss Flower.' When he looked up again his smile was rueful. 'It's nothing but blind charity as it is. There's no work in the garden at this time of year – the

182

Reverend's simply inventing jobs for me. There's a limit to how much potting up and pruning anyone can do. Look at me now, just weeding of . . . I mean, weeding out . . . this wall. Just for the sake of it, I know.'

Victoria stared at him. 'Dan, I hope you're not unhappy here?' She was sincerely shocked. Her little tutorials with Daniel had become a fixture in her life, and she couldn't bear the thought of losing them.

He shook his head. 'No, of course not, Miss. You've been very good. It's been the saving of me, and I won't forget – ever – what you have done for me, helping me to read and everything. But it was only temporary, I knew that at the time, and now there's talk that householders will have to pay these insurance stamps, just for their domestic staff. The vicar told me that himself, last week. He didn't say anything outright, but you can see the way it is. Time I was looking out for something else – though the good Lord alone knows what, the way things are. Don't think that I'm ungrateful, 'cause I'm not, but I can't go on for ever being a burden to the Reverend. Not when everyone has been so kind.'

Victoria felt unreasonably cross, this gardening job had all been her idea. She said quite sharply, 'Well, I hope you find something else that suits,' and went to step nimbly past him on to the stile.

'Here, Miss, watch out, that stone is awfully slippery with those weeds!' he cried, but it was already too late. Victoria's smart little kid boot slid from under her on the freezing moisture on the granite slab, and she would have landed neatly on her bottom on the path if a pair of strong arms had not prevented her. She found herself leaning backwards, looking up at him, for all the world like a swooning maiden in the woodcuts in one of Bella's books. Worse, she had instinctively reached out an arm, and steadied herself by holding on to Daniel.

For a moment she looked into his eyes. He did not relinquish her, and she did not struggle free. Her head was close against his chest. She could hear the pounding of his heart. She closed her eyes and raised her face.

His lips closed gently on her own.

'Daniel?' she said softly, and closed her eyes again. She wanted . . . No! How could she want? This was ridiculous.

'Daniel!' she said. He helped her upright, instantly.

'I'm some sorry, Miss.' He sounded breathless, and she knew that she was breathing fast as well. 'I don't know what come over me. Are you all right? Shouldn't forgive myself, if I'd offended you, or you were hurt, or anything.' His face was crimson, and he looked away.

'Thank you, Daniel, I am quite all right,' she answered primly, but it did no good. Her arm was still circling his neck. His steadying hand was still locked in hers and she was pressing it, as if her fingers were unaware of what they did. Her eyes, too, refused to disengage. She felt that his lips, like hers, were tingling. The world – and they – stood still.

'Victoria?' That was Lionel, appearing from the direction of the church. They jumped apart at once.

'Ah, it is you, Victoria. I thought I heard your voice. Were you coming to look in at the church? I think you said you would. There's a very tricky passage for the sopranos in the second verse, and I think it would be helpful to run over it before the full rehearsal later on.' There was no hint of guile in Lionel's voice and he was smiling pleasantly, though, Victoria thought, he must have seen.

It was Daniel who had the presence of mind to say, 'Miss Flower was just on her way, but she slipped and nearly hurt herself. The stile is very slippery. My fault, with all those weeds and everything. Good thing I managed to catch her as she fell.'

'My dear Victoria,' Lionel was all concern. 'That must have shaken you. You're sure that you're not hurt? Do you feel up to singing, after that? Then take my arm, this path is slippery. Thank you, young man,' he slipped a sixpence into Daniel's palm. 'You did very well. I appreciate your help.'

And Victoria was obliged to take his arm and go. It was perishingly cold inside the church, and although shame is a powerful covering, by the time they'd finished 'running over' the difficult passages she was devoutly wishing that she'd worn something a little less elegant, but a touch more snug.

Daniel watched Miss Victoria as she disappeared out of sight. How could he have been such a clown? But she was a picture, that one, and the way she'd looked at him! He was still breathing heavily and he had to give himself a mental talking to.

'Don't be so damty wet, Dan Olds. Of course she didn't mean anything at all. How could she? Lovely girl like that, and you a gardener's boy at best, in your great boots and working shirt. My hat! What have you been and gone and done? Forgotten yourself and tried to kiss her, like you wanted to! You'll be out of here before you've counted ten! And that curate fellow turning up like that. Poor Miss Victoria won't half get it later on!'

But his inner self refused to be convinced. He could still feel the warmth and weight of her slight body in his arms, the soft pressure of her lips on his. She had returned his kiss, hadn't she? he asked himself. No, you fool, you just imagined it. Just you wait until the Reverend hears.

But the way she rustled when she walked! The rose-scented perfume of her hair! The image of her stayed with him till darkness fell, it warmed him like an inner fire and made the raw cold of the churchyard seem of no account.

He lingered past his usual time, but no one came to tell him he was dismissed and he did not see her again that day. Mollie was there at home and waiting, dressed up to the nines. Striking enough in her new red skirt and blouse.

'You like it, Dan? I bought it specially,' she asked him provocatively.

'Very nice!' But it was a little bright and boldly cut, and when she stepped forward for a kiss she smelt strikingly of carbolic soap and cheese. She must have felt his diffidence and was inclined to be annoyed. 'How've you been so late coming to-night? Hadn't forgotten it was the chapel's magic lantern show?'

He had of course, but he muttered something about finishing

the job. 'Couldn't have left piles of slippery weeds up on the stile. Miss Victoria or somebody might have hurt themselves.'

'Oh, Miss Victoria now! And 'ark at you! Hhave hhurt themselves!!! Like the Earl of Rot. It's all those books she's giving you to read. You'll be too grand to speak to your own self in the mirror, next.'

She was teasing, tugging on his arm, but Dan found that he was not amused. 'If you want me to come with you,' he said, 'you'd best let me go and change out of these working clothes. They're damp, and I'm half-frozen as it is.'

He turned and went upstairs, but not before he had time to overhear Mollie's mocking mutter, 'Froz*en*!', and see her pull a comic face at Ma. Perhaps he should have said 'froze' as usual; generally he did try to speak in the old ways at home.

The magic lantern show was interesting, all about elephants and Africa, and afterwards there were paste sandwiches, jam tarts and buns. Dan quite enjoyed himself and – feeling apologetic for his earlier mood – he chatted cheerfully to Mollie as he walked her home. It wasn't her fault, after all, if all she had to talk about was dairy factories, and how Stan and Eadie and the child made life cramped and difficult at home.

'Course they're still thinking to be moving on. Get somewhere of their own. Be a bit more room home, then.' She gave him a sideways smile.

She was always going on like this, these days, he thought. Trying to press him into things, hinting that they could marry and move into Eadie's room. He tried to change the subject by asking after Jamie, but she brushed that aside.

'Working in the dynamite works up Hayle this week, but that won't last. First sign of trouble and they'll put him off. It's the same with any job he takes. In and out like Auntie Annie's clock.' Because of his shoulder, she didn't have to say, and they both knew that it would be the same for Dan. She took his arm. 'Let's talk about something a bit cheerfuller. How many days you get off Christmas time? Giving you Boxing Day are they? We could go out for a proper bit of a walk, if so, supposing that it's fine.'

186

And she prattled on. But when they reached the door to number nine, she turned and forced herself into his arms, pressing her body firmly against his. He knew that he should welcome it, but the whiff of cheesy carbolic half-defeated him. His heart was lost to rose-scent, and dainty pale-blue coats.

Mollie nestled closer.

He held her to him in the foggy frost, stroking her shawled head thoughtfully. She turned her face towards him and he grinned down and pressed her nose with a playful finger, but he couldn't bring himself to kiss her, as he used to do, and as she very clearly hoped he would.

Lionel put away the lantern and returned the song books to the vestry shelf. But though the church was dark and chilly, he did not hurry home, but lingered at the altar where one lone candle burned.

The truth was, he was wrestling with his soul. Not that he was suffering from doubts; he was as convinced of his calling as any man could be. Nor was it unworthy thoughts, exactly; he prided himself that he had learned to control the inner workings of his conscious mind. It was his dreams that troubled him.

He had done his best to put them away: suppress the memory and lose himself in parish duties and musical affairs. He had even agreed to get up a series of little Advent concerts with the choir, after the success of the one they had done before the Harvest Home.

Not that he approved of it at all. He'd hated the Harvest Festival. Decorating the church in that vulgar fashion with marrows and string beans, like some kind of pagan carnival! And now they were proposing a dreadful Christmas pageant, with a model stable in the sanctuary and children dressed in towels and dressing gowns.

He poured out his feelings to his diary: 'I cannot feel that this is permitted by the prayer book or sanctified by the real traditions of the church. A hundred years ago, no one would ever have thought of such a thing.'

Yet when Reverend Doctor Flower had proposed 'a proper Christmas concert and Nativity this year, now that we've got a choir and organist to help', Lionel had agreed, without a single word of counter argument. It was a deliberate act of clerical obedience, a penance he could impose upon himself.

But it didn't seem to help. If anything the dreams were getting worse.

He had been kneeling in front of the altar, but now he got awkwardly to his feet again. He had achieved no sense of absolution. Ironic, he thought, he offered it to others, perhaps he needed someone else to offer it to him.

The idea gave him comfort. Yes, of course. He would go and ask Dr Flower for advice. That would be real penance, if you like. Lionel sighed. Confessing his sordid little dreams to the vicar face-to-face, was more daunting than hair shirts and rigid fasts.

He genuflected to the altar and crossed himself. He was soothed by the familiar rituals, and he was feeling a little more confident as he snuffed out the altar candles and blew out the lamps. The verger was waiting in the porchway with the key, and muttered, 'Goodnight Reverend', as he passed. Lionel murmured a blessing, and went out into the churchyard, trying to look as worthy of his calling as he could.

The vicar was out with a parishioner, but next morning at breakfast Lionel raised the question of an interview.

Dr Flower said, 'Yes, Lionel, of course, at any time. This afternoon would be convenient. Mr Pencarrow was due to come today, but I understand that he has not returned from London. He was delayed by these railway strikes. Straight after lunch would suit me very well.'

So, that had not been difficult. Yet now that Lionel was standing here, outside the study door, his courage very nearly failed.

But it was too late now. A voice called out 'Come in!' and Lionel obeyed to find his vicar sitting at his desk, with a decanter of port and two glasses on a tray, regarding him with warm benevolence. 'You wanted to see me about something, Lionel?'

The moment for humble confession had arrived. Lionel found it impossible to do. 'It's . . .' he began, and then words deserted him.

'Something of a personal nature, I presume?' Dr Flower smiled and pressed his fingertips together as he leaned back in his chair.

Lionel swallowed. This was to be his penance; he must face it like a man. He forced himself to articulate the words: 'It's a little delicate. The truth is, Father, I've been subject to –' he hunted for the words – 'lascivious thoughts.'

The vicar cleared his throat. 'I understand. Well, Lionel, since we are speaking man to man, I will be frank with you. These "thoughts" are not, perhaps, as rare as you suppose.' He glanced away, studying his hands as though they were fascinating, then suddenly: 'We men are given urges for a higher good, but Satan has a way of twisting them to our discomfiture.' He put on his glasses – simply, it seemed, for the purpose of looking at Lionel again over the top of them. 'Are you – forgive me – confessing this because Victoria figures in these dreams?'

Lionel was shocked by this idea. 'Not Victoria. Not any young woman . . .' There it was out. Dr Flower was looking very stern. Lionel felt overwhelmed by what he'd said. Some little personal fiend was whispering in his ear and Lionel added, weakly, 'Not any young lady . . . in particular.'

The vicar nodded wisely. 'You do yourself credit, Lionel, to be so disturbed. You are wise to take temptation seriously.' He hooked his thumbs under the collar of his coat and, addressing the bookshelves on the wall as if they were his congregation, went on in a gravely earnest tone: 'If you find yourself . . . embarrassed . . . in this way, take a brisk walk, or better still a swim. A cold bath is said to be efficacious too. Keep occupied, and keep your thoughts on higher things. I'm sure I have no need to tell you that.' He looked at Lionel again. 'Or you could find a proper outlet for these drives.'

Lionel felt himself blushing uncontrollably.

Another smile. 'Perhaps it is God's way of telling you that it is time you found yourself a wife.'

Lionel felt a burden lift from him. Of course! Perhaps Dr
Flower hadn't wholly understood, but this – surely – was the
guidance that he sought? It was so simple, why hadn't he thought
of it himself? Victoria! There so was much to be said for it. She
was amiable, pretty, sensible – not given to silly giggling and
flirtatious ways – and she liked him, he was sure she did. She
would make a first-class clergy wife. And it would do him good:
it would be manly, proper, salubrious. He found himself stum-
bling out, 'You think Victoria . . .?'

The vicar twinkled at him. 'I think you should ask Victoria
herself. But you have my blessing, Lionel, my boy. In fact –' he
gestured to the decanter on the tray – 'I rather hoped that's what
you'd come to say. But I'm glad you trusted me with your self-
doubts. I appreciate your honesty in that. Believe me, Lionel,
love is not a sin. These urges are quite natural, and not as unusual
as you might suppose. Now, time for a little celebratory drink, I
think. I hope to welcome you to the family soon.'

Lionel went downstairs in a dream. Some of the advice was
excellent. He would go for brisk walks and cold early-morning
dips. Above all, he would spend time with Victoria, as her father
had so obviously hoped. And when he judged the time was right,
he'd speak.

When he went into the drawing room, she greeted him with
such a dazzling smile that it gave him confidence. Obviously, he
wasn't odious to her; perhaps she always smiled at him like that.
Had he been ridiculously blind?

He didn't say anything to her that night, of course, but duly
devoted the next hour to practising duets. Victoria seemed to like
it too, and that encouraged him. He found himself mentally
rehearsing a proposal speech. This would not be too difficult.
Perhaps he could learn to love her as he should, and free himself
once and for ever from those disquieting dreams. The dreams in
which Mr Ralph Mills – with or without his jacket and cravat –
played such an unhealthy and exciting part.

Two

L ionel spent the next few days plucking up the courage to propose. It seemed a simple enough thing, until the moment came to say the words, and then it was suddenly ridiculous. He knew – he had a helpful little book – what was expected on the wedding night. There was a lot of manly talk of 'mastering your urges', but he didn't really have any, as far as he was aware; at least not as far as Victoria was concerned. It seemed simply preposterous to think of her that way. Almost actively unpleasant, actually.

Yet he knew that marriage was the proper thing to do. The very prospect had controlled his dreams. Since his little heart-to-heart with Dr Flower his night-time fantasies had been, if anything, about Victoria: waiting for him in a long white dress, all disconcerting female bumps and curves. He had woken sweating once or twice. That was a good sign, he told himself, it was the sort of thing the book alluded to, although there had been one disturbing night, when his dream bride stripped off her dress and revealed the lithe, tanned body of a boy. It still gave him goose-pimples to think of it.

But enough of that. He was taking Dr Flower's advice: going for brisk walks and even taking a cold tub once or twice, though it was freezing at this time of year. He'd even written to the Rural Dean (who, with his Anglo-Catholic views, had regularly offered his curates the confessional), and received a hearty letter by return: 'Of course you must go ahead, my son. Matrimony is ordained by God.' So what was he waiting for?

He looked across to where Victoria was now, sitting opposite him by the fire, looking as demure and sensible as usual in fawn. He smiled.

She looked up and caught his eye, and smiled uncomplicatedly back. A woman without guile, he thought.

He braced himself. 'What are you reading, Victoria, my dear?' He moved his chair a little closer as he spoke.

She made a face. 'Oh, an old copy of the *Girl's Own Paper*. The print is not too small to read by lamplight, and Miss Boff thinks it respectable. She brings it sometimes to me from Penzance. But I find it very dull these days. I hear there's a brand new penny paper now, *the Woman's Weekly*. Perhaps it would be more suitable than this!' She read aloud in a mock-stern voice, ' "D. H. The expression you mention is not blasphemous, but it is vulgar slang. Also your handwriting is execrable." ' She put the magazine aside and laughed.

It was not a romantic opening and he said, absurdly, 'You are fond of books, I know.' He paused, and added in an attempt to find a common bond, 'As I am myself.'

Victoria gave a rueful smile. 'I have finished all the proper books I have, and I have not seen Bella in an age. She lends me a new one, now and then.'

'Shared interests are important in a friend,' he said, with emphasis. 'Between men and women equally.' He had her attention now; she was gazing at him. He pressed his advantage. 'I have seen you many times, helping that young gardener boy to read. No, do not be embarrassed, I cannot help commending your devotion there.'

'Truly?' Her eyes were shining and alight. 'I was afraid you might have disapproved.'

'Disapproved? My dear Victoria. Nothing could be a greater joy to me. Is that not what the Bible recommends: loving one's neighbour as oneself and not turning aside because a man is poor? I am not one who believes that because a person is of the inferior . . .' (He was going to say 'sex' but delicacy prevented him from doing so, and he sought for an alternative.) '. . . kind . . . they should not use the talents that God blessed them with.'

'You think so?' She was hanging on his words. 'I fear the world would not agree with you.'

He came a little closer. 'When God brings a man and woman together, He shows them how they can work in partnership.' There, he had done it. He was firmly launched upon his declaration now. 'And if there is affection – as I think there is – on both sides . . . then I believe that they should grasp the opportunity – whatever the "world" may think.'

He reached out, greatly daring, to squeeze her hand. To his astonishment she seemed to welcome it, capturing his hand in hers and raising it impulsively to her lips.

'Oh dear, darling Lionel. What a sweet, understanding friend you are.' She was gazing raptly in his eyes. 'I was afraid that I was merely following "the devices and desires of my heart", as the prayer book says. You think that this might be, after all, God's will?'

Dear Heaven! She was going to accept him. And she was still clinging to his hand. He fought down a wave of unworthy panic, and said guiltily, 'Of course, you must not think of rushing into things. It is a tremendous step to contemplate. You must give it careful thought and prayer.' He extricated his fingers gently as he spoke.

She said meekly, 'Yes, of course. It would be foolish to do otherwise. But I do appreciate this talk with you. You don't know how glad I am to have you as a friend.' She sighed. 'Of course, there is still Deedee to convince.'

He got to his feet. 'Your father is aware of how I feel.' He made a little bow, ridiculous, like a Prussian soldier in a play.

When he got outside the door, he leant against the wall. His heart was thumping and his palms were damp. Despite the drizzle and the lateness of the hour, he put on his cape and hat and went for a long brisk walk along the lanes.

Victoria sat as if she had been welded to her chair. She could not believe her ears. The will of God? When one thought of it like that, of course it was. And she had been avoiding Daniel for a week! Yet surely Lionel was right. Destiny had contrived to bring her close to Daniel, and the attraction that they felt – she had only to remember that unexpected kiss to know that Daniel experienced it as well – was meant to be. 'Whatever the world may think' as Lionel had said.

She hugged the knowledge to her when she went to bed that night, and it was her first thought when she awoke. It was her day for parish visiting, and there was no escaping that, but she longed to be home again to talk to Dan, and she whisked from house to house, delivering her pots of jelly like a whirlwind in disguise.

Then it seemed to take forever before lunch was served and cleared, but at last Victoria found herself alone. Miss Boff had set off with Deedee's mail to post, Lionel was off to teach his class of confirmees, while Deedee himself was busy with a parishioner, though Mr Pencarrow was expected later on.

The afternoon was damp and overcast, but Victoria went into the garden all the same. There was no sign of Daniel anywhere, but she located him at last, potting up hydrangeas in the shed.

He turned to greet her. 'Miss Victoria!' He turned scarlet with embarrassment. 'About the other day – I'm that sorry. I don't know what to say. I don't know what came over me. I had no right . . .'

She went up to him boldly and would have grasped his hand, if it had not been grimed with earth. Instead, she took him gently by the arm. 'Don't apologize. You had every right. You only did what we both wanted at the time. And I'm not sorry, not one little bit. Are you?'

He looked at her doubtfully. 'You sure, Miss Victoria? It's been on my mind. I hardly slept a wink because of it.'

'I haven't slept much either.' She seized his other arm. He tried to draw away but she held him fast, forced him to meet her eyes, and suddenly he was smiling back. She found herself giggling, just as Bella would have done.

'This is madness. We can't be doing this,' he murmured, but there was no conviction left.

'Doing what?' she murmured, and he met her lips again. This time it was a long and lingering kiss. She seemed to come up from

194

a deep abyss. He was breathing heavily again, and so was she. His eyes seemed very beautiful and dark.

He shook his head. 'It's no good,' he said. 'We're making trouble for ourselves.' He let her go. 'There can't be anything between the likes of me and a proper lady like yourself.'

'But surely, if you're fond of me . . . You are, aren't you?'

He looked at her. 'I think you're the most lovely thing I ever saw,' he said simply. 'I'd lie down and die for you, if it would do you any good. But you can see – it isn't any use. What kind of future can there be for us?' He gave a bitter laugh. 'If your father ever heard of this, he'd have me out of here before you could say "knife".'

'Well, Lionel doesn't think so,' Vicki said. 'He thinks our meeting is the Hand of God.'

'More likely the hand of Other Fellow, seems to me. Destroy the both of us, this will, if we don't look out. Of course I want you, Miss Victoria, a man would want his head read if he didn't. You're clever, witty, knowledgeable, kind – and prettier than a picture in a book. But this isn't Charles Dickens now, and it isn't going to come out neatly in the end. Think of the ordinary things. You know what your house is like, and you've been to mine. Honestly, can you see yourself down there? Scrubbing the floors and doing mangling? And that's all I've got to offer you – not even that, with these damned legs of mine.'

'But my father—'

'Will have his own ideas for you. Believe me, Miss Victoria, he will.'

'But you are decent, moral, kind, respectable. These are the things he praises from the pulpit every week!'

'Enough to get me into Heaven p'raps. But not to get me inside the vicarage. Now, please, leave off and leave me be. Old Roseworthy'll come and find us, else, and then I won't even have a job.' He shook his head. 'It's all my fault, I know. I lost my head – and now I've led you into losing yours. Try to forgive me, Miss Victoria. Try to forgive me, and let me be!'

There were hot tears standing in her eyes. She was shaking her head furiously. 'I can't,' she murmured.

'Else I shall have to give my notice in,' he said. 'Here, don't cry. I can't bear to see you weep. Here, listen! Someone's calling you.'

It was Miss Boff, of course. Who else would it be? Victoria jumped guiltily away at once, and Daniel said, 'You see? You know I'm right, deep down.'

'It wouldn't matter who you were, Miss Boff would disapprove! She would think it the height of impropriety for us to be alone, if you were the Rural Dean himself,' Victoria retorted but she did move to the door. 'She's out there looking daggers as it is,' she reported, from the crack. 'Now what are we going to do?'

For answer, Daniel moved past her and threw wide the door, holding it open so that she could pass. 'By all means, Miss,' he said, loudly enough for anyone to hear. 'I'll let you have some for the Christmas fête. I'm sorry they won't be ready earlier.'

'Thank you, Daniel.' There was nothing to do but take his quick-witted cue and walk out with her head held high. 'Ah! There you are, Miss Boff. I thought I heard you calling me just now.'

Miss Boff scowled at her ferociously. 'I was indeed. Here's Mr Prowse come to call, and your poor father still occupied upstairs so there was nobody to greet him but the serving girl! It is as well I came back when I did, so I was able to repair the breach. It is most unfortunate. What, pray, were you doing in the shed, closeted alone in there with that rough young man?'

'Daniel has promised to put up some plants for me, that's all.' She was not an accomplished liar and the half-truth troubled her.

Miss Boff sniffed. 'So you say! It is to be hoped that that is all, indeed! I'm surprised you don't know better, at your age. It's more than unbecoming, it's unsafe. You don't appreciate the dangers that you run. They are not raised as we are, Victoria! Now come inside.'

'Yes, Miss Boff,' she murmured meekly. She was suddenly aware – even if Miss Boff was not – of Daniel's fingermarks on her pale blue sleeve.

*   *   *

'Miss Boff?' Edward regarded his visitor doubtfully. Since Victoria's words about the governess mooning after him, he had always been a little nervous of Miss Boff. 'I fear I am a little occupied this afternoon. I have a funeral at two and Mr Pencarrow's looking in a little later on.' He gestured to the papers on his desk. 'But, of course, if this will not take long . . .?'

Miss Boff gave a thin little smile. 'I'm *so* sorry to interrupt you, Dr Flower. Naturally, you're a very busy man, but I do need to have a private word.' She paused and pursed her lips. 'I've been meaning to talk to you since yesterday about Victoria.'

It always was 'about Victoria' of course, but today she seemed particularly tense, and there was an excited brilliance in her eyes. He waved her nervously towards a chair.

She sat down stiffly and burst out at once, 'I hardly like to tell you this, but I felt that you should know. I should be failing in my duty otherwise. That lad you took on to help with the gardening . . .'

'Daniel?' Edward was surprised. He had been bracing himself for more exhortations about the impracticality of pale-blue coats. 'I thought that had worked out very well.'

'Far too well for some!' Miss Boff exclaimed. She leaned forward confidentially. 'I've been concerned about that friendship for some time, as you know. I've mentioned it to you before. All this unhealthy interest in encouraging him to read, and getting him to aspirate his aitches. I don't know what good it's supposed to do . . . a youth of his type—'

He felt he had to interrupt, 'Rather commendable, I would have said. An interest in parish work . . .'

Miss Boff gave him that little smile again. 'Doctor Flower, that's just what you said before. And that's the point, you see. You always see the good in everything. I should have spoken out more forcefully. But since you didn't seem to mind, and it *could* be seen as Christian charity, up to now I've held my tongue – though I always thought no good would come of it. But just yesterday afternoon I went out to look for Victoria, and where did I find her? Alone in the garden shed with that

197

young man. There, what do you think of that!' She folded her own arms triumphantly.

Edward stared at her. His brain refused to accept the picture this had conjured up. 'You must be mistaken there, Miss Boff. There's some explanation, I am sure. Shall I discuss it with Victoria?'

'Oh, I know what she will say. She said it at the time. They pretended that he was putting up some plants for her. But they were there for minutes before she answered me. I happened to glimpse them through that broken pane, and there they were, gazing into each other's eyes. I can't be sure of it, but I believe she might actually have been in his arms. Dr Flower, it's up to you, of course, but I'd say that it was time to nip that so-called friendship firmly in the bud.'

Edward frowned. It couldn't be! His daughter and a common labourer! It was unthinkable. Of course it was! Miss Boff was always prone to exaggerate. Victoria was overeager that was all. Though perhaps it had been unwise to allow her to take such an interest in a gardener boy. 'I'm sure . . .' he murmured doubtfully.

Miss Boff sniffed and said, 'Well, vicar, I'm sure that you know best,' in a tone of voice which suggested quite the opposite. 'I felt I simply had to mention it.'

He tried to look masterful and concerned. 'Leave it in my hands.' He would have a little paternal chat to Victoria when he'd finished at the funeral. After Pencarrow came, perhaps, though he didn't want to cut that visit short. Stephen had been in London for two months, and visited the antique bookshops there. He'd wired his friend only last week to say that he was back and promising to bring Edward a surprise. Who knows what delightful treasures he had found?

'I leave you to your sermon, then.' The governess brought him from his reverie. She gave a tight-lipped smile, and left, but the vicar did not get straight back to work again. Instead, he found himself worrying about Victoria. The sooner Lionel made a move, the better. Perhaps he would have a little word to him as well. And as for the gardener boy . . . Edward had thought already that in the spring he would have to find some other position for the lad, and he made a note to do it now, as soon as possible. Though, of course, it was only Victoria's passion for teaching the young man to read which had caused all this embarrassment. She'd always shared her father's weakness when it came to books.

That set him dreaming of fine bindings and old woodcuts, until he had to rush to be ready for the burial in time, and then for Stephen's visit.

But Stephen hadn't only brought a book. He'd brought a far greater surprise with him than that.

Three

Victoria was sitting in the morning room.

The afternoon was cold and wet and damp, one of those dank and misty Cornish winter days when it seemed that half the Atlantic had risen as a fog and was settling moistly over everything. Deedee had been soaked through, taking the funeral, though he was upstairs with Pencarrow now. Stephen must have been half-drenched when he arrived – she'd heard a slight commotion in the hall, though she hadn't gone out to investigate. Lionel had gone off in the drizzling rain to take the confirmation class, so she was lucky to be snug and warm beside the fire. She looked out of the window at a world of grey, and wondered if Daniel had managed to find somewhere dry to work – she hadn't seen him anywhere today. She rather thought he was avoiding her.

The memory of Daniel made her smile. She had a gift for him. A copy of *A Christmas Carol* to give him for his very own; not just to borrow as the other books had been. But it was hard to know just how to manage it. She thought for a long time before she picked up her nibbed pen and wrote inside: 'To Daniel, with warmest wishes for a blessed Christmas from Victoria Flower.' That would make it quite respectable and he'd understand the 'warm' though it meant she couldn't give it for a week or two. She blotted the inscription carefully and began to wrap the present in the piece of tissue paper which she'd brought down specially.

She was so engrossed in tucking in the ends that she hardly noticed Ruby at the door. 'Excuse me, Miss Victoria, but you have a visitor.'

Victoria looked up. 'A visitor?' She wasn't expecting anyone today.

Ruby came a little closer and whispered urgently. 'It's that Miss Cardew, Miss. And she don't half look poorly – though it's not my place to say.'

Victoria got to her feet, but before she had a chance to speak, Bella was already in the room. Ruby was right. Vicki hadn't seen her friend for weeks, and she was horrified at what she saw. Bella was not a bit her laughing, fashionable self. She seemed to have got pale and gaunt, her skirts were drenched, her hair was all awry and her face was streaked and swollen in the rain. Or perhaps, when she looked closely, it wasn't rain at all.

'My dear Belle, whatever has occurred?'

Bella made a little sound that might have been a sob, and signalled with her eyes towards the maid. 'Good afternoon, Victoria,' she ventured, in a quavering voice. And then, with an attempt to seem controlled that would not have convinced an idiot, 'Very inclement weather, isn't it?'

Victoria saw what was required of her. She turned to Ruby. 'A little tea, I think. And some toasted muffins, if that can be arranged.' When the girl had disappeared, she went across. 'My dear Belle, tell me! Is everything all right?'

This was too much for Bella. She shook her head, flung herself down on to a chair and buried her face hopelessly in her hands. 'Oh, Vicki! No, it's not. Everything's all wrong!' she sobbed wretchedly.

Victoria knelt beside her. 'There's been an accident?' If anyone had died, she thought, she'd certainly have heard. Bella shook her head. 'Someone in your family? Your horse?' And then with sudden inspiration, 'Petroc's come?'

But Isabella shook her head again. 'It's S-S-Stephen,' she stattered through her tears.

'Mr Pencarrow! But he is perfectly well. He's back from London at last, and is here with Deedee this very afternoon.'

Bella turned away and stared into the fire. She made an effort and controlled herself, and there was only the faintest quaver as she said, 'I know he is. I saw the trap outside. I have to see him, Victoria. Privately. I must.'

Victoria gasped, 'But Bella, you can't accost him here! Whatever will Deedee and everybody say?'

Belle shrugged. 'I don't care what they think. It will be worse if I don't see him soon. And at least, if your father's there, Stephen can't avoid me any more. That's what he's been doing, Vic. Ignoring my letters, keeping away from where we used to meet.'

Victoria fought down an unworthy urge to say 'I told you so', and patted her friend's arm awkwardly. 'Stephen did not come home when he hoped. He was delayed in London, that is all.'

Bella shook her head. 'No, it's isn't that, at all! I hoped it was at first. I thought with these awful strikes perhaps he hadn't had my notes, and he was still away. I hadn't heard, of course. But then I actually saw him in St Just last week, and . . .' She gave a shuddering sob. 'Oh, Vicki! He turned deliberately away, just to evade me in the street. Then, this afternoon I gave up and went to call on him at home. Told John to drop me in the wagonette, and not come back for me till five o'clock – said I was going shopping in St Just.'

'And?'

'Stephen sent down his maid to say he wasn't in! Although I know for certain that he was! I wasn't halfway down the lane before I heard him, driving off in the trap – in the opposite direction, naturally.' Another hiccoughing sob. 'It occurred to me he might be coming here – I walked for miles, before the horse carriage came.'

So that explained the damp, bedraggled hems! Vicki hardly knew how to respond. 'Perhaps you are not wise to think of it,' she said, at last. 'It seems that Stephen's changed his mind. Perhaps he hasn't managed to disengage himself, and has decided that his friendship with you is not, after all, appropriate.'

'It's very fine for him to think that now!' Bella burst out with surprising vehemence. 'It's too late for him to change his mind . . .' She broke off, as there was a timid knock and Ruby appeared, bearing the tea and muffins on a tray.

There was a short silence, while she put it down and left, and by then Victoria had worked out the dreadful truth. 'Belle! Too late? Surely you can't mean . . .?'

But she did of course, you could see it in her eyes. She sounded despairing as she said, 'It looks like it, though it's too early to be absolutely sure. I didn't mean to tell you, but it seems you guessed. No doubt the whole of Penwith will do the same. So there you are. I'm ruined – shamed!'

It was so shocking that for a moment Victoria could find no words. Then she said, helplessly, 'Oh Belle! Perhaps when Stephen knows, he will consent to marry you after all.'

Bella's voice was full of angry tears. 'But Vic, that's just the point. He knows! I told him weeks ago when I first suspected it. I thought . . . I thought the same as you, that he would extricate himself and marry me, the way he always said he would. Papa would have threatened horsewhips when he heard, but even he would have come around in time. But it didn't work out like that at all. Stephen was actually furious at first, and then he got all frosty and remote, and the next thing I heard was that he'd gone away – much sooner than he'd intended to. Now he won't even talk to me. Oh, Victoria, what am I going to do?'

For once, Victoria was lost for words. This was outside her experience, and none of her cleverness was going to help. 'You'll have to tell your parents, it's the only thing to do. After all, they'll find out in the end.'

Bella burst into another flood of weeping. 'And what will happen then? Papa will drive me from the house and I'll end up in the workhouse, with all those dreadful tramps! Or worse! They'll lock me up, like they did Lily Penge.'

Victoria felt herself go cold. That had been a local scandal, a few years earlier. A young woman from a good family had got herself with child and they'd hustled her off to hide her in a home for the insane. It hadn't even saved her from disgrace: the whole sorry story had emerged when she fell from the roof and dashed her brains out, trying to escape. It was a fate too horrible to contemplate.

'You could talk to Deedee,' Vicki said.

Bella rounded on her, tearfully, 'And what good is that? He would only go and tell Papa – and that would be twice as bad as telling him myself!'

'Of course he wouldn't—'

But Bella cut her off. 'And Petroc's coming in a day or two! To think that I turned down that good, kind man – for this!' She looked up at Vicki, suddenly, 'I don't suppose he . . . no . . . of course. No one will ever have me now.'

'Well, talk to Lionel then! He is an ordained priest, after all – and he favours confessions every week. After all, you've just confessed to me.'

'You're different!' Her friend took out one of her little handkerchiefs, already screwed into a ball and soaked with tears, and said between deep shuddering breaths, 'Anyway, it's much worse than I'm telling you. I've . . . God forgive me . . . I've tried everything I know. I've drunk pints of cod liver oil, and I've gone out riding every day. To try to . . . get rid of it, you know.'

'Belle!' Victoria was appalled. So that was the reason for the ashen cheeks. She had only the dimmest idea about things like this, but she knew that it was dangerous. 'You can't do that. You might have killed yourself.'

'I don't care if I do kill myself. I would be better dead!'

Things were spinning out of Victoria's control, and she cast around for something . . . anything . . . practical to do. 'Belle, you mustn't talk like this. You came to talk to Stephen, didn't you? He can't escape you here, so perhaps there's hope. But you can't see anyone in the state you're in – there would be a scandal instantly. I'll send for some water for you to sponge your hems, and you can rinse your face as well. And you have drunk hardly any of that tea. Give me your cup and let me pour some fresh. It will help you to collect yourself.'

Her friend meekly did as she was bid, and by the time Victoria rang the bell for Ruby to take the tray and bring some water in, Bella was looking a little more composed.

'Now,' Victoria said, a little later, as she helped her friend to rearrange her curls, and pinch a little colour into her cheeks, 'you're looking more yourself. Listen, I can hear them on the stairs. That'll be Mr Pencarrow leaving now. If we hurry, you'll be just in time to catch him in the hall. I'll try to distract Deedee when he comes – I have an urgent message for him anyway from the sextant – and give you a chance to speak to your friend alone.'

But even as she spoke the words, she saw that it was impossible. Deedee was already in the hall, and Ruby was standing by with coats and hats, but it was clear that Pencarrow had not come alone. He was assisting a handsome woman down the stairs, offering his arm.

When he saw Victoria and Bella he turned. He didn't seem abashed. Indeed, he smiled his most ingratiating smile. 'Miss Flower . . . ah, and Miss Cardew too! What a doubly happy circumstance. Now I can introduce you both. Emily, my dear, this is the daughter of the house, and this is her friend, Miss Cardew. Ladies, may I introduce my wife.'

Shock hit Isabella like a thunderbolt. Victoria could see it in her face. She had put out an automatic hand, but drew it back to steady Bella, who looked as if she might faint on the spot: she had turned deathly white and was shaking uncontrollably. It was as well that Lionel chose this moment to arrive in a flurry of wet umbrellas, hats and sticks, so attention turned momentarily to him.

Suddenly Bella pushed Victoria's arm away and bolted through the open door, brushing past the curate as she went.

There was a moment's startled pause: Mrs Pencarrow looked at her husband in surprise; Lionel stopped brushing raindrops from his hat; Deedee, like Victoria, seemed frozen to the spot.

At last he said, in clear bewilderment, 'Victoria?'

'Forgive us. Bella isn't well,' she gasped, and went out after her. To no avail. She found only the dripping branches and the rain. She rushed out to the gate, but even Dan, who was outside working in the lane, had not set eyes on Belle.

It had only been two minutes at the most, but Isabella Cardew had disappeared.

'Here, Mollie! Where you off to? Wait for me?' Harry Varfell came panting down the lane outside the factory and caught her up as she walked down the hill. 'Wet leaking you're going to be in this, with just that thin cape over you. 'Ere, take my coat.' He stripped it off his shoulders as he spoke and wrapped it round her own.

She had to smile at his good-naturedness. 'What about you, then?'

'I'm so wet, a bit more makes no difference. Been out delivering some spades – always some reason to send me out, sure as it comes on to rain. But they was wanted urgent, and these strikes have made it 'ard. Waggoners still want a fortune to carry anything.'

'I thought that was all over now? Didn't Mr Churchill have the army in?' She knew about the strikes. They'd been the talk of the dairy factory for weeks. 'Some of the girls were certain it would spread down here, and we would lose all our deliveries, and that'd be the end. Haven't happened though – suppose we're too far away. Though, come to think, there's miles of stuff down at the quarry still, waiting for a chance to ship it on.'

Harry grunted. 'Had me out walking in the rain, that's all I know.' He grinned at her, the rain streaming down his pink, kindly face. 'Not that I mind, seeing as 'ow I met you on the way. Carry a thousand shovels through a thunderstorm for you.'

She laughed. 'I b'lieve you would.' She let him take her arm. It was getting dark and cold.

'I'd do more than that.' He pulled her to him, huddling her towards his massive frame so that he was a shelter from the rain. 'But what's the use. Sooner have Daniel Olds, you would. And where's he, when you're caught out in the rain?'

'Busy up the vicarage, I expect,' she said, though she had been asking herself much the same for days. Weeks, even. It seemed an age since Daniel had called up to meet her at the dairy gate. Of course he had a job to do, but he might have timed his comings and goings to match hers once or twice. Never suggested meeting any more. And, then, when she did run into him – usually by going to call in at the house – she couldn't get him to talk any sense. Not about anything that mattered, anyway. His head was too full of those stupid books – and Mollie knew who to blame for that!

It made her more than usually cross, and she did not pull away – not even when they heard hurrying footsteps in the gloom, and Harry said, 'I 'spect that's Daniel now.'

He would have reluctantly let go of her, but Mollie clutched his arm and leant against his shoulder even more. 'What if it is?' she said. 'Aren't doing anybody any harm, are we? You're only sheltering me from the rain. He didn't bother doing it 'isself.' Serve Daniel right, she thought, remind him that other folks were interested in her, even if he'd got too stuck-up to care.

But it wasn't Daniel. It was a young woman, dripping wet, half-running and half-hobbling up the lane – straight through the puddles in that lovely coat – and sobbing her heart out as she went. When she saw the two of them, she stopped.

Mollie stepped forward, impulsively. ''Ere, Miss. You all right, are you? Oughtn't to be out here, night like this.'

The other woman didn't answer her. She looked at them a moment, shook her head, then gave a wail like a mad thing and set off again.

Mollie looked up at Harry anxiously. 'Whatever's up with her? Do 'erself a mischief, she will, careering round these old lanes in the dark. Where d'you think she's off to, anyhow? Nothing up that way but the factory.'

Harry shook his head. 'See who it was, did you? That young Miss Cardew up St Evan House – the one that gave the prizes May Day just gone. Course she looks a proper fright, tonight, but that's who it was – I'd put my shirt on it. Should we go after her, you think?'

'My lor', Harry! I dunno, I'm sure. Can't well go interfering with the likes of her. But . . . p'raps we ought to do. She looked

207

so wild, like she might do anything.' She found that she was trembling. 'She frightened me. Gave me quite a turn.'

Harry's arms surrounded her at once. They were wet, but warm and comforting and she allowed herself to press against his chest. 'There, there,' he said. 'We can't have you cry. We'll go tell Fayther, he'll know what to do. Oh, hang on, 'ere's someone coming now. Looking for her, most probably.'

Mollie turned her head to look, but she knew at once. She'd recognize that slight limp anywhere. 'Hello, Daniel,' she said, but she didn't move from Harry's arms. It would have been too late in any case.

She waited for Dan's anger, but it didn't come. Instead he said, 'Hello, Moll. Evening, Harry.' He looked them up and down. 'So that is how things are. No . . .' he said as Mollie made a gesture to explain, 'don't apologize. It wasn't working out in any case. I wanted to say so, myself, weeks ago. I should have done, perhaps, but you were so good, offering to wait. I didn't want to hurt you, that was all.'

Mollie stared at him. He didn't seem jealous in the least. In fact, he was relieved if anything. It was true then. He had been turning cool. She should have been upset herself, or shocked, but she just felt empty like a broken pot. And furious – though, what could she say? He'd caught them, fair and square. 'Now, Dan—!'

He cut her off. 'Don't fret. I aren't much of a catch these days. If you want Harry then I'm pleased for you. And for him – he's wanted you for long enough.' He looked at the other man, and actually grinned!

Harry's arm tightened around her waist. Dear Harry, always there when you needed him. She raised her chin and said defiantly, 'Like I'd have waited for you, if you'd wanted it. But that isn't what you want, so certainly, Harry's more than good enough for me. At least he hasn't got above himself, thinking he's the blumming Earl of Rot, because some vicar's daughter bats her eyes at him.' It was unkind, but at that moment that was how she felt.

Daniel did not snap back at her. He just said patiently, 'Then we're agreed. Good luck to both of you. I'll leave it to you, Mollie, to explain to everyone.' And he turned and walked away along the lane.

That was the moment when she knew she'd lost him, finally.

But Harry was hugging her until she thought she'd break. 'You mean that, Moll? You'll have me, after all?'

And when she murmured wearily, 'Yes, Harry. I'll have you, after all,' he picked her up and tossed her in the air, as though she weighed no more than a leaf.

'Come on,' he said. 'We've got things to do. And then we'll go and tell them all at home!'

Neither of them gave another thought to Isabella Cardew until they heard the news.

Daniel was too shaken up to go straight home. Instead, he turned left at the stile and wandered aimlessly towards the sea. He had disengaged himself! Just coming upon Molly and Harry like that, by chance. It was so much easier than he deserved.

He'd made up his mind he'd do it, this very afternoon.

He had been sitting outside the front of the vicarage, huddled on his stool. He was soaked through, but he preferred to be out here, cutting back the briars, where nobody could see him from the house. He was still half-waiting for the axe to fall: that governess woman hadn't been fooled the day before, a bit. She knew what they'd been doing, in the shed. But here, he was out of temptation's way, and not likely to do anything else ridiculous.

At least, he thought that was the case. He had been idly watching the callers come and go all afternoon, but suddenly there was Miss Victoria running out (without even an umbrella in all that rain), and looking wildly up and down the lane.

He was hidden from her sight behind a bush, so he got slowly to his feet. 'Miss Flower?' Then, greatly daring: 'Victoria?'

She turned to him, and he could see her face. She looked – he hunted for the word – distraught. 'Oh, Daniel! Thank God. Did you see which way Miss Cardew went?'

He shook his head. 'I saw her coming in, Miss, but I didn't see

her go. Must have gone over the back stile and out the churchyard way.'

Victoria nodded, and the tension left her face. 'If that's the
case, she's probably gone home. I'm glad. It was the only thing to
do – the coachman will have missed her long ago.' She gave him a
swift smile. 'I was afraid she'd gone out to St Just.'

None of this made very much sense to Daniel, so he just said,
'Yes, Miss Victoria.' She was still looking worried, so he added,
'Is everything all right?'

This time the smile was genuine and warm. 'I'm all right,
Daniel. Poor Miss Cardew is a bit upset. She's had a disappointment of the heart. The man she loved – someone of whom her
family did not approve – proved to have an entanglement elsewhere, and now he has married someone else. I shouldn't really
tell you, but you are the only one on earth I *can* confide in over
this.' She looked at him suddenly. 'You wouldn't do that, would
you Daniel? You haven't got another girl somewhere? I saw you
with someone, on May Day, didn't I?'

Daniel felt himself go hot, despite the rain, because, of course,
he had – though naturally it wasn't the same thing at all. He said,
'There is a girl, Miss, down in Polvidden Row.' He saw her face
and added hastily, 'But that's all over now.'

It wasn't quite a lie, he told himself. Things were not right
between himself and Moll. The more she tried to press him into
marriage, the more he'd pulled away. He'd tried to tell her,
several times before. Not that there was anything wrong with
Moll, it was just that, alongside Miss Victoria Flower, he
couldn't feel the same about her any more.

There was a voice. 'My dear Victoria, what are you doing
there? Come in at once, you'll catch a chill, and we shall have you
in the sickroom for a month.' That was her father calling.

Victoria smiled at Daniel again. 'I'll see you tomorrow then,'
she said, and touched his hand. 'I'm glad there isn't anybody
else.'

He watched her go back towards the house. She was so
beautiful – and unobtainable – even with her face and ringlets

wet and raindrops dripping down her neck. *I'm glad there isn't anybody else.* That's when he'd made the promise to himself: to see Mollie the first chance he got, and make it true.

And it had happened, fallen in his lap. It was almost too much to believe. He had reached the end of the lane by now, and he leaned there on the stile, watching the sullen shimmer of the sea against the dark. He was wet through, but he didn't care. Perhaps it was divine will, after all. He was so wrapped up in his thoughts that he hardly heard the cry.

'Help! Help!'

It was coming from somewhere down the cliff. He went across the stile and over to the edge, walking carefully as the cliffs were treacherous. He lay down and looked over cautiously, scanning the wet uncertain dark.

'Help!' There it was again. A woman's voice. 'Oh, help me! Help!'

He could see her now, perhaps fifteen feet down, wedged between the cliff-side and a clump of something dark. Looked like a little furze bush; some of them found root down there, sometimes, in an inch or two of soil too small to be a ledge. Awful thing to fall into, but lucky it was there. Sheer rock face fell away on either side. There was a bit of the top cliff-edge missing too, as if it had given way beneath her feet.

He looked down. There was no way he could reach, and the cliff was far too steep to climb – even in daylight, and with two good legs. 'Stay there!' he shouted, unnecessarily, 'I'll be back with ropes!' He wriggled back and hauled himself upright.

Then he set off towards Polvidden at a limping run.

Four

The Pencarrows had left, somewhat in disarray, and Victoria had retired to her room, obviously concerned about her friend. A bad moment, Edward thought, to insist on that paternal little chat he'd planned, about behaving appropriately with the garden boy. Instead, he waited until after Evensong. Then, instead of retiring to his study till supper was announced, he motioned Victoria aside into the morning room.

'Deedee?' she murmured in surprise. The room was chilly at this time of day. 'Should I get Ruby to make up the fire?'

'This won't take long.' He lit the lamp, and sat down facing her. He selected one of the two upright chairs, and straddled it backwards, chin leaning on his hands. He used to sit like this with Vera, once.

The informality startled Victoria. She said, and her voice was rather sharp, 'Deedee, is this about Bella by any chance? The way she bolted out like that?'

It wasn't, but he could not ignore it now. He cleared his throat. 'It was unfortunate. And discourteous, under the circumstances.'

His daughter gave a sort of snort. He said, reproachfully, 'Victoria!'

'I'm sorry, Deedee, just as I'm sorry we embarrassed you. As I mentioned, Bella's been unwell. And as for being discourteous, shall we just say that her discourtesy is rather less than his? Indeed, I think he's behaved shamefully to *you* – not even to inform you that he planned to wed, and then to turn up here with his wife like that. It was a shock to all of us.'

It was an apology of sorts, and he might have left it there.

212

Edward had felt rather snubbed, in fact, but he felt obliged to offer something in his friend's defence. 'The lady followed him to London, and Pencarrow had to take out a special licence and marry her in haste, simply to protect the lady's reputation. He murmured that to me this afternoon, while she was occupied with other things. And of course, with all the railway strikes, there's been no post for weeks. He couldn't well let anybody know.'

Victoria made that snorting noise again.

Edward was feeling out of sorts and he pounced on that at once. 'Victoria, if you disagree with what I say, I would be grateful if you'd express yourself in words, rather than making that unseemly sound. I take it, that, for some reason, you do disagree?'

She flushed uneasily but did not reply.

'Well?'

The blush was deeper now. 'I'm sorry . . . I can't . . . I'm not at liberty to say.' She shifted her glance away from him, and – seeing something on the table top – moved it rather guiltily away.

He couldn't let it pass. 'And what is that? Pray don't say nothing, since that's patently untrue!'

'It's . . . it's a little present, that is all. It's a book. For Daniel, for Christmas – you know, the garden boy.'

He felt a tide of helpless irritation rising like a blush. 'So, Miss Boff was right! She said you had an unhealthy interest in the boy.'

'Unhealthy?'

'Well, unsuitable. Unhealthy was her word! She said that she'd chanced upon you in the shed with that young man, alone and behaving in a too familiar way. I could not bring myself to believe it then, but now I find you wrapping private presents for him as if he was an intimate of yours. I'm sure your motives have been of the best, Victoria, but I see Miss Boff is right. You have allowed yourself to become a little too involved. It would be best to keep your distance more, and give up these reading sessions once and for all. It's one of the things I came here to discuss.'

She got to her feet, her cheeks ablaze. 'Papa! I can't. It means so much to both of us. You can't mean that.'

213

He hated it when she called him 'Papa' so formally. He said, 'I mean it, yes. And from your reaction, only just in time. I'm coming to believe that you actually are developing a ridiculous fondness for this boy – under my very nose. I must have been blind. Just when you're half-promised to Lionel, too.'

'Lionel!' She stared at him as though one of them were mad.

Well, he knew better. He had asked Lionel only this morning how things stood. 'Don't pretend, Victoria. Lionel came to see me weeks ago, and asked for my permission for your hand. He tells me that he's voiced his hopes to you, and urged you to take a little time to think. But you encouraged him to hope, he said.'

'Lionel?' she said again, and then her face dropped. 'Oh, I see. The will of God. That's what he meant! I thought . . . I might have known. So he wasn't on our side, after all?'

' "Our side", Victoria? And who are "we"? Are you telling me that you have entered into some . . . undertaking . . . with this gardener fellow? A boy from the lowest sort of family? I can't believe what you are telling me.'

She swung to face him. 'And I can't believe what you're telling me! You, who are always preaching how we are all equal in the sight of God. That's just what Daniel said. "Perhaps I'm good enough to get to heaven, but not good enough to get into the vicarage." Well, I'm appalled. What's happened to your Christian charity?'

That stung. He stood up. It wasn't very dignified, because of the way he'd sat down on the chair, but he pulled himself upright angrily, and straightened his attire. He was still in his cassock from the service earlier. 'And where is your duty and obedience? I'm not just your parent, I'm your vicar too – and yet you dare to speak to me like that! Now, I'm warning you, Victoria, and I won't tell you again. I forbid you – forbid you utterly – to have conversation with that boy again. I have done my best for him – at your suggestion – and this is my reward! He'll have to go, of course.'

'And what is to become of him, since you take this tone? It's all right to dismiss him, I suppose, now that you've done your

Christian charity? I thought I knew you better – but he was right, of course, and I was wrong. Who cares if his family starves, or ends up in the workhouse in the end? Not you! As long as your precious social standing's safe. Well, what will the parish think of that? Not much, vicar, I can tell you that.'

She said 'vicar' with so much vehemence, he flinched. He clung to the dignity he had left as he said, 'You should have thought of that before. Of course I have no option, after this. You could hardly have imagined I'd approve? I . . .' He broke off. She was crying now: he never had been proof against her tears. 'Victoria!' He took her elbow, rather awkwardly. 'It's your best interests I have got at heart.'

She brushed him off, her eyes still bright with tears. 'How do you know what my best interests are?'

He felt in his pocket for a clean handkerchief, but he didn't have one. There was one – presumably of hers – crumpled beside her on the chair. He picked it up to give it her – and stared. This was no ordinary handkerchief. It was of finest lace and lawn; a love token perhaps? And he had one just like it in his bedroom drawer. He remembered where he'd found it, out in the rumpled hay, and a dreadful, impossible, suspicion dawned. Surely not his daughter and that garden boy, out there on the cliff? And what were those letters supposed to represent? He seized Victoria's arm again, more forcefully this time. 'This handkerchief –' he thrust it before her eyes – 'tell me at once. Where did you acquire it from?'

'I didn't "acquire it" from anywhere. It's Belle's. She left it here this afternoon. She's got a set of them. It's got her initials on it, look: I.L.C. Isabella Lucinda Cardew. Let go, you're hurting me.'

He let go, in a daze. 'Isabella's?'

'What does it matter whose it is?' Victoria cried. 'We were talking about Daniel and myself—'

But she was interrupted by a thundering knock on the front door. Father and daughter stopped and stared at one another in surprise.

'You're wanted,' Victoria said grimly.

He nodded. Somebody was dead. What else could it be, at this time of night? But when Ruby hurried in, it was to say, 'It's Colonel Cardew and his coachman, sir, wanting to know is Miss Cardew 'ere. I said as how she'd been and gone, but perhaps you'd like to speak to 'im yourself.'

'She's not been home?' Victoria exclaimed. 'Oh, gracious heaven! She said that she'd be better dead. Oh, Deedee! She's done something desperate.'

Her father looked at her, and all at once he saw the whole dreadful business. 'Pencarrow, is that it? I suppose that she had hopes of him herself?'

His daughter hesitated, and did not reply.

'Victoria, this is no time for games. If your friend is missing, we must know – it will help to teach us where to look.'

She seemed to think for a moment, then nodded, helplessly. 'She has been meeting Stephen. For months. He . . . he led her to think . . . That's why his marriage came as such a shock.'

He nodded, thinking about that handkerchief again. Surely it wasn't possible. But, yes. Pencarrow had been 'delayed' that afternoon, and Isabella had been out there on the cliffs, he'd even spoken to her as she passed. But surely Stephen was too much of a gentleman . . .? He shook his head. 'I see. Yes, Victoria, I see. I can only sincerely hope that you didn't encourage or abet her in this foolishness. And take this timely lesson to your heart. You see where unsuitable attachments lead?' He saw her flinch, and knew the point was made. 'Now, I must go and see the Colonel.'

He did more than that. After a hurried consultation in the hall, he called for Lionel, put on his hat and waterproofs and had the hurricane lamp brought out and lit. Five minutes later, they were struggling down the lanes, in the general direction of St Just, searching for Isabella in the streaming dark.

Miss Boff stood at the turning of the stair and watched them go. She'd been keeping a discreet eye on the hall, ever since Edward –

216

Dr Flower – had taken Victoria aside. She knew what that was all about!

She gave a thin, approving smile. Victoria paid little attention to her governess these days, but when her father told her any-thing . . . That would put a stop to those clandestine smiles, and accidental meetings in the shed!

She would have gone on upstairs to her room, but then there'd been that knocking at the door. She'd only paused to find out what it was, but naturally – once she'd overheard the shocking news – she'd stayed put and took in every word. So, that Isabella child had not gone home. Miss Boff sniffed. She was not entirely surprised. Not a very proper girl at all. The kind of young woman who could bring such unbecoming books into a vicarage was capable of any indiscretion. Oh, those girls thought Miss Boff didn't know about the books, but of course she did! She'd seen them under Victoria's pillow, several times – she'd even read a page or two, all about women with no moral sense at all – though, as she had no business in the room, she'd had to hug her disapproval to herself.

And now look what Isabella had done! Abandoned her coach-man in St Just, and failed to go home at all. So Lionel and dear Doctor Flower were obliged to go out in this dreadful rain to look for her! Well, it was all the parents' fault. They had let the girl run absolutely wild. With company like that, no wonder Victoria had got herself into scrapes. No doubt Miss Cardew had encouraged her. Not a suitable friend at all, however well-connected she might be.

Miss Boff pursed her lips. She must have another word to Dr Flower.

She was still contemplating this necessity, when the door of the morning room opened without a sound, and Victoria came out into the hall. Miss Boff instinctively moved back into the shadow of the stair. What was the girl up to now?

She was not left to wonder very long. Victoria sat down on the stair, pulled on her boots, slipped her thick cape over her and, taking a candle from the candlestick, went out into the night.

'Victoria!' Miss Boff called after her, a little feebly and a lot too late. She came downstairs herself. She went to the front door and opened it. A blast of cold air gusted in, with raindrops on its breath, and threatened to blow all the candles out. She closed the door hastily again.

But she had glimpsed what she had really hoped to see. Out there towards the churchyard stile, a dark silhouette against the sky: Victoria, vainly attempting to shield the candle with her hand.

Well, there was only one thing to be done. Miss Boff had boots and bonnet too, a fine wool cloak and a walking cane. It was a matter of moments to put them on, and then she too was out there in the chilly dark, hurrying towards where Victoria had been. She had no candle or umbrella, but she didn't stop to look; from what she'd seen, it was a waste of effort in the wind.

It was difficult crossing the stile and graveyard with no light. Wet nettles clutched her skirts and stung her legs, miry puddles squelched beneath her boots, and low-lying gravestones lurked at every turn.

'Victoria?' She called in earnest now. 'Victoria!!'

But there was no answer. Only the wind moaning in the spire, and the persistent patter of the rain. She stumbled through the lychgate to the lane, but there was no sign of anyone. She paused. If Victoria had gone anywhere, she thought, it would be in the direction of Polvidden Row, where that wretched gardener-fellow lived. Sneaking out to meet him, probably, while she knew that everyone was out, and thinking she would never be observed. Well, in that case, she was in for a surprise.

It wasn't too bad, out here in the lane, provided that you walked with care and used the cane to test the ground and so avoid the holes. She was getting pretty damp, of course, but this should not take long. Once she had caught up with Victoria . . . She set off as briskly as she could.

She had gone a half a mile or so and reached the big fork in the lane, before she paused. Which way could Victoria have gone? There hadn't been a single sign of her. Miss Boff peered anxiously into the dark. Nothing either way, that she could see. Of course, that candle would have blown out long ago, but there was no movement, other than the wind. Suppose Victoria hadn't come this way at all? A tryst in the garden shed, perhaps? That was not impossible. Why hadn't she thought of that before? And it was really pouring now.

Suddenly she felt foolish and afraid. She was not accustomed to being out at night. And she was soaked – she could feel the dampness right through to the skin. Her boots were full of water, her hands were ice, and her soaked bonnet ribbons drooped. Even her cloak dripped with rain from head to toe.

She shivered. This escapade was not of the slightest use! She did not usually give up, but tonight she turned and made her way back to the vicarage. It seemed to take her twice as long, and when she did arrive, it was enraging to find Victoria answering the door, amazed to see her governess half-drowned, when she herself was drier than a bone.

'Miss Boff?' she exclaimed. 'I thought that you were Deedee coming back. Whatever were you doing in the rain? Ruby!' she called out to the maid. 'We need some towels here, and some hot tea, as soon as possible.'

Miss Boff took off her dripping, ruined hat. 'I think I might ask you the very same. Where did you go? I saw you sneaking out.'

Victoria looked at her. Her eyes were red, as if she'd been in tears. 'I wasn't sneaking anywhere. Did you know that Isabella's lost?' And then, as Miss Boff answered with a nod: 'Well, it came to me she might be hiding in the church. I know we were there for Evensong, but she might have been there – somewhere – all the same. There are lots of nooks and crannies, and the spire. I just took a light, and went over there to look. I thought she might have . . . well . . . repented of something that she'd done. Felt the need to pray.' She shook her head. 'She wasn't there, of course.'

'You were in the church? When I went past?' Miss Boff could hardly frame the words. The cold and damp had got into her bones, and she was shivering.

Victoria shook her head. 'I didn't know that you were even there. What were you doing out there, anyway?'

Miss Boff said, with an effort, 'The same thing as you. Looking for Miss Cardew, naturally. Only I didn't . . . ahh . . . ahhh . . . choo!' She finished with a sneeze.

'Miss Boff, I think you'd better go to bed. I'll have Ruby bring you up a tray of tea. And some lemon cordial perhaps. It seems to me you've caught a nasty chill. It was immensely good of you, but you shouldn't have gone searching in the rain.'

Miss Boff felt an embarrassed flush suffuse her face. 'Really, I'm quite all right, Victoria!' she tried to say. But she was shivering again, and feeling distinctly odd.

So much so that when Ruby came, with towels that had been heated in the range, Miss Boff found her teeth were chattering. She had to allow herself to be led upstairs, stripped and dried off like a child, and put unprotestingly to bed.

Victoria turned out to be right. It was a very nasty chill indeed.

Dan had done a good job raising the alarm. Every man in Polvidden old enough to help was out there on the cliffs, armed with ladders, ropes and lanterns of all kinds. One or two had even come with spades or picks – anything that was to hand. Jimmy was dispatched to Penvarris village to: 'knock on the policeman's door and fetch him, quick.'

The rain was falling still – worse, if anything – and a stiff breeze was rising on the sea, slapping the salt spray in their faces and turning the ground slippery underfoot. Four quarrymen (who had a leaky rowing boat between them and went out now and then with lines and home-made lobster pots) put on their oilies and sou' westers and led the way, while the others straggled along behind, turning their coat collars up and their hat brims down in misery, but undaunted all the same. Nobody was talking very much.

'Whereabouts was she then?' one of the leaders turned to call, over his shoulder, to Dan who was limping along as best he could towards the rear. The man was obviously hollering, but the wind almost whirled his voice away. Dan hurried up to indicate the place.

'Somewhere over there a bit,' he shouted back. 'There, where the ground has slipped away. Shouting for help, she was. That's how I found her first.'

She wasn't shouting now. He saw men glance at each other in the lantern light, their faces running with the rain. You could see the fear and tension in their looks. One of them – it looked like big Stan Tregorran – went towards the edge, leaning against the wind, but the others called him back until they'd tied a stout rope round his waist.

Old Tom, standing next to Dan, said, 'If some of that there edge is fallen in, more of 'er might go any time. No point in losing anybody else.'

Tregorran had been roped by now, and reached the edge again. They saw him lie down, just as Dan had done, and lean over the precipice. 'I see her!' Tregorran shouted triumphantly. 'Can you hear me, down there?' There was a faint scrabbling from somewhere down the cliff, and – even over the wind – Dan heard a little avalanche of stones pinging on to the rocks below.

'No!' Tregorran cried. 'Stay still, for 'eaven's sake! We got some ropes. Just 'old on tight – somebody's coming down.' He edged back and scrambled to his feet again. 'She's still there,' he murmured to those close enough to hear. 'Though how we're going to reach 'er heaven knows. Can't even get down the path to run a line – all that's part's fallen in. Just have to pray that bit of gorse bush holds and that the girl 'olds still – she'll have the rest collapsing otherwise. She 'eard me, though – that's one good thing about it, I suppose.'

There was a little ripple at the news, and suddenly everyone was chattering at once – everyone with his own idea of how this should be done.

It was Old Tom of all people, who took control. He put two fingers in his mouth and let out a piercing whistle, and the uproar stopped. 'Seen this once before, I 'ave,' he said. 'Main thing is to get a man down there, and steady 'er – get a rope around her, save her falling any more. Then we'll think how to get her up.'

'Right!' Stan Tregorran said. 'Who's going to take hold of this rope, and let me down a bit?' There were a dozen willing hands, but Tom intervened.

'Got a rope ladder 'ere. Might as well use 'un, if we can. Make her fast against that standing stone, and let down her down as far as she will go. Then you got something to hang on to, Stan. One or two of you better take a hold of it as well, make sure it doesn't get away.'

There was a murmur of assent. Eager hands were already dragging the ladder to the edge and securing it with half a dozen ropes. Tregorran lay down and wriggled to the end.

'But how we going to get her up?' said someone in the crowd. 'She's never going to climb. You can't just tie her to a rope, she'll bash 'erself to death. Stan'll just 'ave to carry her, supposing he doesn't fall and kill them both.'

'Let down the solid ladder, separate.' Daniel was remembering a stretcher case he'd seen. 'Stan can lash the girl to that, and help to guide it up – keep it away from banging on the cliff too much. T'isn't perfect, but . . .'

A cry from Tregorran interrupted him, 'Have to do something, blurry quick – and better be two of us, besides. I'll never do this on me own. This blurry rope ladder's not a bit of good, tonight. Banging about something awful in the wind.'

Dan found himself saying, 'I could go. I'll put my head and arms through it – don't need a pair of legs for this.'

There was a snort of disbelief. 'You?'

He was tying a rope around himself. 'I'll be more use down there than here – still got all my strength in the top half of me. You let me down on the ladder – gentle-like – and I can fend off as I go. I'll take the line, and Stan will be free to guide the solid ladder down. Come on, what are you waiting for.'

He was already halfway towards the cliff-edge as he spoke, and there was no lack of willing hands. The rope rungs were passed around his neck and he wriggled arms and shoulders through.

222

The he inched back towards the top, and over it. Sickening darkness opened at his feet.

It was uncomfortable, the rope bit fiercely underneath his arms, but it was secure, and there was still the line around his waist.

It was frightful, even then. The wind was biting and the rain was fierce. He did need both his legs, of course, and every time he fended off a sharp pain shot up to his thigh and little flurries of pebbles showered down. Then, Tregorran was beside him, blowing in the wind, making little avalanches of his own and cursing mightily. It seemed to take forever in the dark.

Then, when at last they reached the girl, they had the devil's job to get a rope secure. Dan had the line, but he kept swinging in against the gorse, and threatening to dislodge everything. Stan did get one foot on the little ledge, but it crumbled under him, and there was a sickening moment when the furze-bush rocked.

The girl moved slightly, whimpering, and then Dan managed it. He couldn't have done it without the rope ladder underneath his arms, allowing him to use his hands. But with a desperate effort he held in, tearing himself against the gorse, passing a loop around her waist. He felt it tighten with her weight.

There was a general murmur of relief. At least she was now supported from above. He hung there panting, bracing with his torn arms.

But there was no time to rest. A dark shape hung a moment in the air, and came slithering down towards them, banging and showering them with little stinging stones. He had to look downwards to protect his eyes, and it struck him sharply on the arm.

That made him slump against the rope, so he didn't see what happened next, only heard a shriek and felt the most tremendous tug. One of the rescuers almost toppled from the cliff. The girl had somehow roused herself and launched herself at Stan, clutching at him wildly. There was cursing and threshing, and then it stopped. She seemed to have gone limp. The solid ladder rocked and swayed. Dan grasped the lower end of it and held grimly on, using his own weight to hold it vertical. Above him, Stan struggled in the dark with ropes. Dan thought his arms and heart would burst, until finally Stan hollered, 'All right. Haul her up.' He let go and inch by inch the ladder drew away.

Dan was bruised and bleeding by the time they got him up, and it took half a dozen men to help him on to land. Another group had brought Stan up as well, and the girl had been laid gently on the muddy ground. Men held the lanterns over her to see.

Dan tried to get to his feet, and staggered painfully. He had to be supported by a man on either side, but they helped him over to look. He almost sobbed with weariness and disappointment at the sight. It was Miss Victoria's friend – the one who'd gone running off like that – and it seemed that she was dead. Her dress was stained with something dark that looked suspiciously like blood, she had been scratched to pieces by the gorse, her face was white, and one foot stuck out at an angle from her leg. She didn't move or make a sound.

But before he could catch his breath to speak, Stan Tregorran crawled across to see. He looked half-dead himself. He placed his battered fingers on her lips. Then he nodded. 'She's still breathing. She should be all right.' He gave the ghost of a smile. 'Had to punch her on the jaw to shut her up – or she'd have killed the lot of us.' Then he rolled over and was copiously sick.

'What's going on? What's happenin'?' came the cry of Mollie's voice. She and Harry were pushing through the crowd. People drew back to let her see, and she clapped both hands to her face. 'Oh, my lor! Harry! Look what's happened here. Dear God – it's Daniel!'

'Missed all the excitement, 'aven't you?' someone said to Harry sourly. 'Woman 'ere has fallen down the cliff. Pity you weren't here earlier to 'elp. We could have done with it, great strapping lad like you.'

'We weren't home, me and Mollie,' Harry said. 'Out for a bit of walk.' It sounded ridiculous, on a night like this, even to Daniel who knew that it was true. 'We had a lot of things to talk about.'

'Never mind all that,' Daniel gasped out. He didn't want an inquisition now. 'It's that Miss Cardew from St Evan House. Somebody ought to go and let her family know.'

'Well, 'ere's the policeman from St Evan now!' And there he was bumping along the lane on his bicycle, his bull's eye lantern flickering. Ironically, the rain was easing now. The constable (he seemed extremely young) came down to have a look.

'Broken her ankle, and some ribs, by the look of it. But she's still living, thanks to you. Take her somewhere more sensible than this. I'll let her parents know.' And he cycled off again.

Harry and another man picked the ladder up and began to carry it. Stan Tregorran was on his feet by now and shrugged off any help, but Daniel couldn't walk without support. The little procession made its way across the stile and back towards the dim lights of the Row.

Dan looked at the injured girl. Her eyelids fluttered and she moaned and stirred.

Harry shook his head. 'We saw her earlier,' he said. 'Running all peculiar down the road – wailing like a witnik in the rain.' He shook his head. 'Didn't fall down there on purpose, d'you suppose?'

'Don't be so daft, Harry.' Mollie kept glancing towards Daniel, but he wouldn't meet her eyes. 'With 'er money, why would she do that? Besides, you saw that clifftop's given way. Went out there to 'ave a cry, that's what, and went too near the edge.'

'Yes, I 'spect you're right, my love,' Dan heard Harry say.

They'd reached the shelter of the houses now.

The women were out standing on the street and, on the doorstep of the nearest house, ready with hot tea and hevva cake for the rescuers. Jimmy was already there and tucking in ('Run all the way there and back, I did'), and soon the other men had followed suit, taking off dripping coats and boots and crowding in, steaming, to warm up by the fire

They carried the unconscious girl upstairs and laid her gently down upon a bed, and that was where the Cardews found her when they arrived.

Five

Victoria spent a miserable night. She had gone to bed, but couldn't sleep. Her father's words kept coming back to her. 'I can only sincerely hope you haven't encouraged or abetted her in this.'

Yet that was exactly what she'd done. She had suggested how, where and when Isabella and Pencarrow might contrive to meet – and secretly prided herself on her cleverness. And what had come of it? Bella was ruined, shamed, disgraced – had been so desperate she'd run away – and now she was even dead, perhaps. By her own hand, too, which was even worse. To be a suicide! Not even to have a Christian funeral or be laid to rest in hallowed ground. And in the next world – what then? Victoria shuddered at the thought.

Because, in a way, it was really all her fault. That realization had come to her tonight. It was not only the search for Bella which had led her to the church: she'd gone to light a candle for herself, but she'd found no comfort in her prayers. The church had been as cold and adamant as Deedee's angry face, and at last she'd had to face the chilling truth. Without her 'encouraging and abetting' there would have been none of this. She had been meddling as Miss Boff would say.

That thought too, filled her with remorse. Look what had happened to Miss Boff! The poor soul had got drenched in the search, and had gone to bed unwell, looking very poorly, Ruby said. And Deedee and Lionel were still out in it. Thanks to her 'encouraging and abetting' – all of it!

But even that was not the very worst. The very worst was what she'd done to Daniel Olds. It was the thought of that which filled her with despair. All her own fault, again. She had encouraged him. Deliberately! Manoeuvred him and sought him out. Invited him to hold her, kiss her lips, confident that it would be all right, presumptuous enough to speak of divine will. And now? Deedee would dismiss him, she had no doubt of that, and then what would become of him? What other employment would he ever find for all the hours of lessons which they'd spent – mostly, she now realized for her own benefit? A young man with no money and a crippled leg! What would become of his whole family? She had brought ruin and trouble to them all. Dan had tried to warn her, but she'd refused to listen to his fears; sure that she knew better, selfish, arrogant, and – yes – foolish person that she was.

Victoria groaned and thumped her pillow for the hundredth time, trying to make her head lie easily. But it did no good. It was not discomfort keeping her awake, it was remorse, and guilt.

In the end she gave it up and went downstairs. She wandered into the kitchen, seeking warmth – the fires had gone out in the other rooms. Mrs Roseworthy must have been wakeful too, and heard her come, because she came padding from her quarters at the back, resplendent in rag-curlers and a dressing robe, and made a cup of cocoa for them both.

'Couldn't rest a wink till that dear man comes home,' she said, and they sat – as though Victoria were still a child – and drank in silence by the kitchen range, drawn together by anxiety.

It was a long, uncomfortable night. The hands on the clock above the mantel seemed to crawl. A wild night, too. Although the rain had eased, the wind still roared and moaned around the chimney pots and rattled all the windows in their frames. Victoria caught Mrs Roseworthy's glance, and knew that they shared the same unspoken thought. This was no weather to be out searching in the fields.

It was almost dawn before there was a rattle at the door. Both women rose and rushed into the hall, and Deedee and Lionel came in.

They looked exhausted, cold and worn and wet, their faces smudged and drawn with tiredness.

'Deedee?' Victoria exclaimed.

'They've found her,' he said shortly. He didn't seem surprised to find them up. 'Taken a tumble down the cliffs it seems – she's badly hurt, but they expect she'll live.'

Lionel was stripping off his dripping coat and hat. 'It happened on Penvarris cliffs – right down the other way. Colonel Cardew sent a man around, to let the searchers know, but he took a little time to find us all. They think she's broken quite a few bones, but she's come round and seems to be all right. They've got her home, and the doctor's on his way.' He gave her a strained smile. 'Well, I'm all in. I'm off to bed. Goodnight.'

'Goodnight.' Victoria didn't move. Relief had almost made her knees give way. Not only for Bella but for the menfolk too. After Miss Boff, she'd been afraid for them. Thank God that Deedee, in particular, was safe. She glanced at him. He looked so weary and so soaking wet, a good man who had been out half the night, searching for a girl he hardly knew, a man of courage and of principle. So why was he so angry about Dan? Surely she might persuade him after all? She had gone the wrong way about it, certainly. 'Honour thy father and thy mother', that was the commandment, and she had not obeyed. She had done things of which he disapproved, and when he sought to check her, she'd lost her temper and insulted him.

'Deedee,' she began uncertainly, 'about the things I said . . .'

He looked at her. He sounded infinitely sad and tired. 'Go to bed, Victoria. It's late. Go to bed and say a prayer of thanks that nothing worse has come of all this foolishness.'

He was implacable. She turned away, but he called after her, 'Goodnight, Victoria. Thank you for waiting up.' A pause, and then, 'We'll talk about all this another time.'

But when she came down for breakfast, he was gone.

It was the task of any parish priest to call upon his flock, especially in times of accident or grief. And this, Edward assured himself, was such a time.

All the same, as he trotted Bluebell and the cart up to St Evan

House, he couldn't help a little feeling of unease. This was no ordinary accident. Very well, the ground had slipped away, and that is why Isabella Cardew fell, but what was she doing out there on the cliffs? Especially on a rainy winter night? It must be – mustn't it? – to jump, 'do something desperate' as Victoria said. So what had driven her to this extreme?

He turned in through the gate. The questions troubled him – they'd troubled him all night – but it wasn't the answers that troubled him, because only one answer was possible.

Pencarrow – his friend – had behaved appallingly. Taken advantage of Victoria's friend, who could only have met him through the vicarage. Pencarrow! A snake that he had welcomed into his home. A man who – he now saw – had flattered his own weaknesses, and wormed his way into his confidence with a knowing look, and a capacity to search out old books. In fact, come to think of it, to search out almost anything. Whatever a man needed, Stephen could be relied upon to 'know a little fellow in the trade'. And always at a profit to himself.

All the shutters of the house were closed. He sighed. A house of mourning. Thanks to his so-called friend. And yet, when he thought about it, the signs had always been there: Pencarrow could never pass a pretty girl. He, Edward, had blindfolded himself – sold his soul – not for a 'mess of pottage' but for a shelf of fine bindings and attractive colour plates.

He drove round to the stable block, and – almost without a thought – handed Bluebell over to the boy. Not the same boy, surely, as he'd seen before? This lad was bigger, stockier and a little less refined. The habits of a lifetime's visiting prompted Dr Flower to say, 'You're new here, aren't you?'

The boy grinned, pushing back his cap. 'Not 'zactly new here, Reverend. Always b'longed to work here, in the yard. Only I got promotion see – they've made me up to groom. Going to learn me how to drive the carriage soon, then I can be under-coachman, too. Gave that John his notice, haven't they, for losing Miss Isabella yesterday.' He made a face. 'Poor lad, wasn't 'is fault, as

I could see, but there! Colonel had 'im out within the hour. And I aren't complaining, that's a certainty.'

Edward slipped a sixpence in his hand – a kind of penitence – and made his way round to the front again. The house looked so forbidding he hardly liked to knock, but hardly had he done so than the maid came to the door, and he was welcomed instantly inside. The Colonel, who had been breakfasting, came out at once, and shook him by the hand.

'My dear Dr Flower. How good of you to call. I understand you helped to search last night! Everyone has been so good. I can't thank you enough.' He led the way back to the breakfast room. 'Here's the vicar come to call, my dear.'

The formidable Mrs Cardew gave a startled smile. 'Won't you join us, Dr Flower? Somewhat unorthodox, I fear, but we're rather late this morning, I'm afraid. A little kedgeree? We've been up all night, as you can understand.'

In the interests of civility Edward permitted himself to be served with toast and tea. Now that he was here, he found, this was a little difficult. He said, 'Your daughter, how is she today?'

'Doing very well indeed,' the Colonel said. His bluff face beamed. 'Broke her right ankle and a rib or three, and of course she's very scratched about – you heard she fell into some gorse? Nothing short of a miracle, I'd say – though I suppose you're used to it, in your line of work.' He motioned to the footman for the marmalade. 'There was some nasty bleeding at the start – that had me worried, I can tell you – nearly thought we'd lost her for a time.'

His wife said crisply, 'It was nothing serious! That's all stopped long ago and now the doctor's been. He says that Bella will do very well. Of course, she's weak – not well enough for any callers yet, but in a week or so . . .' She gave a practised smile. 'Please tell Victoria we'd love to see her then. How is she, by the way?'

She was changing the subject! Yet she clearly knew. Edward looked at her. 'Oh very well, I'm glad to say, though very much disturbed by this, of course. You know that Isabella came to see her yesterday, before this . . . incident? I didn't have the chance to speak to her. She seemed a little . . .' He hesitated. 'Anxious and distraught.'

Mrs Cardew fixed him with a smile that didn't reach her eyes. 'Yes,' she said. 'It's most regrettable. Some sort of mental megrim it appears. The product of the fever, possibly. Bella has not been feeling well for days. The last thing the poor girl can recall is being set down shopping in St Just, and after that, there's nothing but a blank. She must have lost her memory and wandered aimlessly, until she ended up too near the edge.' She met his eyes. 'I do hope she didn't say – or do – anything terribly unfortunate? She may have been hallucinating, too. Though I'm glad to say that's over now. There's no more risk of that, you understand?'

Oh yes, he understood. He was not a father and a priest for nothing, after all. 'I'm glad to know she's out of danger, then. If she should need to talk to me . . .'

Mrs Cardew gave a little laugh. 'I'm certain that she will. As soon as she is on her feet again. And on such a delightful topic too. You know her cousin Petroc's coming here next week? For the Christmas season, naturally. I think he came to see you once before, about the banns, but Belle wasn't really ready for him then. She promised him an answer when he came this time, and – Horace, I'm not sure if you've heard this – of course she's set her heart on having him. Sooner rather than later, too, now that she's had time to think it through.' She gave that little brittle smile again. 'More tea?'

'I say, that's jolly festive news!' The Colonel sounded both surprised and pleased. Edward looked at him. 'Horry will be home by then, as well. Calls for a little party, I should say, as soon as Isabella's up to it.' Yes, it was evident. The mother clearly knew: the father had no inkling of the truth – the awful scandal that had passed so narrowly.

Edward said slowly, 'Colonel, there is something else. Something, I feel I should discuss with you.'

Mrs Cardew's eyes grew very bright, and she sat very still.

The Colonel looked at him mildly. 'My dear fellow, yes?'

'I understood last night, from your messenger, that you were thinking to reward the rescuers? The two men that pulled your daughter from the cliff?'

Cardew's round face lighted in a smile. 'I am indeed!' And Mrs Cardew gave a little sigh, as though a tightness in her chest had eased. 'One of them was that gardener boy of yours.'

'Yes, so I heard.'

'Deuced brave of both of them, I'd say, but that lad in particular. Over that ledge with no thought for himself. . . .' He stopped. 'You were going to ask?'

'Only what form you thought that your reward might take?'

He frowned. 'Was going to give them money. You think otherwise?'

Edward drew in his breath. 'I wondered, if you might be persuaded – as an act of charity – to do something else? Something more permanent. I tried to give the boy a chance, myself, after that business at the pit. He saved a man's life there, as well, you know. A decent type, and a good brain as well, but with that leg of his . . .! He's wasted as a gardener's boy, and I can't keep him on for ever, anyway. I wondered, with those business friends of yours in Hayle? You know the owners of several factories. If you were to mention Daniel to them, help him through an apprenticeship perhaps? He'd never manage it, left to himself. Apprenticeships cost money, and he's bringing money in, but if you were to sponsor him? That would make a real difference to his life – and to his family too.'

There! Whatever Victoria accused him of, she could not say that he'd abandoned Daniel. If this apprenticeship could be arranged, it would be a real step forward for the lad – and separate him from Victoria too.

The Colonel was looking doubtful, though. 'Well, I don't know. I can see the force of what you say. But I never cared for pulling strings like that, especially for somebody I hardly know. And it could be years. More of an undertaking than I meant. And, you know, he was not the only one. There is the other man to think of too.'

What Edward did next cost him sleepless nights. But he was desperate. He turned to Bella's mother with a smile. 'And what does Mrs Cardew think? Perhaps it is too high a price to pay? But, perhaps, for Bella's sake? She came so near to such a dreadful fate.'

Mrs Cardew looked him in the eyes; she understood what he was suggesting: his silence in return for her support. She gave him a smile of pure complicity, and then she said, 'But Horace dear, of course we must. Nothing could be more fitting in the world – give this young man his life, as he gave Bella hers. How good of Dr Flower to think of it. And, as for the other lad, don't I recall that they were having lay-offs at the pit? You were discussing it at dinner recently. We could do as Dr Flower has done, and give the fellow a position here. We have one vacant, now the coachman's gone, and there's a little cottage with the job. No doubt the young man would jump at that. And that needn't cost you anything at all.'

Her husband looked at her. 'I suppose . . '

'Of course!' She motioned for a footman with a tray. 'So regard it as quite settled, Dr Flower. Now you must try one of Horace's special oranges. He has them shipped in from the South of France . . .'

He felt like Judas as he took the fruit.

It was a wonder Mollie didn't lose her job that day. If there was one wrong way to do a thing, she did it, sure as fate, from dropping the paddle in the tank, to letting hairs get in the cream. Her mind wasn't on it, that was what was wrong. Her brain was out there in the lane again, with Harry and Dan last night, playing over and over like one of those new-fangled gramophones.

Had she done right to let Dan go like that? Sometimes she thought yes, and it served him right, and sometimes she thought no. Should she go down and try to sort it out, or should she let it be? And so it went, round and round. The more she asked herself, the less she knew. And the longer the blessed butter seemed to take to 'turn'. It seemed that going-home time would never come.

Then, when it did come round at last, she slipped out the side in case Harry should be waiting at the front. Somehow she couldn't face all that today. Then she wasn't satisfied until she'd looked, and she was disappointed that he wasn't there.

Want your head read, Mollie Coombs, you do. No more sense than a pickled whelk, she told herself, but it didn't stop her loitering in the lane, changing her mind a score of times about calling down the Row.

Of course, she did go down at last, but there was a great carriage right outside, with little tassels on the blinds and all, and a young coachman lolling in the seat. He wore an ill-fitting uniform, and whistled insolently at her as she approached. 'Got visitors in there,' he told her cheerfully. 'But you can come and sit up 'ere with me, and wait.'

So she went straight back home to number nine, after all, not in the sunniest of moods. When she got in, Eadie was upstairs.

'Putting little Stan to bed,' she called. 'There's a few potatoes in the bucket there, and a bit of swede and onion in the pot.'

Mollie rinsed off the dishes in the sink, wiped down the sticky table, swept the floor and was just putting the peeled potatoes on the hob, when Big Stan came up behind her, like he often did. She shoved her elbow sharply in his ribs.

'Here, Stan Tregorran, none of that! Mind where you put your 'ands. That's private property. I've told you that before.'

But he didn't let her go, the way he usually did. Instead, he pinched her bottom playfully. 'Be even more private in a minute, then. Me and Eadie and the boy are moving out next week. Then you and Fayther can have this to yourself.'

She whirled to face him, the poker in her hand, 'How's that then, with quarry jobs so poor? Never thinking to go to Australia, like Jamie did? Don't know where the fare'd come from, if you were.'

He backed off, grinning. 'Nothin' so common! No, I got a place. Won't pay like quarrying, perhaps, but it's secure. And no rent to pay. Proper little two-roomed house and all – might be a uniform and everything, if I turn out to suit.'

She looked at him. 'You been out drinking down the Tinner's Arms again?' She turned back to the stew.

'No, I mean it. Start next week, down at St Evan House. All Colonel Cardew's doing, see – reward for hauling up that girl of his. Just got to work my notice out with Prowse. He's doing the same thing for Dan, as well, only he's sending him up Hayle.' He laughed. 'Just as well you two called it off last night, or he'd have been in two minds whether he should go.'

She put down the saucepan with a bang. 'How do you mean, "sending him up Hayle"?' She didn't turn around.

'Oh I dunno – it's some apprenticeship. Up to the dynamite works, I think. He didn't rightly tell me everything – just came down to the pit, and let me know. Went into Penzance this very afternoon, to use the telephone, that's all I know. How's that for fancy, if you like! And he's arranged for Dan to see a man about his legs, because he couldn't go to work today, so there! Cost you half a crown to speak to, very soon.'

There was a silence.

'Moll?'

She didn't answer.

'I thought you would be pleased. About the house and everything.'

She slammed the lid down on the saucepan, hard. 'Well, so I am. Delighted. Thrilled to bits. For you and Dan and blooming everyone. There! Is that enough? Now will you leave me be?'

She couldn't eat a morsel of the stew, and when Harry came, a little later on, she buried her head against his chest and cried. He was a little baffled, but he didn't seem to mind.

Six

Victoria had waited in for Dan all day, but he hadn't come. Even though she'd walked halfway down the lane, and hunted for him almost everywhere. True, her father had forbidden her to talk to Dan, but she hadn't actually given him her word. Surely Dan deserved an explanation at the least – especially if he was going to be dismissed, as she was fairly certain that he was.

In fact, as the afternoon drew on, she began to believe the worst. Perhaps Deedee had already been down to Polvidden Row, first thing, and paid him off. Perhaps she would never see Daniel again.

It was Old Roseworthy who gave her the news at last, when she found him sharpening a hoe. 'Dan'l? No, he isn't 'ere today. Hurt 'isself, didn't he, last night, saving that young lady on the cliffs. Right as a trivet in a day or two, they say. Brother came here first thing to bring us word.'

That was the first she'd heard of it, but it was comforting. More than comforting. Daniel had not been sent packing yet. On the contrary, he had been a hero, it appeared. Even Deedee would have to be impressed by that. She would make sure to tell him when he came, though she would have to be careful how she handled it.

She hadn't seen her father all day. Nor Lionel – he had gone out on the cliffs to see Ralph Mills about an anthem for the Christmas choir. The carollers would be starting very soon. That would be nice, she'd always loved that, going out round the lanes, warm breath misty in the air, faces and fingers tingling with cold. Pity, she thought, that Daniel didn't sing. Perhaps she could persuade Lionel to ask? It would be all right, then, for them to meet, and it wouldn't exactly be conversation if they sang.

She pulled herself together with a jerk. This was how Bella's troubles had begun. If she was to meet Daniel, she'd do so openly. Deedee would just have to come around in time. Although she quailed at the thought of that. She had argued with him, yes. Stormed at him once or twice. But she'd never disobeyed him in her life.

She walked slowly back into the house, oddly at a loss for what to do. She even wandered up to see Miss Boff, but Mrs Rose-worthy was there, just tiptoeing gently from the room, and shook her head at Vicki warningly.

'I shouldn't go in there, my dear. She's taken bad. Ought to have the doctor to her, when your father comes.' So Vicki wandered back downstairs again to wait. Then when Deedee and Lionel did get home, they were so worn out with being up all night, that all they wanted was to go to bed. There was no time to talk to anyone at all.

And the next morning it was just the same. Lionel and Deedee busy, Miss Boff in bed; no one to talk to, and nothing much to do. Her old boredom stared her in the face.

There *was* a scribbled little note from Bella, brought by a cocky little coachman with a wink. It read:

I can't have callers, I am in disgrace. I'm sorry, Vic. I meant to do it, but I lost my nerve, and then the cliff gave way beneath me anyway. But it did get rid of you know what, the doctor says, and I'm to marry Petroc in the Spring. I don't care any more. P.S. They don't know I'm writing this, so don't reply.

Victoria read it twice, then screwed it up and threw it in the fire.

In the end, she went out with the chicken jelly pots, just to find something to occupy her time. Really, she hadn't meant to go down to the Row, but somehow she found her feet were taking her there. Well, it was all right, wasn't it? Daniel was still an employee, and he was hurt. Who deserved a pot of jelly more? She didn't even have to speak to him.

Suddenly, a voice interrupted her thoughts. 'Well, if it's not Miss Flower, as I'm alive! What brings you here again? Come to see what more trouble you can cause?'

It was that frightful red-haired girl again. Clearly looking for an argument. She was looking furious, and standing, hands on hips, defiantly in Victoria's way.

Victoria attempted to be dignified, and sidestep the girl without a word, but Mollie Coombs was far too quick for her. 'What's the matter then, cat got your tongue? Or just too grand to bother with the likes of me? I meant it, what I said. What brings you here? Come down to gloat, have you? Make sure he's gone?'

'Gone?' Victoria framed the word, but no sound escaped her lips.

Mollie made a bitter little sound. 'Oh come on. Pretend you didn't know? Don't make me laugh. This was all your doing, wasn't it? Not enough for you to let us be. I've seen you look at him from May Day on. Why did you have to do it? Haven't you got enough? Just because you couldn't have him for yourself!'

Victoria found that she was trembling. 'I don't know what you mean.'

'Stealing him away, that's what I mean. Building him up and giving him ideas. And when that Colonel Cardew turned up here, and offered him an apprenticeship up Hayle, what was the poor lad supposed to do? How could he turn it down? Even supposing that he'd wanted to? Never get a job again, round here. But, of course, he never wanted to – you took good care of that. Drove all the spirit out of him. Well, you've got your way, he's gone – gone in a horse and cart this very day. And, if you know what's good for you, you'll do the same. We don't want your type round 'ere. You don't belong here, and you never did. You and your blumming jelly jars, as if you were some angel in disguise. We can look out for ourselves, you hear?'

She was panting with the force of it. Victoria felt almost sick with fear. A girl like this could hit her, anything. She backed away.

'Moll?' It was that very large young man she'd seen her with before. 'Thought you were coming out with me, seeing you're off this afternoon. Is something wrong?'

'This woman 'ere's what's wrong. Tell her to go away. Tell 'er, Harry, make her go, before I forget myself entirely.'

He had put his arms around the girl. 'It's all right, Mollie girl. She's going. You are going, aren't you, Miss?' He flashed Victoria an embarrassed smile. 'Only you can see how it is. It's been upsetting here. With Dan going off so suddenly like that, and everything.'

'Yes,' Victoria said, quietly. 'I'm going. There's nothing here for me.' She turned and walked slowly up the Row, into a world more empty than she'd dreamed possible.

The cart lurched doggedly towards Penzance. Dan shifted on his seat. His leg was paining him, though not a fraction as much as his aching heart.

He'd understood the way it was, of course, the minute Cardew came with all this talk of apprenticeships in Hayle. It was the vicar's doing, naturally. Decent of him, in a way, not to have simply thrown him out on his ear. But clever, too – it would have been impossible to refuse or to call at the vicarage again – that was an implied condition, he understood that too. 'There will be a ticket arranged for you, on the up-train tomorrow, ten o'clock,' the Colonel said.

Ma had been so pleased and proud to have the Colonel call, and Jimmy had been cock-a-hoop. This was security for them – no threat of the workhouse any more. And Merelda too. She could get married now and never mind. And himself? Six months ago he would have said it was a miracle. But now – perhaps it was just the best that could be hoped.

He would work hard, study, make a go of it. He could send money home, make something of himself. And perhaps, one day, who knows? Victoria would be proud of her pupil, if she heard.

He slipped a hand into the cardboard box that was all the luggage he had. His fingers felt the cover. *David Copperfield.* He would read it till the pages fell apart.

Crowdie, whose cart it was, looked at his face and must have seen the tears that threatened him. 'Your leg bad is it? Won't be too long now. We're nearly in Penzance.'

And they jogged on towards the station and the train.

It was Christmas Eve; fine and starlit, but extremely cold. Lionel's fingers tingled in his gloves; he shouldn't have held them so close to the fire, he'd get chilblains again which would make it difficult to play an instrument. He gave the song sheets to Victoria and clapped his hands together as he walked.

'A lovely evening for it, anyway,' he said, trying to make her smile. She seemed to have stopped smiling recently. That accident to her friend had sobered her.

'Yes, very nice,' Victoria replied.

'We'll sing all the traditional carols first,' he said, 'and save the others for St Evan House. It's flat out there, and we'll have time to catch our breath, and I believe they sometimes serve a drink?'

'Yes, usually,' Victoria said, 'and cake. And a fruit cordial for the children too.' There, he had done it. The faintest little smile. 'No doubt Bella and Petroc will be there – there's to be quite a gathering, I understand.'

'Ah yes, of course. I quite forgot. They announced their engagement yesterday. Though she was still swathed in bandages, I hear.'

'Yes,' Vicki said, and then nothing more.

He tried again. 'We've quite a little choir tonight, if they all come. At least a dozen adults, and the boys. Ralph's lent me another lantern too.' Mistake! He had been avoiding thinking about Ralph.

'Of course, you went to see him yesterday.' Worse and worse. 'I hope you found him well?'

Oh yes, he longed to say. Quite well. Too well, in fact. The smile too hearty and the hand too firm. It had lingered on his shoulder, he could almost feel it now, and the gentle pressure of Ralph's palm against his own.

'My dear, dear fellow, do come in,' he had welcomed him. 'A little drink, perhaps? What will you have? I'll have to pour it for you – we are quite alone. It's Young's night off.' There had been a little tray beside the fire with whisky and mince tarts, and Ralph had waved towards it as he spoke. But he hadn't moved, just stood there, very still. 'It's times like this that I miss Matthew so.'

He had been close, too close. It was electrical. Lionel had felt the panic in his soul. He should have moved. This was a sin. It was not meant to be. But he had said, helpless. 'Yes. Yes, you must.'

And Ralph had said, 'Yes, I do.' He had taken his hand and led him over to the stool. 'There's something here for you – a little gift. Matthew gave it to me once.' He had taken a little package from the mantelpiece and tenderly closed Lionel's fingers over it.

It was a piece of stone, most delicately carved. Two men, looking into each other's eyes. Lionel had felt his heart begin to pound. 'I couldn't . . .' he had protested.

'David and Jonathan, they say. The greatest friends of all,' Ralph had murmured softly. 'Such a pretty thing.'

Lionel had then felt stifled. His blood was singing and his nerves had turned to twanging mandolins. He had stood up and said, 'That's kind of you.' If he did not escape, he knew then, the devils on his shoulder would win for evermore. 'But really, I must go.'

And it was over, suddenly. Ralph had said, 'Not just a little drink?' in such a normal tone, that he had begun to think that he'd imagined it. But deep down, really, he knew otherwise.

'Lionel?' Victoria startled him. 'You seem lost in thought?'

He smiled. 'Yes, I am.' Suddenly it came to him what he must do. 'The thing is, Victoria, I spoke to you a month or so ago, made my intentions clear. Have you had a chance to think about what I said?

'You mean, will I consent to be your wife?'

For a moment courage nearly failed him, but he managed it. 'I'm no great orator or poet, I'm afraid. But I'm honest, decent, sober, Christian.' It was true, all true. He had fought against temptation and had won. 'I'll do my best for you.' He took her hand, her woollen glove in his.

She didn't pull away. 'I know you will.'

'So you accept.'

'I think so, Lionel, yes.'

He should have kissed her, but he bungled it. Instead, he pressed his frosty cheek to hers. 'You won't regret it, Victoria, I promise you.'

'No.' Then, after a minute. 'There's no hurry though? To be actually man and wife, I mean.'

He could have hugged her with relief. 'None at all. A long engagement's best, I always think.' He kissed her then; a gentle little peck.

'Deedee and Miss Boff will both be pleased.' She smiled. 'And so will everyone. It's the best thing, all round.'

She was quite right of course. Her father was waiting with the carollers, and when Lionel murmured in his ear, there was no mistaking his sincere delight. 'Lionel, my dear fellow! Wonderful. And you, Victoria!' He hugged his daughter, there in view of everyone. Then he boomed it out. 'We have an announcement here to celebrate!' and soon the choir was crowding round, full of congratulation and surprise.

There never was such singing, after that. Down Polvidden Lane, one or two doors already decked with holly-wreaths, down to the bottom of the Row, where children were visible indoors by candle-light weaving hoops of greenery to hang, up to St Evan House at last for wine and cake.

'*God Rest Ye Merry, Gentlemen, let nothing you dismay,*' they sang, the little lanterns bobbing in the dark.

And so, reluctantly, down the hill and home.

Epilogue

July 1917

Victoria walked very slowly down the street. There was at least ten minutes before the train arrived, even supposing that it was on time. But there was little of interest in the shops these days. Grey sheets, grey bonnets, even greyer bread. This wretched war had made the whole world drab.

When she reached the station, it was packed, as usual. Women mostly. Some with anxious faces crowding on to the platform – perhaps they had menfolk coming home on leave. A group of nurses by the waiting room. Salvation Army girls with tea. Two Land Army women, and a nun. Even a woman in the ticket office now. Half the country was in uniform.

Then, with a whistle and a huffing hiss of steam, there was the train. It clanked and sighed and clattered to a stop, and passengers came streaming out of it. Old men, young women, soldiers, clergymen. For a moment Vicki felt alarmed. How could you hope to find anyone in this?

She need not have worried. The door to a compartment opened further down the train, and Bella and her brood were handed down. Victoria spotted them immediately. Bella, in her coat of pretty pre-war blue was a jewel of colour in that mass of brown.

Vicki elbowed her way through the crowd. Bella was fussing with bags and reticules, but she turned and seized Victoria's

hands at once. 'Dearest Vicki, it's been such an age! It's wonderful to see you. I've so much to tell! And such a journey, you have
no idea! I almost wish we'd come down in the cart with all the
baggages. It's so good of you to call for us like this. Transport is
so hard to get these days!'

Victoria smiled. 'Deedee was coming to Penzance today, in
any case. He'll meet us at the tea shop later with Primrose and the
cart.' She laughed. 'Poor little Primrose. Almost as old as
Bluebell used to be, and twice as slow. But we were lucky to
get another animal at all. Most of them were taken for the army,
long ago.'

'Yes, I know. It's been the same for us. Petroc did buy a motor
car, just before the war, but that's been put away – out in the old
barn collecting dust – there isn't the petroleum to be had. And no
one to drive it anyway. Poor mother has no coachman; one
simply cannot get the servants any more. That's why I decided to
close up the house and come. Hilda – that's the nursemaid over
there – is the only staff I have.' She smiled. 'I was lonely anyway,
with Petroc gone. Though naturally I knew he'd have to, in the
end. He's gone as aide-de-camp to General Murray, did you
know? Papa managed to pull a string or two.'

Still the same old Bella, Vicki thought, burbling on while
people struggled past with trunks and bags, and both the
children hopped from foot to foot. 'You must feel it terribly,'
she said aloud to Bella.

Bella was instantly contrite. 'Oh, Vic! How thoughtless of me.'
She glanced at the broad black band on Vicki's sleeve. 'Poor
Lionel! I was so sorry when I heard. And just when you had fixed
your wedding date at last! Do you still miss him terribly?'

Victoria heard herself reply, 'Oh, yes.' And it was true. Lionel
had become a sort of anchor in her life: a gentle, steadying,
persistent tug, though at a little distance from herself. 'Though of
course, Lionel went away almost at the beginning of the war. He
felt that chaplains were desperately needed at the front. And the
men did appreciate him, you know. He gave a lot of comfort in
his quiet way.'

She didn't say what Lionel had said, the very last evening he was home, that he had found no comfort for himself. She was glad, though, that he'd managed to confide in her. He'd told her everything. Why he had volunteered at first – put himself deliberately in danger's way – trying to escape his inner self. And how temptation was even worse out there. She could see him now. 'Can you forgive me?' he had said as tears welled up in his eyes.

'Of course I can. What is there to forgive? They are only thoughts.'

He had shaken his head. ' "Whoso commits adultery in his heart . . ." Perhaps I shouldn't think of marrying.' He'd looked at her. 'Or perhaps I should, the next time I come home, if you'll still have me, after this, Victoria.'

'Of course I will.' She could not find it in her to be shocked. It was almost a relief, to know that she too was a second choice.

But he never had come home. Had he, she sometimes wondered, done it deliberately? Chosen to go out into that hell of fire, knowing he could not help the wounded man? She would never know. They'd made him a hero for it, afterwards. Poor Lionel.

'Anyway,' she said briskly, 'that's all over now.' She turned to the children in their little hats and coats. 'This must be your little James. And this is Peter. My word, how he's grown.'

'He's almost five now,' Bella said. 'Petroc says we'll have to cut those lovely ringlets soon. And send him off to school, I suppose, though I don't want to do that, yet.'

Tow-headed Peter scowled ferociously. The younger child clung to his nursemaid's skirts and sucked his thumb.

'Time for a cup of tea, I think,' Victoria said. She led the way. Bella followed, flanked by both her sons, leaving Hilda – a skinny girl, with teeth – to find a porter and cope with baggages.

The tea shop was a rather grim affair. 'No sandwiches. No cake. No jam. No more bread today' the notice in the window warned as they went in. But there was tea, and milk and cordial, even two rather grey and lumpy rock cakes for the boys.

While they were engaged in eating these, Bella leant forward

246

confidentially. 'Do you see anything of the Pencarrows now?' she murmured, with a blush.

Victoria shook her head. 'Still farming over at St Just, I think. I haven't heard. We're not on calling terms with them any more. Why do you ask?' She was surprised that Bella had raised that painful memory.

· 'I saw a fellow on the train, that's what reminded me. He looked a bit like that young man you used to like. The one who had a limp. What was his name?'

'Daniel Olds,' Victoria said. Too quickly.

Bella looked at her. 'What's become of him?'

'I don't know. I haven't seen him since.'

Married, probably, like that Coombs girl who'd shouted at her twice. Victoria had seen her several times, struggling with babies up the lane. Once with that young giant of a lad, bigger than ever in his uniform.

Bella seemed to read her thoughts. 'You knew that Mollie person, didn't you? The one whose brother-in-law came to work for us? Is she reliable, do you suppose? With all of us coming home again, Mother is looking out for someone else to scrub – and she's applied. It might work out, her sister's very good. Mother's even let her stay on at the house, even though her husband went off to the war.' She took a sip of tea. 'I don't know what's going to happen in the end. He lost a leg at Ypres. I suppose they'll have to go when he comes back.'

'I'm sure that Mollie Coombs – or whatever her name is now – will suit you very well. She always struck me as a hard-working girl. Though, of course, I don't know her very well. I've only spoken to her once or twice. Rather a sharp tongue, that's all I know, but that won't matter if she's scrubbing floors.' Victoria said, feeling forgiving and magnanimous.

'I only wondered,' Bella said. 'Jamie, don't put your sticky fingers on my coat. Oh, and look Victoria, there's your father with the trap. Hilda, go out and tell him that we're here.'

'I'll go,' Victoria said. 'I've got to get back to my desk in any case. You know I'm working for the government, helping to keep this national register of theirs?'

'The one where they send people off to help the war? Into the forests and that sort of thing, even if they didn't want to go?' Bella made a face. 'I don't think I should care for that, at all.'

'Someone's got to do it,' Victoria replied. 'The country can't work without supplies. Or railways, or buses. And the men are all away! There is a war on, after all.' She smiled. 'Besides, I'm on the list myself, of course. They'd have sent me somewhere, if I wasn't doing this! But you needn't worry, Belle, they're not registering wives and mothers yet!'

Bella laughed. 'I should think not indeed!' But she was getting to her feet, assembling her little purse and gloves. Hilda was buttoning the children in their coats. 'So, you're not coming with us in the trap? I see your father's bought a larger one.'

'Not yet. I'll come home later on, when I've finished work. I've got a bicycle these days, you know. Quite like those pictures of Americans! Anyway, larger trap or not, I don't think there'd be room. Deedee's already got Miss Boff with him. Though she doesn't take a lot of space, these days, poor soul. She's getting to be very frail, I fear. Hello, Deedee, everything all right?'

For answer her father waved the reins at her.

'Well, make sure you come and see us very soon,' Bella said, as the little party got themselves aboard. 'And thank you for taking us for tea, just what we needed after that crowded train. One can't even order a cold hamper now!' She grinned. 'And look – since you're staying in Penzance awhile – there's that man I was telling you about. The one who looks a bit like Daniel Olds.' She nodded at a man across the street, with baggy brown trousers and a battered hat. Ridiculous, he didn't look like Dan at all. Bella smiled. 'Well, we must go. Promise you'll come to dinner. Saturday perhaps? Mother would simply love it if you did!'

Victoria stood at the kerb and watched them go. It was quite exhausting, having Bella back. Life had been very quiet since she went. She stole another look across the street. Whatever had Bella been thinking of? There wasn't the remotest resemblance to

248

Dan. She was annoyed to find her cheeks were flushed, and she had experienced the strangest little thrill. She was also making herself conspicuous; there was a gentleman in an overcoat and suit who was looking at her most peculiarly.

She went to turn away, but he came across the road. He'd come quite close before she realized that this must have been the person Bella meant! He did look like Dan, too, or would have done, if it had not been for the smart clothes and overcoat. Dan had never worn kid gloves and polished shoes.

'Miss Flower?' Even then she could not believe her ears.

She looked him in the face, and saw his eyes. There was no question, then. They were the same as always: smiling, shrewd and grey. 'Daniel?'

'It is you then?' he said, and smiled, and she realized for the first time that he had doubted too. "You looked so different – with your hair like that – I wasn't sure.' He gestured to the mourning band around her sleeve. 'I hope . . . not Dr Flower, or your governess?'

It was absurd. She was a girl again. She wanted to laugh, to smile, but she answered with proper soberness, 'No. No. A man I planned to marry – he was killed.'

He looked away. 'I'm sorry.'

She said impulsively, 'It was the curate. Lionel Smallbone. You may remember him.'

'Him?' he said sharply, and then met her eyes. 'I'm sorry, that was very impolite. I'm sure, if you were fond of him . . .'

'Yes,' Victoria said. (I've never been fond of anyone, but you, she admitted inwardly, and his eyes replied, I know.) Her lips said, brightly, 'You are looking well. That job you went away to must have suited you.'

'Yes, I believe it has. I studied hard – I even came out top in the exams. I was working with explosives anyway, and of course I knew a little about that. They made me a supervisor straight-away. They were quite pleased with me, and then there came the war. A lot of workers volunteered and went. I couldn't go, of course – my leg. So, here I am, a manager, with a whole new factory under me. We're making ammunition for the army, now. It's been a blessing for my family.' He smiled. 'All down to Colonel Cardew and your father, I'm aware.'

She caught her breath. 'Your family?' She forced herself to smile. 'You have a family, then?'

He grinned. 'There's only my mother and little Lucy now. And my youngest brother, Jimmy. I'm putting him through school. The others have all grown away and gone. I never married, if that is what you mean. I never felt inclined to . . . afterwards.'

'You've never called on Colonel Cardew then? To let him know what had become of you?'

'You think I should? To thank him?'

'I think he would be very pleased to know what a success you'd made of things.' Dear heaven, his eyes were looking at her so! He might as well have seized her in his arms and kissed her, right there in the street. 'I'm sure my father would like to see you, too.'

She prayed that it was true. It was a risk, but life was different now. The war had changed so many things – and she was older, more determined, too. 'Oh yes, call on my father, certainly.'

'And I may call on you, Miss Flower . . . Victoria? Soon?'

She thought her heart would burst for joy. 'Oh yes, Mr Daniel Olds, please do. Call on me very soon.'